THE FINAL MILE

A SAM POPE NOVEL

ROBERT ENRIGHT

For Sophie and Olivia,

CHAPTER ONE

ELEVEN YEARS AGO...

'Private Matthew McLaughlin, sir.'

The young man stood firm, his back straight, his shoulders wide. Although a wiry man by design, he'd certainly taken his exercise routine seriously, and had packed on a visible layer of tight muscle. Sergeant Carl Marsden always kept an eye on the newest wave of Privates as they joined the rest of the armed forces, each stepping off the plane with an excitement bouncing around them like they were headed to a music festival.

A few weeks into their first tour, with the Afghanistan heat beating down on them relentlessly and their backs aching, they soon adopted the usual grimace of a soldier.

Proud. But in pain.

Marsden had been in the UK Armed Forces for over two decades, serving as part of an elite squadron battling a corrupt government in South America. It had earnt him a few medals and the respect of everyone he came across, but to him, it was the bullet wounds and battle scars he carried that proved he'd fought for the betterment of the world.

1

Now, he was stationed at the base, tasked with identifying the potential of each brave soldier and highlighting the elite. Those who showed capabilities beyond the average soldier would be guided down specific paths, where elite task forces would recruit them for missions Marsden knew were strictly need to know.

It was why he'd called Private McLaughlin to his office. The thick canvas walls of the tent flapped gently in the harsh breeze. While they did well to protect them from the sweeping sand of the dusty floor, it also locked the heat in like an oven and Marsden sipped his bottle of water to quench what felt like an eternal thirst.

With the temperature soaring, Marsden had removed his jacket, grateful for the short sleeves of the T-shirt that stuck to his clammy body. While his dark skin was a blessing in the scorching sun, he could still feel the heat emanating from his forearms. Beside him, Corporal Sam Pope had gone one step further, his camo-green vest strapped to his muscular frame. Sam had caught his eye six years ago when he was just twenty-one and had since blossomed into the deadliest sniper he'd witnessed in all his time serving for Her Majesty.

Not only was Sam a gifted and deadly soldier, he was a man of integrity and Marsden had forged a wonderful relationship with the man based on respect and their commitment to doing the right thing. While it risked the wrath of those higher up, Sam had proven himself a few times in a combat situation to value the lives of his comrades and civilians above his own.

Sam would die for the cause if he believed in it.

The UK needed soldiers like him.

Men like him.

Which is why, as Private McLaughlin stood, sweating in his full uniform, Marsden had asked Sam to join him.

'How long have you been in the army, Private?' Marsden asked, pretending to read from notes he'd long since memorised.

'Two years, seven months, and four days.' McLaughlin's voice quivered slightly as he stared straight ahead. 'Sir.'

'How old are you?'

'Twenty-two, sir.'

'Please,' Marsden said calmly. 'Sit.'

Mac nodded and then rigidly sat in the chair opposite the desk. The mismatching furniture gave the office the look of a charity shop, but Marsden was grateful for the privacy.

The last thing he wanted was to share with General Ervin Wallace, a man who was as bloodthirsty as he was boisterous. While Marsden didn't agree with the bulldozer-esque approach of the man, he knew that when push came to shove, there wasn't anything Wallace wouldn't do to protect his country.

The young soldier, sat nervously picking his nails, had been on Marsden's radar for an entire year before Wallace deployed him to the same base as them. Wallace's orders were for McLaughlin to be integrated into the unit, with Sam Pope to mentor him. McLaughlin had been several levels ahead of the rest of his class when it came to accuracy and distance shooting, stats which Sam had raised his eyebrows at when presented with them.

They didn't measure up to his but considering Sam Pope's marksmanship had been the stuff of legend, it was never likely to be.

'Would you like a drink?' Sam broke the silence, offering the young recruit a smile.

'Yes,' McLaughlin stammered. 'Yes, sir.'

'Please, just call me Sam.'

As Sam walked across to the fridge in the corner, McLaughlin smiled nervously. Sam wondered what it must feel like. For him, there was never any doubt he would be a soldier. His father, William Pope, had been a senior ranking officer and with his mother leaving when he was a toddler, Sam had followed him from outpost to outpost. While it had contributed to a somewhat fractured childhood, Sam had blossomed into a bright, brave man built with unscrupulous integrity.

But reading through McLaughlin's file had painted a different picture. Sat before them was a lippy kid who had been kicked out of school for his bad behaviour. A young man who had had a few run-ins with the law and probably saw this as his last chance to turn his life around. Sam applauded the choice he'd made, knowing that the

3

British Armed Forces wouldn't so much as beat the bad attitude as reshape it.

Mould him into more.

Into a soldier.

Sam pulled open the fridge, the shaky old machine humming loudly as he pulled a couple of bottles of water from within. He tossed one across without warning.

'Catch.'

McLaughlin rose to the challenge, his instinct and reflexes working in tandem as his hand shot up, snatching the bottle from the air. Sam nodded his approval and McLaughlin smirked, feeling relaxed for the first time.

Marsden waited, his hands linked and resting on the unread notes that papered his desk.

'So, you ready to step up?' Marsden's calm voice carried such authority and McLaughlin quickly guzzled his water to reply.

'Yes, sir.'

'You say that a lot.' Sam joked. McLaughlin smiled, their friendship already blossoming.

'Now, while I know you're keen to get behind the scope, no sniper worth his salt pulls the trigger without spotting for a while. I expect you to listen, to learn, and beyond everything, Private, I expect you to ask.'

'Ask, sir?'

Marsden turned to Sam, who put his bottle of water down before fielding the question.

'If you don't know, you ask,' Sam said bluntly. 'I know what it's like in the barracks and when you guys all first get here. Everyone stays quiet, nobody wants to look like they don't know what they're doing or that they don't belong. But not with me. As far as I see it, if you need to know something, you damn well better ask me. It could be the difference between life and death. You do that and I promise, I will do everything in my power to keep you alive.'

'Yes, sir…I mean Sam.' McLaughlin corrected himself with a wry smile.

'Brilliant.' Marsden clapped his hands together and stood. 'Then tomorrow at 0600 hours, you officially join the sniper division.'

'And by division, he means you get to tag with me.' Sam joked, drawing a shake of the head from Marsden.

'Quite. Dismissed.'

'Thank you, sir.' McLaughlin nodded, before scrambling from his chair.

'Sir.' Sam wrapped his knuckles on the desk as he followed, walking quickly to catch-up with his protégé as they exited the tent.

'So, private, what do I call you?'

'Umm…Matt. Matthew. My friends call me Mac.'

'Then Mac it is.' Sam smiled, clapping his hand onto the young soldier's shoulder and banishing any nerves. 'Mac it is.'

———

EIGHT MONTHS LATER

Somewhere behind him, Mac could almost make out Sam's voice screaming through the blind panic and relentless thudding of the helicopter.

They had been on an outlook, casting their eyes out over the dilapidated town known as Chikari, when their cover had been blown. While Sam had been focused on the dusty road that peered off into the horizon, awaiting the safe return of one of their convoys, Mac had been negligent. He hadn't been watching as the Taliban mobilised, launching an air strike on their location and sending a helicopter to chop them down.

Sam had told him to stay put.

It was the last thing he remembered before the panic set in.

Survival.

Fight or flight.

Mac decided to fly.

As he pushed himself off from the ground, completely revealing

5

their position, he'd turned on his heels and began to run as fast as he could.

Sam yelled after him, his cries for his friend to remain calm dying in the sheer noise of the aerial assault.

As Mac ran, his heart raced too, his body shaking as the very real threat of death began to reach for him with its unforgiving clutch. The echo of a sniper rifle shook through the sky as Sam attempted to take down the chopper, but it was to little avail.

Mac continued to run, his boots pounding the weeds and dust of the mountainside, his movements erratic, his direction clueless.

Sam called out for him.

Then his entire world changed.

The whoosh of the rocket being launched sounded like an airplane taking off, and it clattered onto the ground a few feet behind him.

The explosion was instant.

As Sam was rushing towards him, it must have blown him backwards, with Mac not realising it had sent Sam spiralling down the uneven cliff face to the unforgiving ground below.

His survival was unlikely.

The blast itself had sent a shockwave through Mac's entire body, the pain, as uniform and skin were disintegrated by the flames, had been overwhelming. The pain was immediately replaced with a strange numbing sensation, as the shock began to take control. It felt like parts of his body were there only in spirit. His entire right side felt absent. As he lay in the long grass, gasping for breath and any semblance of clarity, his skin was still bubbling from the immense heat of the flames.

The right side of his head was charred, the hairs of his head and eyebrows gone, the layers of skin beneath charred.

As he called out for Sam, his voice caught in his throat, his body trying to reserve its energy as it fought diligently to survive.

'Sam.' His voice rasped, no louder than a whisper, and his left eye managed to shoot a glance to his right hand.

The skin was gone, the smooth pink muscles beneath were as visible as the relenting sun.

6

While the remnants of his right ear hung from his mangled skull, he could hear the faint crunch of footsteps on the rocky cliff face.

Sam.

Come to rescue him.

He had promised he'd look after him.

That he would keep him safe.

Get him home.

Despite the pain, he arched his head up, his left eye squinting in the harsh glare of the sun.

The smell of burning hung in the air like a thick fog and somewhere in the distance, he could hear the thudding of the chopper as it flew away.

The footsteps doubled and it was only when he caught the outline of a thick beard and a white cloth wrapped around the head, did he realise that his prayers hadn't been answered.

It was the very opposite.

A few more figures emerged, darkened by the shadows of the burrowing sunshine.

As the Taliban soldiers mockingly joked at his expense in their native tongue, he felt hands grasp his legs and slowly, he was hauled across the rough terrain, hoping that he would succumb to his wounds before his captors could reach their destination.

With his chances of survival diminishing, he felt a tear roll down his left cheek as he was slowly and painfully dragged towards his living hell.

———

NOW...

Wallace was dead.

When it had been reported on the international news channel that his mentor and saviour had been murdered by Sam Pope, Mac had felt the rage rise to the surface once again.

Ever since Sam had given him the slip in Rome three months before, Mac had been waiting for Wallace to reach out.

To give the orders to fight back.

But they never came.

After the years he'd spent in captivity, the relentless and brutal torture he'd survived, he'd thought of nothing more than his revenge.

Sam had left him to die.

Wallace had liberated him and nursed him back to health, continuously repeating to Mac that he was a soldier of the British Armed Forces and in his mind, it meant he was an asset.

True soldiers don't leave men behind.

With the limitless funding extended to Wallace and his Blackridge organisation, Mac spent over a year battling through extensive reconstructive surgery and stomach-turning physiotherapy.

While it fixed his damaged body and rebuilt him as an elite, killing machine, Wallace paid no attention to the psychological damage years of brutal torture had caused. In Wallace's eyes, it made Mac a unique asset.

A man without anything to lose.

Through the years, Mac had asked Wallace repeatedly for his revenge, but Wallace kept him away from the United Kingdom, insisting that Mac use his considerable talents and his penchant for violence to help him save the world.

Mac had killed multiple targets for the man, all in the name of the blind loyalty he showed to the man who not only rescued him from his horrific existence but had guided him to a life of meaning.

There had been bloodshed.

But he'd shed it gladly.

While he'd failed in his mission to kill Sam in Rome, he

now knew that it was time to return to the UK and finally exact his revenge on his supposed friend who had left him for the wolves.

Sam had eventually gotten married.

Had a son.

Lived the life that Mac never had the chance to.

Seven years. Seven years trapped in a cell in a desolate terrorist training camp in the middle of nowhere.

Beaten.

Tortured.

Raped.

All because of Sam Pope.

And now Sam had killed the man who had pulled him back from the brink.

As the unremarkable man on the TV spoke about Sam Pope's trial and his inevitable life behind bars, Mac felt his fists clench, the charred skin tightening across his murderous hands.

Staring at himself in the mirror, he wasn't ashamed of the scars that run roughshod across his face.

He wore them with pride.

It was time to thank Sam for them, and with Wallace not in place to keep his leash tight, Mac promised himself that he would choke the life from Sam and enjoy every second of it.

The right eye, a beautiful white from the blindness incurred by the devastating blast, stared vacantly ahead. His left eye, an olive green, was watering, a tear of rage falling from it as he mourned Wallace and vowed his revenge.

As he began to pack the small number of possessions he kept in the dank hostel room in the south of Austria, he gritted his teeth and urged himself to keep everything under control.

It would take more than a prison to keep Sam Pope safe.

But it would take all his focus to force the UK to hand him over to him.

With revenge driving his every move, Mac marched to the door, threw his black overcoat over his wiry frame and slammed it shut for the last time, and began his long and unplanned journey back to the UK.

Back to Sam.

Back home.

CHAPTER TWO

Sixty-eight years.

The rest of his life behind bars.

That was what Sam Pope was looking at. The holding cells at West Hampstead Police Station had been his home for the previous nine days, ever since he was pulled from the High Rise in Dulwich, his back sliced open from the brutal fight with 'The Hangman of Baghdad'. As DI Amara Singh had helped him from the building, he barely registered the Armed Response team trained on him, their guns aimed, their fingers ready.

The rain had been beating down, the freshness of the water seemed to douse some of his pain, but not much.

Singh's boss had been quick to get in his face, sneering as she sent him to the police van to be locked up and, most likely, the key thrown away.

After being rushed to the local hospital to have his body stitched back together, Sam had been taken to West Hampstead station, where he was booked in, told what he was being charged with, and then sent to his cell.

It had been one of the best night's sleep he'd ever had,

which was sadly interrupted in the early hours of the following morning by Singh's irate superior.

Assistant Commissioner Ruth Ashton.

A career woman if ever Sam saw one, her sharp features and well-groomed attire gave off an attractive, yet fiercely professional aura, and she regarded Sam with complete malice. She'd demanded he be taken to an interview room, where she alone would interrogate him.

Sam refused the presence of a lawyer.

There was nothing for him to hide.

Nothing he wanted to fight.

To him, the fight was over.

They would read back to him the laundry list of crimes he'd committed ever since he'd embarked on his one-man war on crime, and unless they were inaccurate, he would gladly admit to them. While he knew taking the law into his own hands was a crime, he wasn't ashamed of what he'd done.

The people he'd stopped.

The lives he'd saved.

He was proud of what he'd stood for and while he knew that he would likely spend the rest of his life behind bars, he didn't regret it.

It had given him a purpose.

Something he'd been missing for over three years, ever since his beautiful son, Jamie, had been taken from him. Killed by a drunk driver who Sam should have stopped, Jamie had been Sam's pride and joy. He had been the pinnacle of his love with Lucy, his ex-wife who left him when he never recovered.

Jamie's death had broken Sam.

And while taking down criminal empires and killing sex traffickers wouldn't change what had happened, each one gave Sam a bit of that purpose back.

Ashton didn't see it that way. Without holding back,

she vehemently ripped into Sam, comparing him to the criminals he'd eradicated. When Sam had countered that he'd done more to fight organised crime in a year than the police had in a decade, he thought she was going to strike him.

As she rolled out the list of his crimes, Sam sat listening, his cuffed hands resting on top of each other, and his badly beaten face a picture of bloodied and bruised calm.

After the London Marathon had been bombed the year before, Sam had investigated the death of a young officer, stumbling along a conspiracy that linked a high-ranking inspector to one of the most dangerous criminals in the country. As Sam had unpicked the horrible truth, he'd left a trail of bodies in his wake, all to save an innocent psychiatrist, Amy Devereux, who had been caught up in the disgusting cover-up.

It had seen Sam break his promise to his beloved son. A promise that he wouldn't kill anymore.

With fifteen deadly and highly decorated years as the UK's most lethal sniper, Sam had promised his son that he would shed no more blood.

That and he would read as many books as possible, just to placate his son's insatiable thirst for the written word.

Memories of his son sitting in his beanbag reading were some of Sam's fondest, but as with all memories, they begin to fade and it hurt Sam to acknowledge that those treasured moments were starting to lack the finer details.

The colour of Jamie's T-shirt.

The title of the book.

Soon, the very image itself would fade, a generic representation of what he thought his son looked like.

Sam may not have kept his promise to not kill, but he'd intended to keep his promise when it came to the books.

His mission to save Amy also cost him the life of his best friend.

Theo Walker.

One of the most respected medics in the forces, the two men had been firm friends as they toured Afghanistan, with Theo eventually stepping away from the army as Sam transitioned into General Wallace's elite team. Although no longer a medic, it was engrained in Theo to save people and he began a warmly received youth project in Bethnal Green. As a black man who had turned to the army to get away from a life on the streets, Theo was driven to help as many young children walking in similar shoes as possible.

Theo had given his life to protect Amy, a sacrifice that Sam refused to be in vain as he stormed Frank Jackson's High Rise and brought his, and the corrupt inspector's, empire crashing to the ground.

Several men were killed along the way, many by the pinpoint accuracy of Sam's trigger finger.

Sam would serve time for every one of those deaths.

As Sam had continued his war on crime, he soon stumbled across a desperate father, Aaron Hill, searching for a missing daughter the police had ignored.

When Sam pointed out that fact, Ashton dismissed it, adamant that everything possible had been done to bring Jasmine Hill back.

It was Sam who eventually did.

With the horrific future of sex slavery at the hands of the Kovalenko crime family, Jasmine would have ended up as another statistic and another lost soul in a brutal trade. Sam had taken on the Metropolitan Police himself, engaging in a shootout with an Armed Response team before his all-out assault on the Kovalenkos.

Several more were killed, including Andrei Kovalenko and his brother, Oleg.

Sam took responsibility for their deaths, but also of the locating and successful rescue of Jasmine Hill and three other girls.

Ashton refused to comment.

With the destruction of the Kovalenko's sex trade, Sam had also helped uncover a link between them and a leading mayoral candidate, which led Ashton to suspect that DI Adrian Pearce was working with Sam. It was an allegation Sam strongly denied, although his mutual respect with the detective had blossomed as they took down Frank Jackson and brought in Inspector Howell. Pearce had become a strong ally, not only offering Sam help from the inside, usually against his better instincts, but also guidance.

Pearce had reminded Sam several times he was a good man.

A good man doing bad things for good reasons.

While Ashton couldn't charge Sam with the subsequent assault on the Kovalenko's Ukrainian hub, she assumed it had been his handiwork. She discounted it as an international issue, along with the incidents in Berlin and Rome.

According to her, they didn't matter. A statement that Sam refuted.

Sergeant Carl Marsden, his mentor, had been murdered in Rome.

Murdered by General Ervin Wallace.

That mattered.

Ashton scoffed at the accusation, her affection for the fallen general betraying her neutrality. Sam noticed it in a split second, the flicker of her eye as his name was mentioned. He was trained to absorb everything, drink in every detail, and use it to his advantage.

Whether it would help him kill a man from a few kilometres, or aid his escape by a matter of seconds, there was no detail that was inconsequential.

Ashton had history with Wallace.

That much was clear.

Ashton soon brought the conversation back to the

panic Sam had caused at Liverpool Street Station two days prior, with the video footage of him being hurled from the promenade to the ground floor spreading across the social media platforms like wildfire.

Sam calmly deconstructed her narrative, indicating his attacker was Farukh Ahmad, an assassin and associate of Wallace, who had elicited his help to track Sam down.

Again, Ashton dismissed Sam's besmirching of Wallace, but Sam countered with explicit details about the files he'd been given.

The files that Wallace had killed for.

That Marsden had died for.

As Ashton's face drained of colour, Sam painted the true picture of Wallace, a war monger who had more blood on his hands than Sam, Farukh, and any killer or soldier in the country. It was why Sam had been made target number one by Wallace and his Blackridge outfit, and why Sam staged the assault on Wallace's motorcade.

Slowly, pieces began to connect for Ashton, who had been told by Pearce that Wallace had had Singh abducted.

She didn't want to believe it, but Sam confirmed it.

Wallace wanted to use Singh as leverage against Sam, who captured Wallace in return.

It was a violent, dangerous game of one-upmanship, one which eventually cost Wallace his life. After Sam had handed over the files in exchange for Singh's safe release, Sam had revealed the wire under his shirt, recording the confession of Wallace and one that implicated Farukh. Abandoning his usual repertoire of hanging his victims, Farukh impaled Wallace by the throat, slashed his jugular open, and sent him hurling from the top of the High Rise.

Ashton refused to believe it, tears forming in the corners of her hate-filled eyes.

Sam killed Wallace.

She was adamant.

Sam accepted his fate, that he'd killed a number of people, all of them criminals. That included Farukh, who, after slashing open his back and beating him to within an inch of his life, Sam had brutally killed by impaling him on a pole before ramming a blade into the man's skull.

The brutality of the death was not lost on Sam, who agreed that he should be taken off the streets.

Killing criminals had been a necessity.

To save lives.

But the barbaric deaths of some of his opponents had worried Sam that he may be enjoying it. With each criminal he put in the ground and with every empire brought crashing down, whether it was the Kovalenko's human trafficking business or Wallace's stranglehold on global terrorism, it had all been for the greater good.

It had restored something in Sam, something that had been lost ever since his son was taken from him.

But there was never any enjoyment in it.

Now, with the fight over, the truth exposed, and Wallace dead, Sam was ready to put the gun down and accept his punishment.

He confessed to killing all those men, except Carl Marsden and Ervin Wallace.

Irate, Ashton told him she'd make sure he never saw the light of day again.

She took his signed confession and the next day, Sam was taken by armoured vehicle to the magistrates' court, where he pleaded guilty to the confession and was given a crown court date of eight days from then.

Those eight days had been as peaceful as Sam could remember.

There was the odd sneer from a prison guard during the arrival of meals, but surprisingly, Sam found a number of the officers approved of what he'd done.

In their eyes, he'd been able to do the things they

wished they could, but the bureaucracy and the judicial system had their hands tied. While they were bogged down with paperwork and minimising the bad press thrown their way for the slightest infringement on a criminal's rights, Sam had kicked down doors and put bullets in rapists, pimps, and crime lords.

One officer even brought Sam a copy of *Jurassic Park*, which he never knew was a book. He read it cover to cover within a day and subsequently read it through once more before his trial date.

According to some of the friendlier guards, his entire case and impending trial had become one of the biggest stories in quite some time, and they were relishing the subsequent let down.

Sam had already confessed.

There would be no dramatic trial with pieces of evidence falling out like a trail of breadcrumbs exposing further corruption within the powers that be.

Sam would be sentenced to life in prison, or to be exact, sixty-eight years behind bars.

He would take his sentence with his head held high, his shoulders straight, and his conscience clear.

Everything he'd done, from bringing down the High Rise, to turning London inside out to find Jasmine Hill, to causing an international incident in Rome to engaging in a fire fight on Tower Bridge, he would do again if he had to.

It was the right thing to do.

Wallace's horrendous misdeeds had been exposed, with Paul Etheridge, and old army friend who had helped Sam when possible, following through on the plan to leak the files and confession to *The Pulse*. Blackridge had been dissolved immediately by the government, with an elaborate search for the rest of Wallace's assets underway.

Word had reached Sam that one of *The Pulse's*

reporters had been murdered, found hanged in his own home.

No doubt just another unfortunate casualty of his war, this time at the hands of the Hangman of Baghdad.

Sam mourned him, the guilt of the man's death along with the subsequent devastation to his family, would hang heavy on Sam's mind.

Another innocent person caught in the crossfire.

As Sam laid back on his uncomfortable bed, he gritted his teeth. The stitches that held his back together hummed with pain and he slowly closed his eyes.

Thinking of his son's innocent smile, Sam drifted off to sleep, ready to face his future in the morning.

CHAPTER THREE

The horrid inevitability of the day hung over the day like an angry rain cloud. DI Amara Singh hadn't slept a wink, emerging from her bed before five in the morning before kicking her coffee machine into life. As the caffeine rumbled out into her mug, she felt sick.

Today was the day.

Sam Pope was going to be sentenced to life in prison.

It had been a strange six months that had changed her irrevocably. As Sam Pope's war against organised crime had escalated, she'd seen it as the biggest opportunity of her career. To be the person to bring him to justice would skyrocket her career within the Metropolitan Police, continuing her sharp rise through the ranks. Ever since she'd joined in her early twenties Singh had been labelled a prodigy. While some sneered at her hastened elevation through the ranks, dismissing it as a quota ticking exercise, she knew better.

The fact she was a female or of Indian descent made no difference.

Her strict Hindu parents had always encouraged her to follow her sister's lead, by marrying into wealth and providing them with grandchildren. While she adored her sister and at times, pined for the devotion and love a family provided, it wasn't the life for her. Spurred on by her now deceased Grandfather Singh soon made them proud in a different way.

Within two years of being a police officer, she'd been weapons trained and joined the Armed Response Unit, undertaking several dangerous missions and catching the eyes of those higher up. She soon transitioned to a detective, with her tenacity and sharp mind making her a valuable asset to the Met. Her work on Project Yewtree had seen her name cross the desks of many a senior officer.

When the opportunity to lead the task force dedicated to bringing in Sam was established by Assistant Commissioner Ruth Ashton at the behest of the then mayoral candidate, Mark Harris, Singh put herself forward.

Ashton backed her to the hilt.

Singh had it made. All she had to do was bring Sam in.

That was when everything changed.

As her hunt for Sam intensified, so did his as he tore a hole through the London underworld to find a missing girl. As the bodies piled up and Singh's grasp on the task loosened, it soon became clear to her that Sam wasn't the enemy. Having dedicated her life to the law, she could never condone his actions.

But he did save four young girls from a life of sex slavery, along with bringing down yet another criminal empire.

That wasn't the act of a criminal.

Singh threw back the coffee like it was a shot of tequila and poured herself another. At three o'clock that afternoon, she would be there as Sam received his sentence and she was sure he would do it without fear.

Without a hint of regret.

She knew she wouldn't feel the same.

As she got dressed into a smart, well-fitted, dark grey

suit and crisp, white shirt, she kept thinking back to ten nights before. Having watched as an innocent man, Helal Miah, had been hanged in his own home, she'd been attacked.

Taken as bait.

Used as leverage against Sam.

There were a number of reasons why that could have been, and Singh allowed herself to speculate that it was because she meant something to Sam. Their attraction had grown ever since Sam had evaded her at Etheridge's house six months before, and it escalated to a passionate kiss in a lift at Liverpool Street. Moments later, Sam was brutally attacked by the very man who would take her hostage.

She wanted to believe that she was taken because Wallace knew how Sam felt about her.

But the crushing reality she'd accepted is that Wallace took her because he knew Sam would do the right thing. As much as it hurt, she couldn't help but admire it.

It was why she felt so guilty.

After the showdown between Sam and her captor atop the High Rise, she tried her hardest to help Sam to his feet, to help him escape. He had suffered serious injuries, with his back bleeding profusely, but she urged him to move. He didn't.

The fight was over.

As the police had surrounded the building, trapping them in, Sam had dropped to his knees, offering Singh the only way out of the situation that wouldn't see them both behind bars. While the thought of Sam living the rest of his life in prison broke her heart, they both knew that a high-ranking detective thrown into prison was a lamb to slaughter.

Sam pleaded with her to arrest him.

Bleeding, beaten, and with his life over, Sam was still fighting for the right thing.

The kiss they'd shared had stayed with her since the passion and sadness that'd passed between them had produced a permanent crack in her heart. While she'd never entertained the idea of settling down, the thought of not being able to have a future with Sam was one that would hurt her until her dying day.

She would watch him proudly walk away once he was sentenced, knowing he was doing it to keep her out of jail.

It may not have been love, but it was certainly something.

Singh tried to distract herself once she got into her car, the feeling of not having a Blackridge tail for the first time in six months felt a little alien, and she still shot the odd cursory glance into the rear-view mirror just to be sure.

There was no one there.

An April shower was sprinkling the road ahead as she pulled out of Canon's Park, through Edgware, and joined the M1. She headed north for one junction, before turning off at Watford and making her way around the outskirts of the town before joining the M25. The orbital motorway was one of the busiest in the country, circling the entire capital city, and was the bane of most commuters' lives. At half ten on a Wednesday, it was relatively clear, and she pressed her foot down, her Audi A4 Sport zipping past the more cautious drivers. The rain clattered against her car, the black paint shimmering under the rain drops and the sun that was mockingly slicing through the downpour. Just over an hour later, she turned off and passed the sign welcoming her to Farnham and ten minutes after that, she pulled up outside the large gate that shielded the large home from the road.

Paul Etheridge's house.

Singh didn't know why she'd driven there and told Etheridge as much when he answered the door. Despite her confusion, Etheridge had welcomed her in with a smile and led her through to his kitchen. Six months before, the house had been overly opulent, with the millionaire tech mogul living the lavish lifestyle his salary could dictate. Singh recalled sending an Armed Response Unit in to extract Sam, only to hear the gunfire and later find her team incapacitated.

Sam had never shot to kill.

Each of his shots had been pinpoint to the legs of her team, and although they all suffered immense pain, none of them experienced anything other than flesh wounds.

The shots were meticulous.

Innocent people didn't suffer at the hands of Sam Pope.

Not directly, anyway.

Etheridge could attest to that. A few weeks after Sam had disappeared to Europe, Singh had sought his help, along with her then trusted ally, DI Adrian Pearce. They had found Etheridge beaten, tortured, and losing blood. While they'd saved his life, Singh knew that Etheridge's ordeal was due to his links to Sam.

A man in black.

The same description Aaron Hill had given after he'd been threatened by the man hoping to find Sam.

Whoever the man was, he was dangerous, and Singh had wondered if the brutish Farukh, whom she'd helped Sam fight, was the man beneath the balaclava.

She wondered.

She hoped.

Since that night, Etheridge seemed to have changed. While he walked with a limp, he walked with purpose. His previously chubby physique had been trimmed down. The house, once perverse in its expensive tastes, was now threadbare.

There was no sign of his wife.

No sign of anything.

24

The metal brace that wrapped around Etheridge's knee would most likely be permanent; the bullet that was fired point blank into his kneecap had shattered the bone beyond repair. While Etheridge had the resources to ensure his life was always comfortable, he would be permanently disabled by the injury.

Innocent people didn't suffer at the hands of Sam Pope.

Not directly.

Now, as she sat on the same patio where she'd first encountered Sam, she listened as the rain clattered against the roof of the gazebo that was protecting them from the water but not the chill of the wind. Etheridge meandered through the open glass door, two bottles of beer in his hand and a smile on his face.

'Here you go.'

He handed a bottle to Singh with a smile. His original offer of a tea or coffee had been rebuked. Singh's mind was on the trial that afternoon and she needed something stronger. As he handed her the cold beer, she wondered if her reliance on alcohol was becoming a problem.

'Thanks,' she said meekly, taking the bottle and imme-diately lifting it to her lips. Etheridge lowered himself down onto the step next to her with a grunt and held his bottle out.

'To Sam.'

Singh nodded and clinked the bottle and both of them took a swig. The wind picked up, rustling through the over-grown garden and the sad silence that sat between them. Etheridge took another sip of his beer before speaking.

'I never got to thank you for saving my life.' He shook his head. 'If you guys hadn't found me, I'd have bled out.'

'Don't mention it,' Singh said, almost embarrassed. 'I guess you returned the favour, huh?'

'How so?'

'You helped Sam, right? When I got taken by Wallace.'

'I just sat here and ran surveillance. It was Sam who saved you,' Etheridge said humbly. 'Sam and Pearce.'

'Pearce?' Singh exclaimed, her eyebrows raised.

'Did you not know that?'

'Pearce went behind my back to Ashton and had me suspended. Told me it was for my own good or some bullshit like that.'

Etheridge chuckled, shaking his head.

'You know, when Sam came back, he went to see Pearce. Thanked him for saving me and what not. Do you know what Pearce told him? He told Sam to keep you out of it, that you had a career and a life that was going places. And then, when you were taken, Sam leant on Pearce to help get you back.'

'What do you mean?' Singh could feel the guilt building up inside her, threatening to break through in one of her rare and hated displays of weakness.

'Who do you think drove the car after the ambush?' Etheridge shrugged and looked at his knee. 'Sure as hell wasn't me.'

Singh felt sick.

Her burgeoning friendship with Pearce had been one of the few shining lights during her entire ordeal with Sam, but she'd cut him off due to his apparent treachery. To hear that he'd risked his own career, even his life, to help Sam save her hit her like a sledgehammer to the gut.

Pearce had recently retired, quietly making his way out through the backdoor after a distinguished career as one of the good guys. She'd treated him with such contempt.

But he'd done it all for her.

To keep her safe.

Singh raised her hand to her eye and dabbed away a tear. Etheridge awkwardly reached out and rested a hand on her shoulder. While he had an effortless charm a crying woman had always been one of his biggest fears.

'Hey, don't beat yourself up about it.'

'I was so horrible to him.'

'The guy spent thirty years on the force, many of those investigating his own colleagues. I'm pretty sure he's heard worse.' Etheridge offered her a smile.

Singh took a deep breath and composed herself. She cursed herself for getting upset.

'How the hell did we get here?'

'I'm pretty sure you drove, didn't you?'

Singh chuckled. Etheridge was a good man, and there was something about him that made her feel safe.

He was one of the good guys.

The world could use more of them, especially as one had recently stepped away from his career and the other was facing life behind bars.

'My whole career, I was so hellbent on being the best. I was top of my class in everything I did, and I had a very firm grip on what was right and what was wrong.' Singh stared out into the downpour as she spoke. 'But then I was tasked with bringing Sam in, to stop a violent vigilante from haunting the city. But the further I delved the blurrier things got.'

'Sam can do that to you.' Etheridge scoffed. 'The prick.'

Singh smiled again.

'It just doesn't feel right, you know? What Sam did, taking the law into his own hands, is wrong. But what he was doing it for...I don't know. I guess sometimes people do bad things for the right reasons.'

'I'll drink to that.'

Etheridge and Singh clinked their bottles once more and took their final swigs. Singh placed her empty bottle on the cold, concrete step and stood up, dusting off her trousers.

'Do you need a lift to the trial?' She offered, looking back into the house.

'I'm not going.'

'What?' Singh's eyes snapped back to Etheridge who understandably, hadn't attempted to get up. 'Sam needs our support.'

'I can't go. You're the only person who knows I still live here. As far as the Met and the government are concerned, I sold up and moved abroad after my divorce. A way to deal with the heartbreak and the trauma I was put through. If I turn up at the trial, I'll get nabbed. You and I both know they're investigating who helped Sam.'

'So you're hiding?'

'Yup,' Etheridge replied proudly. 'Because that's what's needed right now.'

Singh shook her head in disappointment and headed back towards the door. As she was about to step back into the sparce kitchen area of the house, she turned back to Etheridge, who was staring out over the garden. The rain and wind were dancing in unison through the overgrowth.

'What Sam needs right now is our support. He sacrificed everything to help those who needed it. I know you have your reasons, Paul, but Sam is going to prison for the rest of his life. The least we can do is be there. What else can we do?'

Etheridge sighed and turned to face her.

'There's always a plan, Singh.' He turned back to look out over the garden. 'There is *always* a plan.'

Singh pondered for a moment, with Etheridge's cryptic response sending a bolt of uncertainty shooting through her body like lightning. She opened her mouth to respond but thought better of it. In her eyes, Etheridge was hiding from his responsibility and it hurt her to second guess him.

With a resounding feeling of defeat, she walked back through the house and out through the front door. As she headed towards her car, the rain crashed against her, chilling her to the bone.

With a sense of dread, she hopped into her car, pulled away from the curb, and headed back to London.

———

With a degree of frustration, Assistant Commissioner Ruth Ashton grappled with her cravat. The black and white chequered garment was a part of her tunic, which she was required to wear on court visits. As one of the most senior and powerful officers within the Met, she knew she needed to look pristine for the photographers who would be swarming around the crown court like vermin.

She hated the press, especially after they'd assassinated Wallace's credibility in the aftermath of his death.

But it was all part of the job and she needed to look as in control and as professional as possible on what was the biggest day of her career.

Despite the detail behind Sam's capture, and the irrefutable evidence that Wallace wasn't who he seemed, she'd still been tasked with bringing the vigilante to justice.

She'd succeeded.

While the news outlets had painted Singh as the super-star who finally absolved the city of Sam Pope, the higher ups were quick to slap her on the back for the part she'd played.

Her ascension to the top job in the Met was somewhat of a formality.

But now, as she struggled with her neckwear, she felt nothing but disgust.

The sound of knuckles rapping on her door broke her concentration and she turned in frustration. Just as she was about to launch a venomous tirade at her intruder, the door opened and she stood to attention, her cravat flopping lifelessly around her shirt.

Commissioner Michael Stout stepped in.

Carrying himself with the assuredness that came with power, he was dressed immaculately. His grey hair was neatly combed to the side, still thick despite approaching his sixtieth birthday. While not a tall man, he cut an imposing figure, his broad shoulders were straight, and he walked with the posture and physical fitness of a man half his age. Commissioner Stout had a distinguished career, from his glory days as a tough bastard on the beat to his phenomenal grasp of office politics.

Many had tried, but nobody had been able to stop his rise to the top of the Met Police, and although he had an air of arrogance from the power he wielded, he commanded respect from every room he entered.

'Ruth.' He greeted her with a firm handshake.

'Sir.'

'Today is a big day,' he began, immediately taking his gaze away from her to study the framed achievements that hung from the wall of her New Scotland Yard office. It was a tried and trusted tactic of his, to make the person work for his attention.

'A great day.' She corrected, before scorning herself immediately.

'Quite.' He shot her a look. 'I'm not here to heap praise on you for a job well done, as I feel that goes without saying. Getting Sam off our streets was our number one priority and you delivered, albeit with significant collateral damage.'

Ashton felt a twinge of sadness. Wallace, despite what had come to light, had been killed and her affection for the man had seen her end up in his bed occasionally.

'A regrettable necessity,' she said, forcing herself to stay as stoic as possible. 'But we do not deal with failure, sir.'

'I must say, I have been alarmed by the information that has been made public over the last two weeks. It would seem that perhaps Sam wasn't the biggest threat to this country's safety.'

Ashton knew where he was going but refused to rise to the comment. She waited patiently for him to continue, as he slowly patrolled the office.

'I'll cut the bullshit, Ruth.' His candour surprised her. 'General Wallace endorsed you to take my seat a few days before he was killed. Now, what with the recent revelations about the man, there have been murmurings about whether his word carries any merit. The last thing we need, Ruth, is another scandal. Last year, it was Howell. I need to know, right now, whether there is anything about your relationship with Wallace that could harm this organisation.'

A trickle of sweat ran down the back of Ashton's neck and she willed herself to show no emotion. Although acting wasn't her strongest asset, she gave a quick thought and then shook her head.

'No, sir,' she replied. 'He had a keen interest in the Sam Pope task force and seemed pleased with the progress we made. His interest is now apparent, but it shouldn't detract from the sublime work of my team.'

Stout regarded her with a ferocious stare, searching for any hint of hesitancy. Seemingly pleased, he nodded.

'Good. Because I echo his sentiments.'

'Sir?'

The Commissioner gave a deep sigh and rubbed the bridge of his nose with his gloved hands.

'I've been doing this too long, Ruth. There comes a time when every leader has to take stock and decide whether it's time to hand over the reins.'

Ashton could feel her legs begin to shake with excitement.

'I think you've done a sterling job leading this organisation through tough times. I've been proud to serve under you.'

'Well, I'm not out of the door just yet. But the ball is rolling, and I shall be retiring in two months. The idea of spending this summer worrying about the world was the straw that broke the camel's back. No, now that the kids are settling down, Cathy and I have decided the time is right to enjoy our twilight years without the stress and the long hours.'

Ashton nodded politely, caring little for the Commissioner's home life. He hadn't seemed to notice, and his candour had caught her a little off guard.

'It will be announced within the next week or so. Make sure you're ready for the call. I'm sure you will make a fine Commissioner, Ruth. But a word to the wise, whatever rumours are flying around about DI Singh, extinguish them. The powers that be want her front and centre. In their mind, you've mentored her and she has fast become a beacon of light for this place.'

As Commissioner Stout headed towards the door, Ashton felt her fist clench in frustration. Despite bringing Sam to justice, Ashton didn't trust Singh at all. There was undeniable proof that she'd aided and abetted the man on his mission, one which had claimed the life of the man she'd potentially loved.

But the greater good was at stake and she knew Stout was right. If she wanted to sit in his throne, she needed to play the game just as well as he did.

Personal preference was not a route she could take, nor could she allow her feelings to override her thought process.

Singh was a valuable commodity.

If she couldn't remove her from the equation, she could at least exploit her.

'In less than two hours time, Sam Pope will be on his way to his retirement home in Pentonville.' Stout smiled at his attempt at a joke. 'Make the most of this opportunity.'

'Yes, sir.'

'And for Christ's sake, sort out your cravat.'

Stout exited the room and Ashton dropped into her comfortable, leather seat. Her exasperation at the conversation threatened to overwhelm her. The past few weeks had been the most trying of her life and having to mourn a man who had been accused of such villainous treachery had almost broken her.

But she'd made it through to the other side.

One that would see her finally take the top chair at the table and become the Commissioner of the Metropolitan Police. After taking a moment to recollect herself, Ashton stood, approached the mirror that was affixed to the wall, and began tackling her cravat once more, doing her level best to stop the smile that was spreading across her face.

CHAPTER FOUR

With the spring showers clearing just in time for the afternoon's attraction, the sun bathed the Crown Court Southwark in a glorious beam of light. The large, beige building stood on the south bank of the famous River Thames and was made up of over fifteen separate court rooms. While numerous magistrate's courts were dotted across the capital, the proud building was only one of three crown courts still functioning within the city.

It took a serious offence to wind up on trial within the confines of the building, and the deluge of press vehicles stationed around the front of the building was testament to the severity of Sam's case.

While the country had been gripped by his arrest ten days before, there had almost been a sense of betrayal in his guilty plea.

The papers wanted the 'trial of the century', for a man who had been painted as both hero and villain to have his story told in painstaking detail. Here was a man who had suffered untold heartache, who due to his own sense on injustice, had used his deadly skills to clean up the streets of London. While a number of publications did their best to stay impartial, they all ended up swaying one side or another.

Many vilified him for his actions, despite the people he'd saved and the criminals he'd brought to justice. It went against the very fabric of the country he'd sworn to protect and while his intentions may have been noble; they were also murderous.

Others portrayed Sam as a hero for the people, hunting down the criminal underworld that had plagued the city. The unravelling of police corruption, sex trafficking, and even global terrorism proved this.

The trial would have stepped through his life in meticulous detail and journalists and editors alike were rubbing their hands at the word counts and potential pay hikes. Some even callously played upon the hideous murder of Helal Miah, who had died in the midst of bringing Sam's fight to life. He had been found beaten and hanged in his apartment, killed by a barbaric terrorist who had been hired by the now disbanded Blackridge.

They had martyred him, using his name as almost a badge of honour for how dangerous their profession was and that the world needed to know the truth about Sam Pope, lest his death be in vain.

It had turned Singh's stomach, as she'd been the one who had brought Miah into the chain of events that had eventually ended in his untimely death.

The whole situation made her feel sick.

As she walked around the corner and stepped onto Battlebridge Lane, she saw the impressive building, the sun shimmering off the large, glass windows. She'd been here before, displayed on the stand to recount the events of an arrest where she'd put a serial rapist behind bars. As the defence attorney had tried to assassinate her character in front of the jury, she'd felt a rising contempt for those who do their best to keep the scum out of jail.

She'd never condoned Sam's actions, but she knew he didn't belong with them.

Back then, Singh had worn her police tunic with immense pride, whereas today, she'd settled on just a suit. While she still protected the city with the same ferocity as before, her pursuit of Sam had caused the lines to blur.

Possibly for good.

As she watched the herd of reporters swarming anyone who approached the building, she stopped and looked up to the sky. The English weather always held the fate of the day in its untrustworthy grip but the rain that had fallen earlier that afternoon had since vanished. It drew a smile from her, as she was happy for the small mercy.

She was still angered by her trip to see Etheridge.

While he'd undoubtedly played a part in saving her life, his refusal to show any support to Sam before he was sent down didn't sit right with her.

As did his final remark.

'There is always a plan.'

Singh had become a damn fine detective due to her curiosity and having something as vague as that dangled before her was already eating away at her. There was no plan.

How could there be?

Sam had been beaten to within an inch of his life and was now awaiting a life sentence. There was no plan.

There was no way back.

'Lovely day for a sentencing, eh?'

The familiar voice broke Singh's concentration and she spun on her heel to come face to face with the warm smile of Adrian Pearce. The retired detective was as casual as she'd ever seen, with his usual resplendent suit replaced with a shirt, chinos, and shoes. He had a jacket slung over his shoulder, the warm breeze removing its necessity. A flurry of thoughts and feelings raced through her body like a shot of adrenaline and she tried her best to wrestle back control. She'd been adamant that Pearce had betrayed her when Sam disappeared to Europe, only to discover today that he'd tried to save her.

With his final act as a member of the Metropolitan Police, Pearce had helped Sam stage a dangerous assault on Wallace's motorcade and sent the police to bring her back.

It may have seen Sam leave in cuffs, but he'd done it to save her.

Without thinking any further, Singh flung her arms around Pearce's shoulders and pressed herself against his solid frame. For a man in his fifties, Pearce had always kept fit and he took the brunt of her weight without shifting, before embracing her in their mournful hug. They stood for a few moments, their sadness for Sam and their reborn bond tightening their embrace.

'I'm so sorry, Pearce,' Singh eventually said as she pulled back, trying hard to mask the tear forming in the corner of her eye.

'You don't have to apologise,' Pearce said warmly, reaching up and wiping it away. 'And please, just call me Adrian.'

'Adrian?' Singh scrunched her face. 'That sounds weird.'

'You can blame my mother.' Pearce looked over to the mob of reporters, haranguing anyone who dared step foot near the court. 'I see the cockroaches are back.'

'I know. It's a shame we can't move them on.'

'Well, I couldn't even if I wanted to.'

'How's retirement?' Singh asked, her eyes still locked on the mob at the end of the road.

'Different. But I guess anything would be. It's not like the last year is something you would get used to.'

They stood in silence for a few moments, their attention drawn to a black Mercedes which rolled past them, the windows tinted black. Behind, a police car followed. They watched as it slowed to a stop in front of the building, the press swarming like a horde of zombies. To a burst of flash photography and a litany of boom mics, the driver stepped out, rudely shepherding the intrusion to the side before pulling open the door.

Assistant Commissioner Ruth Ashton stepped out.

A smile, as smug as a Cheshire cat, was across her face, which she'd accentuated with make-up. Singh had never seen the woman wear anything more than a flick of mascara, but with her impending promotion to the top seat rumoured, she was certainly ready for her moment in the spotlight. Out of ear shot, they both watched as Ashton gave a few rehearsed words to the eager journalists, no doubt commending Singh herself for bringing Sam in.

But Ashton would be sure that they knew it had been on her watch.

This was her moment.

For all the good Ashton had done in a stellar career, her movements behind the scenes had been just as important. Her fine police work had always felt arbitrary to her desire to climb the ladder, and it boiled Singh's blood that she was being lauded as a hero on the same day Sam would be convicted as a dangerous criminal.

What made it even worse was Singh would have to face the same questions and despite her resentment, she'd have to tow the same line.

It was almost as if Pearce could read her thoughts.

'Come on, superstar. Let's get this over with.'

Pearce chivalrously offered his arm, drawing a smile from Singh which relaxed her. She graciously turned it down, straightened her back, let out a deep breath, and marched towards the excited crowd ahead, with Pearce following behind her.

The inside of the courtroom was eerily quiet. Despite the maximum capacity, everyone was waiting with bated breath. Running down the side of the room was a portioned off section, with the seats behind the wooden fence filled with eager journalists, all of them prepping for their biggest scoop of the year. On the other side of the room, where the jury would have been seated, Ashton took her seat along with a number of other high-ranking officials. Many of them were there to witness her crowning moment. Others were there on behalf of the military, eager to ensure that General Wallace's killer was brought to justice, despite the overwhelming evidence.

Singh had been ordered by Ashton to sit among them, wanting the world to see that they'd worked in tandem and that she, as the papers had stated, was her protégé. The idea had made her skin crawl, but she towed the line.

Sam had sacrificed his freedom for her. She wouldn't allow him to go to prison for her to then throw it away.

In the far corner, a small, seated section had been reserved for the public and she noticed Pearce had managed to squeeze through, and he sat calmly, his eyes wandering around the grand chambers.

In the middle of the room, the prosecution team were foraging through their paperwork, their white wigs attached firmly to their heads and cascading down the back of their necks in ridiculous curls.

The traditional attire had always caused Singh an element of amusement and there had been times where she'd had to stifle a smirk when addressed by a bloodthirsty defence advocate.

But today, the levity of their outfits had no effect on her.

A large, oak desk sat atop an elevated platform at the

front of the court room, with an empty leather chair sat behind it like a throne. It would grant the judge a clear view of the entire room, and its current vacancy only heightened the tension. To the side was the witness stand, sectioned off with a thin, wooden partition that wasn't required for today's case.

Just in front of Singh, a middle-aged woman sat, her fingers gently gliding over the keys of her stenographer like a concert pianist.

At the far end of the room, a balcony hung, framed with plexiglass. Sam would be led into the room through the door behind it, put on show for the world to see like a dangerous animal at the zoo. With his plea of guilty, there was no need for any representation and Singh was sure that he would take his sentence with dignity.

As the tension in the room began to reach boiling point, the large clock on the wall struck three, and the court officer's booming voice shook the room. He demanded silence and for the room to rise in respect for the judge. Instantly, the door to the judge's chamber opened, the honourable Judge Alan Barnes made his entrance, the court room obliging him as they stood. While his position commanded the silence of the room, his stature did not. Short and portly, he shuffled towards the large chair, slightly dipping his head so he could peer out over the top of his frameless glasses. All eyes were locked on him and he did his best to return the gaze with authority. He lowered himself into his chair, grunting as he landed, and he made a show of shuffling the documents before him.

Every movement felt like it took forever and seemingly pleased to begin, Judge Barnes peered over his spectacles once more and deliberately cleared his throat.

'Court is now in session. Please, bring in the accused.'

CHAPTER FIVE

'But I didn't do anything.'

Jamie's protests of innocence were bordering on laughable and Sam had always struggled when it came to disciplining his son. Despite his regimented, military upbringing, and legendary career within the armed forces, there was still something about a child's naïve understanding of the world that melted his heart. There had been countless times when Sam had needed to mask a grin or stifle a chuckle, because giving a child an inch would mean you were already miles behind.

'Look, Jamie,' Sam said, forcing the sternness to his words. 'Your mum told you not to go out the front when neither of us are with you and you didn't listen. That's wrong isn't it?'

Jamie's eyes were red from tears, the tantrum of being marched to his room may have faded but Sam knew they were walking a tightrope. Lucy, his loving wife, was downstairs in the living room, her headset affixed to her head and her laptop rested on her lap. Her career as a Marketing Manager meant an awful lot to her, but she'd negotiated two days a week where she worked from home, even when Sam was there. All that would change once Sam began his training to join the Metropolitan Police, but that wasn't happening for a few more weeks.

For now, Sam was playing the parent and he knew he couldn't let his wife down.

By proxy, he would let his son down, too. While Sam idolised his son, Jamie had broken a clear rule set by his parents.

Sam appreciated the sanctity of orders, even if he had broken one or two in the heat of the moment.

It had saved lives.

But now, Sam waited a few more moments before asking again.

'That's wrong, isn't it?'

Jamie was lying face down on his bed, the frame of which was built to look like a race car. His blonde hair, which flopped over his forehead, was splayed out across the pillow, while the rest of his body was outstretched like a starfish. The room was strangely neat for a five-year-old, and Sam commended Lucy for installing a neat and tidy attitude within their son. As Sam looked around the room, he finally settled on the growing number of books on the bookcase.

Jamie loved to read.

It was a love Sam had begun sharing with his son and one which Sam had neglected for years. He had always been so focused on his military career, that spending time losing himself in other adventures seemed moot.

But watching his son devour page after page, Sam had decided to show a keen interest in the written word. When he'd asked his son for a recommendation, his son made him promise to read more.

Sam had agreed.

His son had also made him promise to not kill anyone ever again.

Back then, it had been an easy promise for Sam to make.

Eventually, Jamie pushed himself up from his mattress, rubbed his blue eyes, and stared at Sam.

'I was just trying to help.'

Sam stepped into the room; his brow furrowed in confusion.

'Help? What do you mean?'

'I was trying to help the bird.'

Jamie glanced towards the window of his bedroom, and Sam walked across and peered out. On the grass verge outside their house, the carcass of a small bird was buried among a pile of feathers and blood. A cat was pawing at it, approaching the end of its attack.

Sam felt his heart sink.

While he'd been tasked with setting his son straight, he couldn't help but feel an overwhelming sense of pride. A defenceless animal had been set upon by a bigger, bloodthirsty attacker and Jamie had broken the strict rules of the house to try to come to its aid. Guilt hung from Sam's neck like a lead chain and he pulled the curtains together to protect his son from the sight.

'Well, it looks like it worked.'

'It did?' Jamie's eyes lit up and his shoulders straightened. Sam stepped forward and ruffled his son's hair.

'It sure did, kiddo. That bird has flown away. It's probably gone home.'

'Birds don't live in a home.' Jamie giggled. 'They live in a nest.'

'Is it as big as our nest?'

Sam reached out, grabbing Jamie under the arms and began tickling, his son contorting in a fit of laughter. It echoed downstairs, and Sam knew he would have some convincing to do regarding his disciplinary technique. But as his son laughed and cuddled into him, Sam didn't care.

After a few more moments, Sam stopped, stood, and walked to the door.

'I'll go and tell Mum that you are sorry, but how about you come down and tell her too?'

Jamie smiled.

'Okay, Dad.'

'Good lad. Love you.'

'Love you too.' The words sent a jolt of happiness through Sam.

'Dad, is it really wrong to do the wrong thing if it's helping?'

Sam took a moment, carefully considering his next words. He looked down at the hopeful expression on his son's face and smiled.

'You should always do the right thing.' Sam nodded. 'But if you break the rules, you need to be ready to face the consequences.'

Sam believed every word of it, gave his son a playful wink, and *then hurried downstairs to remove the body of the bird and to save his son from crushing disappointment.*

If Sam had known that just a few months later, his son would be killed, he would have reached out, held him tight, and never let him go.

———

Sam shook away his treasured memory of his son as the door to his holding cell creaked open. The court officer, a broad man with thinning dark hair grunted at him.

It was time.

Taking a deep breath, Sam stood and obligingly held his hands out, wrists placed together. The officer stepped in, flanked by another, and he roughly secured the handcuffs, jolting them needlessly and sneering at Sam. Without breaking his stare, or even twitching in pain, Sam smiled at the man, nodded, and then headed to the door. The other officer, who didn't offer nearly as much attitude, tried to hide his smile at Sam's response. The other officer shoved Sam in the back.

'Keep moving.'

Sam refused to respond. He knew that there were a number of police officers who despised him for his actions, taking his betrayal of law enforcement as a personal attack on their loyalty. He understood and respected it. While he wasn't ashamed of his actions, he knew there would be eventual consequences and he planned on facing them head on.

He had been brought from his cell at West Hampstead Police Station to Crown Court Southwark in an armoured van, flanked by a police motorcade. While he had no visibility of the streets as they passed them, he'd been sure that it would have attracted attention. From the kinder officers at the station, he'd been informed that he'd become a celebrity, and that his impending sentencing was headline news.

It had disappointed Sam that his capture, and the bizarre cult of celebrity that had consumed the country was seen as more important than the truth about General Wallace and his vile acts of terrorism.

It was why he'd been needed.

To set the world straight.

As he approached the door to the courtroom, the antagonistic officer reached out and gripped his shoulder, making the extra effort to dig his nails in. They crunched down into Sam's skin, pressing his navy jumpsuit tight against the skin and Sam felt a sharp pain in his shoulder.

A few months earlier, it had been shattered by a bullet. This was nothing but a lame attempt of intimidation.

'Time to face the music, you prick,' the officer whispered, as the door opened and Sam was led through.

The entire courtroom fell into an eerie silence and Sam felt the eyes of everyone zoom in on him as he stepped through into the glass balcony that overlooked the courtroom. Transfixed, journalists began to write in their pads, no doubt jotting down the bruises that covered his face and the bandage around his broken hand. Sam looked across to the section where the public were seated, locking eyes with Assistant Commissioner Ashton who shook her head in disgust.

A man in a suit leant over and whispered in her ear, no doubt congratulating her. She nodded her head and diverted her gaze.

Sam saw Singh. Her eyes were red, the sadness of his situation hanging over her like a rain cloud and he offered her a gentle nod of the head. A reassurance that he was fine.

Then Sam saw Pearce. The retired detective offered him a respectful nod and Sam felt the corners of his mouth twitch as he fought against the smile. Throughout his entire fight, Sam had come to view the ex-detective as a friend, and his show of support meant more to him than Pearce would ever know.

As the circus of his sentencing began, the judge demanded order, declaring that he is control of the courtroom and despite the heightened interest in the case, he wouldn't tolerate it becoming a sideshow. Sam was impressed by the commanding tone of his voice, despite it being undercut slightly by the man's puny frame and ridiculous attire.

Without delay, the judge opened the sentencing by explaining to his audience that as Sam had already pleaded guilty to numerous crimes, there was no jury nor trial taking place. Sam wouldn't be represented by a defence team, as he'd waived his right to council. Once the formalities of the understanding were agreed by the prosecution, the judge began to run through the crime sheet.

Despite his wishes for the session to be treated as a normal sentencing, it didn't take Judge Barnes long to realise opportunity. With the cameras rolling and the press at the ready, the judge dramatically walked the courtroom with Sam Pope's story. The two men killed in Amy Devereux's flat. Another killed within the archive office of the New Scotland Yard building, a place where Sam had once served the city of London.

The criminals found dead at the late, disgraced Inspector Howell's home. His daring raid of the High Rise, which claimed the lives of multiple criminals, along with Frank Jackson.

The death of Detective Sergeant Colin Mayer.

The continued fight against the High Rise operation leading to the death of Elmore Riggs and his crew, along with the brutal torture and disfigurement of the leader of the notorious 'Acid Gang'.

Multiple deaths at the Port of Tilbury, where despite Sam's brave efforts in saving Jasmine Hill and three other young girls from sex slavery, had claimed the lives of Andrei Kovalenko and his brother, Oleg.

While there were multiple incidents in Ukraine, Berlin, and Rome which had been linked to Sam, they were not being brought against him today.

With each stage of the story, Sam could feel the anger emanating from the police presence in the room. It wasn't due to his laundry list of crimes.

It was because he'd been more effective than they had. His methods, while illegal, had brought down two of the most dangerous criminal empires in the country and having it laid out, eagerly lapped up by journalists, only exacerbated their resentment.

The judge continued.

Sam's re-emergence at Liverpool Street Station less than two weeks ago which had seen three people taken to hospital as well as the shutting of one of the city's busiest transport networks.

An attack on a government issued motorcade, where he'd killed several men in his abduction of General Wallace.

Sam flicked a glance towards Ashton, whose lip tightened and fists clenched.

The judge finally brought his grand story to a close, wrapping it up with the death of a known terrorist, Farukh Ahmad, along with the death of Wallace, which the judge made a point of stating that Sam had not pleaded guilty for.

That, nor the death of Sergeant Carl Marsden or the hideous murder of Helal Miah.

The mention of Miah's name seemed to cause a chill in the room, as his fellow journalists mourned a peer who had died in the name of unravelling a conspiracy. Since his unfortunate murder, *The Pulse* had honoured his memory by printing the story Miah had given his life for, the proof coming in the form of an anonymous recording of Wallace confessing to his crimes.

While Miah may have died, and Wallace may not be around to face the music, the world knew what he truly was.

A monster.

It was the end of the fight, and Sam knew his freedom was a small price to pay to avenge the death of his mentor and expose the man who had left him for dead all those years ago.

Judge Barnes took a moment, sipping from a glass of water, and allowing his articulate story to resonate in the room. While the journalists furiously scribbled on pads, and a number of people stared at Sam in disbelief, the gravity of Sam's actions seemed to have shaken the room.

'Samuel William Pope, please stand.'

The judge's voice echoed through the courtroom and a hush of excitement followed. Sam obliged, standing at once, his shoulders straight, his chin up.

Like a soldier.

'You have pled guilty to the crimes I have just relayed to the courtroom. Is this true?'

'Yes, your Honour.'

Another murmuring of excitement followed at Sam speaking, as if this mythical figure had been made flesh and blood. Sam kept his eyes locked on the judge, who seemed to respect the dignity of the man he was sentencing.

'Before I make the sentence final, do you have anything you would like to say?'

This was it. The moment the entire courtroom had been waiting for and the silence swept across the room like

48

a crashing wave. All heads turned to the box where Sam stood.

'Yes, your Honour.' Sam replied, before readjusting his stance. 'I'm under no illusion that what I did carries a severe penalty. My actions were against the law and I accept that fact and the sentence you're about to give me. I have forfeited my freedom for what I believe was necessity. The criminals responsible for bombing this city, the police officers who helped them. They are gone because of me. Four young girls, and no doubt, countless more have been saved from a life of sex slavery. General Wallace, a man who is wrongly revered by a number of people in this room, had been exposed as one of the most dangerous men this country has ever known.'

From the corner of his eye, he saw Ashton shuffle uncomfortably in her seat. He ignored it and continued.

'While I regret that my actions broke the law, I regret even more that they were needed. So I apologise to those who I've hurt, to those whose lives I changed. To my ex-wife, an incredible woman who fought for me when I wouldn't. And to my son, who I wish every single day I could see and who would have asked me not to do it.'

Sam paused, taking a deep breath as the thought of his broken promise threatened to crack his voice. He recomposed.

'I apologise to everyone in this room that we live in a world where what I've done was necessary. But I do not regret, for one second, that I did.'

Sam's words were met with an uneasy silence, as everyone returned their gaze to the judge who surprisingly, offered a warm smile.

'Mr Pope, while your actions were indefensible, I do admit that your intentions were indeed noble. Before this, I also note that you served your country with dignity and valour. But as you said, you have pled guilty to a number

49

of serious crimes and a lot of blood has been shed by your hand. It is with a modicum of regret, that I hereby sentence you to sixty-eight years at Her Majesty's Prison Pentonville, with no chance of parole.'

Judge Barnes emphasised his point with a stern nod of his head.

'This court is adjourned.'

The court officer demanded everyone rise as the judge exited through the door to his chamber, and all eyes turned to Sam as he was led towards the door. As he approached it, he stopped, as did the officers, as a peculiar sound filled the air.

Clapping.

Sam turned back to see Adrian Pearce on his feet, applauding. Despite the furious gaze of the Assistant Commissioner, another member of the public joined in, followed by another, and within moments, nearly the entire courtroom, along with a multitude of journalists, were clapping.

Sam felt a lump in his throat but refused to let himself break. The recognition of the public hit him like a hammer and he offered Pearce a final nod, threw one final, regrettable glance at Singh and ventured through the door where the thunderous sound of applause echoed down the corridors of the Crown Court.

Taken aback by the approval of the public, Sam blindly followed the officers through the building, ignoring the jibes of one of them and they stepped out into the spring sunshine at the back of the building.

The respectful sound of applause could still be faintly heard from the street and the thick, windowless, metal doors of the armoured van were thrown open. Two armed officers were sat in the back, ready to accompany Sam to his future residence.

Taking one final look at the city of London, Sam took a deep breath and stepped in.

With his sentencing complete and his freedom taken, Sam sat on the metal bench that ran the length of the van, pressed his head back against the metal, and shut his eyes, ready to face his impending incarceration.

The van pulled away in the opposite direction to Pentonville Prison.

CHAPTER SIX

Ten Years Ago…

'Fuckin, eh. Would you look at that?'

Mac stood, hands on his hips, letting out an impressed huff. Sam chuckled at his friend's foul language, but he couldn't help but agree. The sight of Big Ben, the historic clock that stood over three hundred feet tall, had been a landmark for the capital for over a hundred and fifty years. After six months on tour in Afghanistan, both Sam and Mac had been given a month to return to their families, before they would be required to return.

In those six months, their bond had grown.

Mac had matured into a hell of a spotter before Sam's very eyes, fastidiously making notes on everything Sam said, hanging on his every word. While there were still improvements to be made, Sam knew that he'd found his perfect spotter.

In Sam, Mac had found the mentor he'd always yearned for, a man who was not only approachable and fun to be around, but whom had a wealth of knowledge and skill to back it up.

They had only had to fire once in those six months, with Sam almost causing Mac a mini-panic attack by refusing to pull the trigger on a high-profile target until Mac gave him the correct wind readings.

Sam had already calculated and lined up the perfect shot, but he harried the young man to make an assessment.

Sadly for Mac, it had been incorrect and once Sam had eliminated the target with a well-placed bullet to his temporal lobe, he made sure Mac was aware of it.

All the promise in the world, but Sam wouldn't accept him as a sniper until he could spot.

Mac had beaten himself up about it for a while, but Sam was quick enough to rebuild his confidence and when Mac almost beat Sam in a friendly competition at target practice, he'd felt he'd re-established himself in Sam's eyes.

Sam patted him on the back but told him to stay focused and to keep calm.

Panic will kill him before any bullet does.

When they were on the plane home, Sam was saddened to hear of Mac's lack of plans. Estranged from his family and without a secure group of friends, Mac was planning on renting a room for a month back in Manchester and catching up on some TV. Sam knew all about Mac's rough past, his brushes with the law, but he never held it against him. Everyone is born into a different situation and the fact Mac had risen to one of the most promising soldiers Sam had ever met was a testament to the man he was.

Sam had insisted he spend a week in London.

See the city.

Meet Lucy.

When Mac had seen Sam's house, he'd let out a long whistle. A modest three-bedroomed house in Ruislip, but with Lucy's keen eye for detail, along with their healthy combined income, she'd certainly added value to it. Mac was excited to meet Lucy, having heard Sam wax lyrical about her for six months.

She certainly was worth every word of praise.

Not only was she as kind and personable as Sam had described, she was absolutely stunning.

Another part of Sam's life that Mac aspired for and the three of them had spent the evening sat out on the patio, with Lucy enthralling Mac with embarrassing stories of his mentor over drinks. Under the patio lights, they'd laughed until the early hours.

Lucy had been up early to go to work, her job as a high school deputy head teacher kept her extremely busy and fulfilled. Sam had suggested taking a trip into the city once Mac had admitted he'd never been and as they rode the Metropolitan Line from Ruislip Manor all the way to Euston Square, Mac had stared out of the window in a trance.

Although part of the London Underground, the Met Line didn't actual head beneath the surface until it had passed Finchley Road, giving Mac a wonderful view of Wembley Stadium as they approached Wembley Park Station. As a big Manchester United fan, he'd seen his team win multiple trophies at the storied ground but seeing the famous arch soaring proudly into the sky took his breath away.

But now, stood on Parliament Street, surrounded by an army of gawping tourists, Big Ben had much the same effect. The magnificent clock face was shimmering in the sunlight, the rays bouncing off the glass. Sam looked at his friend and smiled. It was nice to see him relaxed as he was always so intense while on tour. Sam understood.

Mac wanted to be the best.

Sam was more than willing to help him get there.

As they stood for a few moments, allowing a group of young tourists by, Mac eventually turned to his mentor.

'Thanks, Sam. For everything.'

'Don't mention it.' He slapped Mac on his solid arm.

'Seriously. When I joined the army, I kind of did it as a last resort. I was out of options and I thought maybe, just maybe, I could make something of myself. But the last six months, you've shown me I can go beyond that. Have the life I never thought I could.'

'Oh, I don't know about that,' Sam replied sheepishly.

'No, you have. When I walked into that tent with you and Sarge, I was bricking it. But since then, all I think about is being a soldier.

54

Being the best damn sniper I can be and now, seeing your life, it's shown me what I want my life to be. Thank you.'

Out of nowhere, Sam swiped his arm over Mac's head, locking him in a headlock to the alarm of a few passers-by. After a few moments, they dismissed it for the tomfoolery it was and Sam let go, both men chuckling.

'Enough of this mushy shit,' Sam said jokingly. He glanced at his watch, assessing whether their hangover from the night before would still be lingering. 'Pint?'

'Good shout.'

They turned and headed back towards the parade of shops that lined the streets as they headed towards Holborn, and they soon found a pub. Before they went in, Mac lit a cigarette with a hint of embarrassment, knowing Sam didn't approve but wouldn't judge. After a few puffs, Sam thrusted a thumb towards the door, indicating he was going to get the drinks. Through a cloud of smoke, Mac spoke one final time.

'In all seriousness, thank you, Sam. You changed my life.'

'Don't mention it, buddy,' Sam said sternly. 'As we always say, we never leave a man behind.'

Sam disappeared into the pub, leaving Mac to beam with pride as he finished his cigarette. With all the carelessness in the world, he stubbed it out and followed his mentor in, with no clue that in a years' time he would be subjected to more pain than he thought humanly possible.

———

Sam's words had stuck with Mac through all of it.

The betrayal.

The tortures.

The rapes.

'We never leave a man behind.'

It was bullshit. Empty words from a man who had left him to die in the hot sun. Mac could feel the anger pulsing

55

through him, and his fists clenched, but he took a deep breath. He needed to maintain his calm.

To keep control.

The road back to the UK had been relatively easy. After stealing a car from a used car showroom in Austria, he'd driven through the beautiful country, evading the German border patrol easily enough before once again helping himself to a car. The sleek, efficient German car made for a smooth drive as he navigated his way through the country, driving up through the wonderous city of Munich, before heading north towards Stuttgart. It had taken him three days to venture to the German border, stopping only to sleep in his car in secluded spots off the motorway, or to eat.

With his finances dwindling, it occurred to Mac that he was truly on his own.

Wallace was dead.

Blackridge had been decommissioned and from the protected message boards that the operatives occasionally visited online, those in the field were now wanted by several international governments for questioning. Mac included.

As Mac approached Stuttgart, he recalled another one of Wallace's 'Ghosts', Brandt, was originally from the city and he wondered if he was lying low back home? It was unlikely. From the messages he'd read, Brandt had been unsuccessful on a Sam Pope operation in London the same weekend Wallace had died.

Idiot.

Mac cursed Wallace out loud, slamming the palms of his hands against the solid, leather steering wheel as he drove. If Wallace had given him another shot at Sam, he would still be alive.

Mac would have killed him.

This time, he wouldn't hesitate.

In the months since Sam had evaded him in Rome, not an hour went by when Mac wished he'd taken a different shot. Instead of shooting to wound and allowing him the chance to kill Sam up close and personal, he would have put the bullet through the back of his treacherous skull.

That time would come.

A few days later, after once again evading the necessary border checks upon entering the country, Mac had made his way across France. He had been caught off guard by the serene beauty of the land as he drove through, passing vast open fields and quaint, pictureesque towns. As he approached Calais, he was running on empty.

Physically and fiscally.

Getting back to his homeland would be trickier, as traversing the English Channel would require a willing transporter. With the stringent checks at either end of the Channel Tunnel, the option of driving was eliminated.

Mac would need to stowaway, but he was hardly the friendliest face. With the burns that lacerated the right side of his face, along with his wiry frame, he was hardly inundated with offers. But now, as he stood in the rickety, wooden office of the Maxwell Logistics Company, he knew he had a chance of getting home.

Although it had been branded as a logistics company, the office was a front for two East London brothers who were importing and exporting as much as they possibly could. While they clearly had ties to the underworld on both sides of the Channel, Mac wondered how many brain cells they actually had between them.

Josh Maxwell was the eldest brother, his thinning brown hair and pale skin gave him the complexion of a librarian, but he spoke with the authority of a man in charge. Beside him, his brother, Eric, was once a power lifter. Now, while the bulk still remained, the extra layers of flab that filled out his shirt told Mac he'd succumbed to the temptations of a life of crime.

As Mac lied about paying them once they'd reached the docks in Southampton, Eric slid a card through the small pile of cocaine on the edge of the messy desk, straightened it into a thin line, and then hoovered it up like an anteater on steroids.

Mac shook his head. Reliance on drugs was a weakness and he already knew how the situation would go.

They would act tough. Already, Josh had started his speech about being a dangerous person. *Not the type of people you want to piss off* and so forth. Eric would eyeball him, hoping for him to make a move so he could explode in a cocaine fuelled rage and beat him into submission. It seemed rehearsed, and Mac wondered how pathetic people must be to fall for it.

Eric stood up, loudly exhaling his enjoyment before dabbing his finger in the cocaine and rubbing it across his gums. Josh sighed.

'Fuckin' hell, mate. You wanna keep it down?'

'That feels good,' Eric said to nobody, shaking away the cobwebs and returning his gaze to Mac, seemingly offended by Mac's lack of interest. 'You got a problem, son?'

'Calm down,' Josh interrupted, a clear act to underline his authority. He turned to Mac and pointed to his face. 'Ugly fucker, aint ya?'

Mac smiled politely. Considering the pain and horror he went through in the Taliban camp being told the scars he wore made him unattractive was child's play. He ignored it and folded his arms.

'So, are you able to take me across tonight, or not?' He demanded, catching both brothers off guard. Eric shuffled on his feet as if to go for him, but Mac just raised his only eyebrow. Josh chuckled.

'I like you. You got some serious bollocks talking to us like that. But we don't do things for free, so why don't you fuck off and find some kind of burns victim charity to take you home.'

'Yeah, fuck off.' Eric chimed in, more for his own self esteem than anything else. Mac stood stoic, staring at them both.

He needed to get back to the UK.

Sam Pope had been sentenced earlier that day. It had been on the radio, which meant he would be in prison by the time Mac arrived in London, but that wouldn't be too much of a problem. Blackridge had their roots in pretty much every part of the government and Mac could call in his final favours to be put in a locked room with Sam. The government would probably thank him once he'd beaten Sam to death, using his death in prison as a political tool for some agenda he didn't care about.

But he needed to get back.

With both sets of eyes glaring at him, and their patience wearing thin, Mac looked at Josh and spoke calmly.

'How about you take me across tonight and at least you can survive?'

Both men furrowed their brow in confusion, and Josh glanced at his brother, then back at Mac.

'What the fuck are you tal…'

The gunshot echoed like a clap of thunder and the back of Eric's head exploded, covering the wall behind in a splatter of blood, brain, and bone. In one swift movement, Mac had slipped his hand to the gun that was tucked in the waistband of his jeans and smoothly brought it up. He had done it a thousand times and the precision was now ingrained in him. Within a second, he'd the gun up, both hands wrapped around it, perfectly in line with his eye, and his finger expertly on the trigger.

Eric crashed to the floor and Josh howled in terror as he gazed into the obliterated skull of his younger brother. As he dropped to his knees, tears streaming down his gaunt cheeks, he wept in fear as Mac took a step forward, careful not to leave a print in the thick, dark blood that was pooling around the large corpse.

'I'll ask you again.' He spoke coldly. 'Can you take me tonight?'

As Josh offered a pathetic nod of his head, Mac slid the gun back into his waistband and headed to the door. He was greeted by a cold slap of wind across his charred face. Any feelings or emotions brought on from killing a man in cold blood had long since eroded.

Mac had killed before.

Men.

Women.

Children.

When Wallace had ordered, Mac had obediently pulled the trigger. Whatever hell was awaiting Mac in the afterlife was going to be a holiday in paradise compared to the living hell Wallace had pulled him from.

But now Wallace was dead.

Killed by the same man who had left Mac to rot.

Giving Josh a few moments to grieve for his recently deceased brother, Mac looked out at the port, at the rough sea that was thrashing angrily in the spring night. By morning, he would be back home.

Back to finish Sam once and for all.

CHAPTER SEVEN

'What a day.'

Assistant Commissioner Ashton hung her hat on the free-standing coat rack in the corner of her plush office, before dropping into her comfortable leather chair. She could feel the untrusting glare of DI Singh following her the entire way, but ignored it. The Sam Pope chapter had been brought to a satisfactory close.

While Ashton had wanted Sam locked away in the darkest hole for his crimes, a lifetime spent in HMP Pentonville would suffice. With her ascendency to the top of the Metropolitan Police all but guaranteed, she now needed to ensure that DI Singh was on her side. While she didn't know it herself, Singh was a valuable commodity and her loyalty would be one of Ashton's most valuable assets.

'Singh, please sit.'

Reluctantly, Singh obliged. It had annoyed Ashton that Singh had decided against wearing her tunic. Was it a statement that she didn't believe in the badge anymore? A pathetic show of unity with Sam? As Singh sat down, Ashton spun on her chair and opened the bottom of the oak cabinet that lined the back wall of the office. The clinking of glass accompanied her retrieving two crystal glasses, along with a decanter of brown liquid. Singh imagined it would taste disgusting, but she knew better than to bite the hand that intended to feed her.

Pearce was right.

Singh had it made. Any connections the Met thought existed between her and Sam would magically be erased and she could now look forward to a blossoming career. But she could feel her skin crawling at the thought, especially as Ashton poured out two half glasses of the pungent alcohol with a smug grin across her stern face. On the walls either side of the cabinet, a number of commendations and certificates were proudly displayed and Singh remembered how in awe of them she was when she first stepped into the office.

Her career had been prodigious, rising through the ranks of the Met swiftly and with merit. While a number of her peers sneered at the 'quota filling', Singh pressed on, leaving them in her rear-view as she climbed the organisation. Her time in the Armed Response Unit had only solidified her reputation and when Ashton had requested she run the Sam Pope task force, she'd jumped at the chance.

Ashton was the most senior female officer in the Met, and to have her holding the ladder as she climbed had meant the world to Singh.

Now, she knew that Ashton was only holding it for her own gain.

'To a job well done.'

Ashton lifted her glass and reluctantly, Singh wrapped her fingers around hers and lifted it. Ashton forced a smile, before raising it to her lips and taking a sip. Judging by the following expression, it clearly burnt, and Singh apprehensively looked at her own drink.

'What's the matter, Singh?' Ashton asked. 'I thought you liked a drink?'

The sly dig was petty, but not unfounded. Ever since being booted off the task force, Singh had found herself turning to the bottle more and while Ashton herself had begun proceedings to hound her out, Singh had wavered dangerously on the line of sobriety for too long. It's what drove Singh to dig deeper, to put herself in Wallace's crosshairs.

It had almost gotten her killed.

Sadly, it had led to the death of an innocent journalist.

It had cost Sam his freedom.

As she stared at the glass, the weight of the guilt hung too heavy for her to drink it. She slowly placed the glass on the table, making a silent vow to never drink again.

The sneer on Ashton's face told its own story.

'Look, Singh. I know we may have had our differences in the past, but that's where they belong. In the past.' Ashton held Singh's stare. 'Things are going to change here very soon, and I need to know whether you're in or not.'

'In?' Singh said, raising her thin eyebrow.

'Where your loyalties lie.' Ashton finished her drink and then plucked the lid from the decanter once more. 'Let's not pussy foot around the allegations that you helped Sam Pope. I know there are many people, officers within this very organisation included, who believed his actions were noble. I mean, saving abducted kids from sex slavery is as noble as it gets. But that doesn't give anyone the power to go above the law. So while I'm willing to let those notions of collusion disappear, I need to know that your loyalty is to this badge and to serving this city.'

Ashton poured herself another Scotch, slamming the lid back on the container before dropping back into her seat. As she glared at Singh, the young DI took a breath.

She'd fought too hard to get to her position to throw it all away, but the thought of pledging allegiance to this woman was a hard decision to stomach.

'Ma'am, all I ever wanted to be was a detective. And I'm a damn good one. Whatever you believe, it doesn't matter.'

'Oh, it matters,' Ashton barked back, immediately scolding herself. Commissioner Stout had made it clear: Singh had to be on her side. She changed tact, offering a warm smile that almost hurt. 'But what truly matters is what *you* believe.'

'I believe in the justice system.'

'So, you believe Sam Pope is a criminal?'

Singh could feel the accusing eyes boring into her like a pneumatic drill and she clenched her fist. Every fibre of her being wanted to drive it into her superior's jaw, but she knew that was career suicide.

A career Sam had handed back to her with his sacrifice.

She unclenched her fist, relaxed her shoulders, and looked Ashton directly in the eye.

'I believe he is a good man who broke the law.'

'Good enough.' Ashton raised her glass again, this time on her own and took a sip. 'As long as we know where our priorities lie.'

'Is that all, ma'am?'

'Yes. Dismissed.' Ashton waved her hand and Singh rose from her chair. 'Oh, and Singh. Next time you're offered a glass of expensive Scotch, I would advise you at least appreciate the offer.'

Singh nodded curtly and turned to the door, pulling it open with a little extra force to convey her anger. Ashton smirked, pleased at her own power play and by executing it exactly as instructed by the Commissioner. While she never expected things to improve, she'd at least made it clear that Singh's success is now linked to her own.

Mission accomplished.

Before the door closed and she could finish her drink, a young administrator politely knocked on the door, poking her head through.

'What is it, Emma?'

'It's Gemma, ma'am.' The young lady corrected sheepishly, nervously tucking her blonde hair behind her ear. Ashton regarded her with annoyance, even though the young lady had exceptional manners. Gemma had been working within the Met for over two years and was a firm favourite with the officers. While her peers commended the young lady's efficiency and cadence, Ashton put her popularity down to her pretty face, full chest, and tight shirts.

Ashton chuckled into her glass. She could be a real bitch sometimes.

'What is it?' she eventually asked, not looking up.

'I have the paperwork pertaining to Sam Pope's prison transfer you asked for?' Gemma stepped in nervously. Ashton waved her in, slamming her glass down.

'Thank you,' Ashton said, snatching the folder and immediately flicking it open. 'Oh, and book me in for a visit to Pentonville tomorrow. I want to look that bastard in the eye.'

'Ma'am,' Gemma said, her voice shaking with nerves and confusion. 'He hasn't been taken to Pentonville?'

Before Ashton could respond to the young woman's query, her eyes lit up with joy. Although it had originally been dismissed, it appeared Commissioner Stout had finally granted her wish. One final act of kindness from a man whose boots she doubted she'd be able to fill. There would be no chance of visiting Sam, not anymore.

With glee, she slapped the file down on the table and shot a smile towards a clearly uncomfortable Gemma.

'Never mind,' she said firmly, basking in the glory of the dark hole that Sam Pope had been sent.

––––––

Ashcroft Maximum Security Prison was located in the wood-lands of Salters Green. A few miles out from the Sussex town of Mayfield, the vast woods provided the perfect location for the notorious building known by those in power as 'The Grid'.

The large, concrete wall that spanned the perimeter of the facility was three feet thick, topped with electrified barbed wire that would fry anything it touched. A dirt path off Argos Hill Road was stopped abruptly by the first of three metal gates, each one needing a security pass and an ever-changing access code for entry. The code was scram-bled every twenty-four hours and delivered within an encrypted message that required a thumb print to open.

There was no breaking in.

No getting out.

Beyond the third gate, which also included a physical inspection by three, armed security officers, the fortress loomed, encased in the shadows of the surrounding trees. A grey, concrete block made up of four floors, two of which had been built into the earth itself. Beneath the ground, it housed a maximum of three hundred and forty-six of the UK's most dangerous criminals.

Criminals who not only required incarceration, but those who could never hope for a look at the outside world again. Each one serving a life sentence, the idea of parole a disgusting joke that was banded about by those on both sides of the law. A twenty-two-hour lockdown was imple-mented, with prisoners kept in their six square metre cells, segregated by thick walls and iron doors. The only daylight afforded was for the hour of 'exercise', regardless of the elements, with no protection offered beyond the trained snipers overlooking the courtyard.

To those inside, the idea of being placed at HMP Wakefield was a holiday.

To those who knew of Ashcroft, it was the hole you buried the worst criminals in, knowing they would die either at the hands of each other, the guards, or from their hourglass running out.

To the public, Ashcroft didn't exist.

Sam knew he wasn't headed to Pentonville the moment he'd set foot in the security van. The short glimpse of a pistol strapped under the jacket of the officers who pushed him in told him that.

The blackout doors of the van permitted him no sunlight, as he travelled in the dark, well aware that the van was bulletproof. After twenty minutes, when he wasn't being greeted by the Pentonville Prison guards, Sam was resigned to his fate. While he didn't swim in the 'need to know' circles, he knew of Ashcroft's existence. His investigations into the organised crime had uncovered rumours of The Grid, a place that even the most hardened criminals were afraid of.

A place where people disappeared.

There were no stops on the hour and a half journey, with Sam not afforded a glimpse of sunshine, a smidgen of fresh air, nor a comfort break. As a prisoner, being carted off to a deep, dark hole, he no longer held any claim to those benefits.

Sam Pope had nothing.

Eventually, he felt the traction under the tyres change from the smooth tarmac of a main road to a gravelley, bumpy terrain, and the vehicle came to a stop. One of the men stepped from the front and after a few moments, the loud clunk of a metal gate echoed, and the van crept forward. Another two minutes and the same process was repeated.

Impenetrable.

As they came to a third stop, Sam was treated to a brief glimpse of the outside world, the gloomy day still held an unnatural brightness as the doors to the back of the van were thrown open. He held a hand up to protect himself from the glare, making a note of the two men who were quickly inspecting the cargo.

They were both well built.

One of them was left-handed, his fingers curled around his pen.

Both carried firearms.

Sam committed every detail to memory. It was a gift he had, which was only enhanced by his training. The smallest detail can sometimes make the greatest impact and his ability to absorb them like a sponge had saved his life countless times, and had ended many others.

The doors slammed shut and he was enclosed in the darkness once more. A voice called for them to proceed and the engine purred into life and the van moved forward. A large clap echoed out as the gate slammed shut, locking Sam inside the grounds of the most terrifying location in the United Kingdom.

Sam sat patiently in the darkness, thinking of his son. Jamie had always been so happy, his mood a default positive despite any problem he faced. Sam had watched him struggle with books, but eventually, his son's keen love of the written word soon saw him reading at a level way beyond his age.

Jamie would have been fast approaching his ninth birthday had he not been taken by the cruel hands of fate.

A moment that had set all of this in motion.

Sam could hear the muffled words of authority outside,

and then the crunching of boots gradually growing in volume towards the door.

They swung open.

Before him, a powerful figure stood, his thick arms pointing out like triangles as he rested his hands on his hips. The daylight poured in around the man, casting him in a complete shadow and Sam squinted towards the broad silhouette. After a few moments, the man spoke.

'Sam Pope. Welcome to hell.'

CHAPTER EIGHT

Deputy Warden Harry Sharp had practically licked his lips when the notice of Sam's impending arrival came through, and while the late hour of it's arrival was unusual, it had caused a stir of excitement in him. The standard process was for Ashcroft to be notified weeks in advance of a new inmate, ensuring the necessary safety procedures were in place for their arrival and successful transition into the facility.

But he disregarded the tardiness of the request.

Sam Pope was his.

Growing up with learning difficulties had made Sharp an easy target during his youth, something which had etched itself onto his psyche like a vulgar tattoo. With his parents' dwindling interest in his schoolwork and wellbeing, his poor diet ensured he was teased for both his mental and physical state. Kids are cruel, which is why Sharp had never wanted the family life, cursing the very idea that he would end up like his pathetic parents. His father left when he was eight years old, which Sharp considered a blessing. The man couldn't hold down a job and didn't offer anything to society other than a shining example of what happens when you have no control.

He drank too much.

Took as many drugs as possible.

Fucked whoever would let him.

There was a real possibility that Sharp had siblings due to his scumbag father's promiscuous lifestyle, but he had no interest in finding out. Anything that would tie him further to the man made his stomach turn. His mother, in his eyes, was weak. She allowed his father to sleep around, and she struggled through on a wave of benefits and cash in hand cleaning jobs.

When Sharp made his way to his teens, he filled out. The puppy fat soon converted to taut muscle and while he may not have been the brightest, he soon became the toughest in his school. When he was expelled for beating a former bully to a pulp with a chair, his mother didn't even realise. Sharp focused his attention on joining the police from a young age, but he didn't pass the entry exams.

He fared even worse at joining the armed forces.

Eventually, he became a prison guard.

The feeling of wielding power over people who thought themselves above the law was a sensation he couldn't find in the arms of a woman, no matter how much he paid her. The feeling of slamming his baton into the back of an inmate's skull for talking back was almost orgasmic.

Twenty years in the game, and now here he was, working as the deputy warden for a secret prison with a very select membership. Every time one of its degenerate population spoke back to him, he allowed the anger and pain of his neglectful parents to flow through him.

The incessant teasing from the kids at school.

The total rejection from the opposite sex.

He had been investigated countless times for excessive

force when dealing with inmates, but his peers stood up for him. He didn't know if it was out of friendship, a concept he was unfamiliar with, or because they were scared of him too. Either one was fine with him.

One hour before Sam Pope's sentencing was due to begin, he received notification that Ashcroft would be his destination. At first, he thought it was a joke and was tempted to hand out a few backhands to his staff to draw out the 'hilarious' prankster.

But with Commissioner Stout's name on the document, he found his anger morph into unbridled excitement.

Immediately, he got on the phone to Warden Geoff Harris, confirming their new guest. Harris was a meticulous man, who had spent over two decades in the army. Although he ruled with a much lighter touch than Sharp, he commanded double the respect from the rest of the guards and the inmates alike.

It infuriated Sharp how a man who showed such little aggression, held such power. Sharp may not have grown up the smartest man in the room, but he knew to toe the line. What he lacked in diplomacy he made up for by leading the line and with Harris slowly heading towards retirement due to his increasing health concerns, he had his eyes on the throne.

And when he sat there, he would ensure that his iron fist was never shrouded in a velvet glove.

Harris, in his usual, polite manner, insisted on travelling into the prison, deviating from his mandated rest day. Sharp had to grit his teeth in response, wanting to give Sam Pope his customary welcome. That would have to wait.

Diagnosed with MS at a late stage of his life, Warden Harris took Wednesdays and Fridays as rest days, allowing

Sharp to show his worth to the powers that be and hopefully help him stake his claim to the top job.

Harris arrived ten minutes before Sam was due, insisting that Sharp still take the lead on welcoming him to the prison and then insisted he bring Sam to his office. Not wanting to look like a lap dog to his subordinates, Sharp made a silent promise to show Sam who was really running Ashcroft.

As the security van pulled through the final gate and slowed to a complete stop, he smiled. His uniform was in pristine condition, his navy shirt wrapped around his impressive frame. His handgun, a SIG Sauer P226, was strapped to his belt, with fifteen bullets ready to go. Despite not being the best shot in the team, Sharp was the most bloodthirsty and wouldn't hesitate to fill Sam with the entire magazine if he got the chance.

The rain had relented, but a brisk wind blew around the van as the officers stepped out, identifying themselves before leading Sharp to the back of the van.

They unlocked the doors and threw them open, the brightness illuminating the van like a flash grenade and causing Sam to hold his hand up to protect his eyes.

Sharp smirked, happy at the discomfort of a man who thought himself above the law.

Above him.

With his meaty hands clasping his hips, he stood, allowing the brightness to bathe him in shadow.

'Welcome to hell.'

Sharp mentally patted himself on the back for his opening line, one which he'd used on a number of new guests. While his colleagues may have rolled their eyes at his dramatics, he was always keen to set the tone immediately.

'Get the fuck out of the van.'

Sharp stepped back, ensuring one hand was visibly on

his sidearm and sure enough, with a little stiffness, Sam Pope stepped out, his eyes still squinting as they adjusted to sunshine once more.

With his hands cuffed, Sam took in the grand structure of the prison, his bruised eyes scanning the building as if searching for an exit point. Sharp allowed him a few moments, wanting the severity of his future to sink in before he cleared his throat.

'Welcome to The Grid,' he began, slowly pacing. 'I'm Deputy Warden Sharp. You will address me as such from now on. You will not speak until spoken to. You will not move unless told to. In fact, you will only breath because I've allowed you to. Is this understood?'

Sharp spun on his heel dramatically, his eyes locked on Sam, who nodded. The lack of fear in Sam's eyes irked him.

'You will abide by the rules which we will make clear. Any deviation from the rules will result in one week in solitary confinement. You will have one hour a day to exercise. You will have three meals a day, one of which will be in the canteen for up to an hour. Any attempt to veer from the designated routes to and from your cell will result in one week in solitary confinement. Is this understood?'

Sam sighed and nodded. Having grown up in the military and spending most of his life as one of the UK's elite soldiers, the drill instructor act was borderline pathetic. But realising he was in no position to question it, he played along. Sensing Sam's lack of fear, Sharp strode directly at him, daring Sam to break his stare. His breath was warm, a stale smell of coffee wafting between the stained gritted teeth that he spoke through.

'You're in hell now, soldier boy. And I'm the fucking devil.'

Sam didn't respond, but he refused to break the stare. The deputy warden suddenly feigned to lunge at Sam, in a

74

lame attempt of intimidation. When Sam didn't move, Sharp shot a furious glance at the other armed officers. To placate his own ego, Sharp drove a solid fist into Sam's bruised ribs, driving the air completely out of him. Coughing and gasping for breath, Sam dropped to one knee, battling the urge to fight back with every fibre of his being.

There was no doubt in his mind that he would easily defeat Sharp. But with his hands cuffed, a number of armed guards trained on him, and his future in the man's sadistic hands, he refused to rise to the bait.

This was one fight he would not win.

After a few moments and a couple of exaggerated shakes of his hand, Sharp turned to his men with a cruel smile.

'Get him up.' He turned back to Sam. 'Let's go see the Warden, shall we?'

Harris sat behind his large desk and peered through the window, the gloom of another spring afternoon hanging over the surrounding woodland with an awful sense of foreboding. A storm was coming, not just outside, but within his prison.

Ashcroft was the most high-tech, secure premises in the entire country, and he was proud to run it. He had spent the last thirteen years overseeing the government's plans to effectively eradicate the most dangerous criminals within the confines of the law. Sure, there were liberties taken by some of his staff. Sharp suffered from 'little man' syndrome, but he couldn't fault his deputy's commitment to the cause.

There hadn't been a riot in over five years.

No deaths in the last decade.

The inmates who resided within his prison were the worst of the worst. Mass murderers. Serial rapists. High profile gangsters. But somehow, Harris had nurtured an atmosphere of peace and for the most part, they all towed the line. Their actions while free men had determined their futures and they'd all resigned to their lockdowns.

But Sam Pope arriving had given him a headache.

Usually, Ashcroft were notified a minimum of two weeks in advance if a sentencing would lead to him welcoming a new inmate to their final resting place. The fact this had come in on the day had thrown him off, but Harris made a concerted effort to stay away from the bureaucracy of the police service. As far as he was concerned, the prison service was its own beast and he'd managed to tame the wildest of them all.

The other cause for concern was the reaction of the inmates.

While each of his prisoners was reprehensible by their crimes, there was almost a kinship between them. When they passed each other during their brief moments of free-dom, there was an acceptance of who they were. A disgusting mutual respect had been forged between them, built on the severity of their crimes.

Sam Pope was a vigilante.

He had systematically taken down criminal empires. While Harris couldn't help but admire the man's cause, he was worried how the inmates would take to having a crim-inal killer among them. He had worked hard to keep Ashcroft off the map, but with so much government and police interest in Sam's incarceration, he knew they would be sniffing around for information.

There was no guarantee he could keep Sam safe.

Nor that his guards would want to.

Without the proper time to prep his team and ensure they were ready; Sam Pope had been dropped on them like an unpinned grenade. Harris grit his teeth as a sharp pain penetrated his mind like a needle and he sat back in his chair and shut his eyes. The MS had been getting worse lately, but now was not the time for his health to fail. With a change in the status quo this big hitting his prison, the last thing he wanted was to hand over the reins to Sharp.

It would most likely end in a blood bath.

Filling his lungs to regulate his breathing, the headache was worsened by a pounding fist on his door. Harris sat forward, rested his hands on his desk and slipped seamlessly back into his well-respected composure.

'Come in.'

The door opened and Sharp marched in, chest out and with a smug look across his face. Harris was in no doubt that he'd put on a show for Sam, his theatrics were just another reason he dreaded the day Sharp took his seat. Behind him, another armed officer followed, and Harris pushed himself out of his chair as Sam Pope shuffled in. Judging by his short, sharp breaths, Harris suspected Sharp had overstepped his welcome. It was something he'd reprimanded his deputy over before, but there was little hope for changing the man. The final officer stepped through and stood watch at the door, his arms folded on his chest and his eyes on Sam.

The tension was palpable, and Harris uncomfortably stepped around his desk and approached his new prisoner. Standing at six foot, Sam was the same height as the Warden, but looked almost twice his weight in muscle. The MS has withered away at Harris, who had once been a strapping soldier much like Sam. But age and the debilitating illness had taken its toll. Sam stood to attention, trying his best to hide the clear discomfort he was in due to Sharp, and he locked his eyes on Harris, who offered a warm smile.

'Sam Pope,' he began, as if regaling his grandkids with

a story. 'I must say, I'm somewhat surprised to see you here.'

Sharp scoffed loudly, but quickly remembered his rank as Harris shot him a thunderous glare.

'I trust you understand the severity of your situation.'

'I'm under no illusions, sir.' Sam spoke calmly, catching the Warden off guard.

'Now, I'm sure Deputy Warden Sharp has run through the procedures but let me make it clear. This isn't a deep, dark hole to throw people into. I pride myself on running a tight ship here, but I also take great pride in the care we give our inmates. This may be your final home, but it is home. Now, the restrictions we have in place are non-negotiable, which means you will have to adhere to the schedules. It also means you need to wear a tag. Sharp?'

Harris turned to Sharp, who eagerly approached, his hands wrapped around a metal anklet similar to those used for house arrest. He snapped it around Sam's left ankle, ensuring it clicked correctly. He smirked at Sam as he stood back up and took a few steps back as Sam turned his attention back to the Warden.

'All prisoners are tagged at all times, so we can monitor your whereabouts. We haven't had a riot here in years, but you can never be too careful.'

'Plus, these bad boys shoot fifty thousand vaults at the click of a button,' Sharp chimed in. 'Not enough to kill you, but enough to make you piss your pants.'

'Quite.' Harris shot Sharp another stern look, reaffirming his authority. 'Now with that out of the way, I understand this is a testing time for you. Do you have any questions?'

'Is there a library, sir?'

The question caught the Warden off guard but drew a snigger from Sharp. Sam surmised that Sharp hadn't read a book in his life and kept his eyes on the Warden, who drew a comforting smile.

'We don't, I'm afraid. However, we do have a weekly shipment of cigarettes, food, and magazines. I'm sure we can get a book or two.' Harris eased himself onto the edge of his desk, clearly appreciating the rest. 'You like to read?'

'I do, sir,' Sam responded. 'I find it helps.'

A few chortles could be heard from the other officers, but Harris nodded approvingly.

'It's not a bad thing. Especially in here, your mind could use the distraction.'

Sam scanned the room, absorbing the details. There were several cabinets, no doubt containing confidential documents, along with a top of the range Mac Book which sat on the desk. On the walls, he noted the fine art that hung from their hooks. A shelf, crammed with books, was affixed to the far wall, along with a small display of medals.

'You served, sir?'

Harris turned and glanced at the medals and returned with a proud grin.

'I did.' He slowly eased himself off the desk and approached Sam. 'Many years ago, now. I know about your record, the incredible work you did for this country. It's not gone missed.'

Sam grimaced.

For years, he'd thought he'd fought for the freedom of the world. Every bullet fired from his rifle had taken the world another small step towards it but less than two weeks ago, he'd discovered it was all a lie. Wallace had used him to tighten his stranglehold over the world of global terrorism, and Sam questioned every mission he'd ever completed.

Project Hailstorm.

It had left him with innocent blood on his hand and two bullet holes in his chest. While the truth had been exposed and Wallace's legacy destroyed, the closing of that chapter in his life had left him riddled with self-doubt and another laundry list of injuries.

Where pride once resided, nothing but regret remained.

After a few moments of uncomfortable silence, Sam forced a smile.

'Thank you, sir.'

Harris patted Sam on the shoulder, and then nodded to Sharp who stepped forward, indicating to Sam it was time to go. Sam obediently turned, following Sharp's lead as they headed to the door and the harrowing walk to his cell. As Sam was about to cross the threshold, Harris, who was lowering himself into his chair, called out.

'Just be careful, Sam.' His words were heavy with caution. 'There are a lot of dangerous people in here.'

Sam stopped, and turned back to the Warden, his face emotionless.

'I know,' he said, before shooting a quick look at Sharp. 'I'm one of them.'

Sharp's nose twitched, a clear *tell* to Sam that he was nervous. Harris returned to his notes, as Sam followed Sharp's march back towards the underground cell block. The officer behind him gave him a firm shove in the back, thrusting him further forward. As soon as they'd cleared the corridor and made their way down the steps towards the heavily locked-down lower levels, Sam waited patiently for the retaliation.

Before they unlocked the gate, Sharp drove another fist into his abdomen, followed by a knee to the face that rocked Sam's skull. As he fell to his knees and shook the cobwebs away, he could hear Sharp laughing as the gates opened and the echoes of hundreds of violent criminals, baying to get their hands on fresh meat, roared through the prison like a mighty crescendo.

CHAPTER NINE

Deputy Warden Sharp hated standing to attention.

While he'd always strived for a career within the armed forces or the police, the idea of rank and abiding by the established hierarchy angered him. He was a powerful man but having to obey orders took him back to his youth, where he was tormented and bullied by those higher up the social food chain.

Although he saw the contradiction with how he ruled when Harris was on his rest days, it still boiled his blood when he was asked to open a door for his boss. But those days were soon coming to an end, and as he watched Harris struggle to walk towards the car door he'd politely, albeit begrudgingly, opened for him, Sharp couldn't wait to make what he felt were necessary changes to the way Ashcroft housed its prisoners.

Harris was a light touch.

Sure, he commanded respect from the inmates, but respect meant there would be room for compromise.

After Sharp had beaten and shunted Sam off to his cell, he'd been summoned by Harris, who once again chastised him for his rough treatment of the new prisoners.

While his beating of Sam had been administered in a blind spot of the building, Sharp's reputation proceeded him and when Harris questioned whether Sam would show signs of a beating should he pay him a visit, Sharp could only grunt and shrug.

'Our job is to govern these men.' Harris had stated coldly. 'Not reign supreme over them.'

Sharp had bitten his tongue.

If he had it his way, Sam would be rotting for the first few weeks in solitary confinement. The quicker he could break Sam, the quicker he would bend to his whims. But there was something about Sam that irked Sharp, a resolute nobility that he both detested and envied in equal measure.

The man was a soldier.

One of the best the UK had ever seen.

Sharp had been as obsessed with Sam's mission along with the rest of the media, following in awe as he raged a one-man war on crime. They had written about how he'd singlehandedly taken down one of the biggest crime empires in London, raided a building on his own, and put several men in the ground.

Then, with the fate of several young girls in the balance, he'd gone to war with a Ukrainian sex trafficking rink, and even went toe to toe with the Met's Armed Response Unit. Only two weeks ago, he'd brought down one of the most powerful men in the UK and staged a daring attack on a government motorcade in broad daylight.

It told him that Sam Pope wasn't just made of steel. But that he was nigh on incorruptible.

But that was fine with Sharp. He didn't need to have Sam in his pocket, nor did he need him to fall in line. All Sharp craved was the fear.

Sam Pope may have been a hero to some, but in here, he was a criminal.

Just another shirt number.

Another man who would eventually walk his final mile in the confines of Sharp's prison.

When the day came for Sam Pope to walk his own, Sharp would be in the chair, watching with interest as the highly decorated, revered man would eventually fall under his watch.

That was power.

Power that wasn't quite his yet.

Harris eventually scraped his limp foot across the gravel beside Sharp and locked on his authoritative stare.

'I trust everything will be in order, tonight?' Harris half sighed.

'Yes, sir.'

'Be on high alert.' Harris awkwardly lowered himself into the backseat of the car. 'There will be a lot of interest in our new guest.'

'I'll keep my eye on it, sir.' Sharp offered a faux smile.

'I don't know whether that's a good or bad thing.' Harris mused out loud. A look of concern spread across his withered face. 'Something doesn't sit right.'

'Sir?' Sharp stood straight, hands clasped and pressed to the base of his spine.

'Such a late transfer. Usually, we get so much notice to make sure everything is in place.' Harris shook his head. 'Just, keep everything tight, Sharp, and I'll handle the red tape tomorrow.'

'Have a good night, sir.'

Sharp slammed the door closed before Harris could respond and the car crawled towards the large, impenetrable gate, beginning Harris's overlong exit from the facility. As the gate slid open and the black Mercedes pulled away, a cruel smile creaked across Sharp's face.

Harris's orders had been clear.

Sharp and his team were to ensure that Sam had an easy first night at Ashcroft. That was fine by him. As far as he was concerned, after getting a few licks in earlier, he'd already laid down the law to Sam. Whether he liked it or not, he would fall in line.

Neither Sharp, nor any of his team, would lay a hand on Sam.

As he turned away from the gate as it began to close, he rubbed his meaty hands together. He marched back to the entrance of the ominous Grid, hellbent on keeping his promise.

He wouldn't lay a hand on Sam.

But Sharp could be very persuasive and there were certainly a number of desperate men, willing to do desperate things when given the chance.

Anything for a crumb of comfort and it wouldn't take much for Sharp to make that happen.

As he crossed the threshold and showed his security pass, a pointless exercise that he would do away with the second he took charge, he afforded himself a small chuckle at the idea forming in his head.

It was time to welcome Sam to Ashcroft.

———

Sam was surprised by how comfortable his bed was.

While every impression he'd had since he was marched through the heavily secure facility was that it was designed for maximum punishment, he expected the bed to fall in line. It wasn't like staying at the Ritz, but as he lowered himself onto the thin mattress, he was surprised to find a modicum of comfort from it. Considering he'd spent many nights asleep outside, hidden within the rough landscapes of the middle eastern countries while on tour, a thin mattress was welcomed.

As he'd been led to his cell, he could hear the threats emanating from the other cells. It was expected.

While the inhabitants of The Grid were predominantly cut off from the world, Sam recognised the very real possibility that his mission would have leaked through. If a building that harboured a number of the UK's most dangerous criminals didn't have some links to the world he'd mercilessly fought for over a year, it would have shocked him.

To the guards, he was a criminal.

To the inmates, he was a criminal killer.

In other words, he was on his own.

His head was still ringing from the cheap shot from Sharp but compared to what he'd been through in the last few weeks, it was nothing. As he shuffled on the mattress, a pain shot from his spine, the stitches from his run in with The Hangman of Baghdad not quite dissolved. Sam's mind raced back to that night, balancing precariously on the slippery scaffold of the once prosperous High Rise, with a murderous assassin looking to slice him to pieces.

Sam had powered through.

Fought back.

Survived.

After slicing open the man's throat and leaving him to die in the rain, Sam had envisaged his fight was over. As he'd dropped to his knees, it was the first moment of peace he'd experienced since he'd lost his son. Despite the horrifying revelations of Project Hailstorm, Sam had put things right.

Marsden's death had been avenged.

Blackridge had been disbanded.

Wallace's reign of terror had been brutally ended.

He had allowed DI Singh to take him in, knowing it

would resurrect a career that his mission had ruptured. It was the least he could do.

After a few hours of quiet reflection as he stared at the dank, grey ceiling of his cell, Sam had tuned out the noise from the rest of the prison. He had already missed the allotted hour for exercise, but he could hear the clanking of cell doors as the staggered mealtimes approached. With each group of fifty prisoners who were herded to the canteen like cattle, another wave of violent promises echoed in his direction. The odd rebuke from a prison guard followed, but Sam was under no illusion that they were interested in his safety.

They were here to watch over the prisoners. Keep them in check.

But he sincerely doubted, judging by the attitude of Sharp, that his safety was top of their priority list.

He was just another criminal.

Right on cue, a fist pounded on his door, filling his room with a sharp echo that caused him to grit his teeth. An angry voice demanded he stood to the far wall and Sam slowly obliged. His cell door swung open and a gruff prison guard stood. Mid-forties and with a gut that told Sam he was well fed, the guard eyed him up down before jerking his neck.

'Grub time. Hop to it.'

Sam stretched as he walked, ignoring the pain in his spine, and he rolled his shoulders, still feeling a tightness in the joint which had been decimated by a bullet in Rome. There had certainly been costs to his fight against crime and Sam put his freedom at the bottom of the list. Compared to breaking his promise to his son and the punishment he'd put his body through, being locked down in a secret prison was a minor inconvenience.

As they strode through the prison, Sam scanned the corridors. They were identical in layout, and every single one of them consisted of ten cells, all spaced out by a few metres. There were no distinguishable features, nothing on the walls, and the desperation of the situation the inhabitants faced hung heavy in the air.

Eventually, they made their way to a set of thick, metal double doors, which the guard opened with his security pass. As they slid open, the noise of the room dropped.

The large room was lit by halogen tubes that hung from the ceiling in perfect symmetry. Ten metal tables were spaced evenly around the room, with an uncomfortable stool bolted to the underneath. Occupying most of them was an assortment of some of the most dangerous and vile criminals in the UK and all of them had their eyes firmly trained at the doorway.

On Sam.

'You got thirty minutes.'

The guard gave Sam another shove before casually stepping to the side of the room, joining a colleague to cast a disinterested eye over proceedings. Sam scanned the room, meeting the hate filled stare of most of the prisoners, all of whom were hunched over metal trays containing unappetising food. As he walked towards the lone food counter, he noted the table at the far corner of the room.

A large man with a thick white beard sat, his hands clasped on the table and an air of authority about him. To his left sat a small, weasely man, with greasy hair pasted to his head and a thin, whispy beard. To the right was a specimen. Despite being seated, the man towered over the other two, and was twice as broad. The sleeves of his jumpsuit were rolled up, and his brown forearms were covered with ink. All three of them watched him, their eyes following his every step.

With the rest of the table empty, Sam assumed that a seat at that table was by invite only.

Sam approached the counter and lifted one of the

metal trays, his stomach rumbling despite the food presented to him. A slab of unidentifiable meat, boiled potatoes, and some discoloured vegetables, accompanied with a plastic spork and a carton of orange juice. Despite the clear lack of care in the nutritional value of the meal, Sam was famished and he walked calmly and confidently to the nearest empty chair, placed the tray down, and sat. The other occupants of the table froze, either in disbelief or fury and Sam shovelled a potato into his mouth before fixing them all with a stare.

A cold, unnerving stare.

Clearly, it took them by surprise and Sam afforded himself a small, inward chuckle as a number of them broke it instantly. He had no intention of causing trouble on his first night, but the prison held no fear to him.

And he was hungry.

As the volume in the room began to grow, the interest in his arrival declined. The meat, which was passable chicken, tasted great and as Sam took his final mouthful, he noticed Sharp enter the room, sending another hush across the room like a shockwave. The deputy warden shot him a scowl and Sam replied with a bored raise of his eyebrow.

But then Sharp nodded to the far side of the room.

Instantly, the large, tattooed man slammed his cutlery down and stood and Sam sighed. As the hushed room watched on in a mixture of shock and bloodthirsty plea-sure, Sam tracked the rising sound of the man's heavy foot-steps as they hurtled towards him.

As expected.

Just as the man's shadow filtered over his plate, Sam could hear the extra emphasis the man placed on his final step, indicating he was shifting his body weight. Sam twisted his body to the left, evading the fist which crashed into his dinner like a sledgehammer. Sliding out from the stool in one, swift motion, Sam turned to face the hulking inmate, whose eyes were wide with fury, as if Sam's evasion was a personal insult.

Sam held his hands up.

'Look, let's not do this tonight.' He offered, but the man growled through his teeth and swung another fist. Sam ducked, before planting a hard knee into the man's ribs, driving the wind out of him. As soon as he did, the entire room erupted into a chorus of cheers, as if they were watching their favourite wrestling show. As the man hunched over to gather his breath, Sam wrapped his hand around his bald head and slammed him face first onto the table.

As the man doubled back in a state of shock, Sam turned around in time for another fist to connect with his right cheekbone. Sam shook the blow, and the other man who had framed the older gentleman in the corner swung another. This time, Sam dropped a shoulder, allowed the man's arm to fall across, before grabbing it with both hands. As he pulled the greasy, runt of a man towards him, Sam lifted his body up, flipping the man over and watching as he collided back first onto the cruel edge of the metal table.

Before Sam could turn his attentions back to his first attacker, a sudden pain erupted from his ankle, shaking his body and dropping him to the floor. As he jolted uncontrollably, he could make out Sharp and his officers surrounding the three of them, to a chorus of jeers from the crowd baying for blood.

While he hadn't pissed his pants, Sam could confirm that Sharp was right.

The electric shock hurt like hell.

As Sam's breathing slowly returned to normal, Sharp loomed over him, a cruel smile of crooked teeth across his face.

'Trouble on your first night, eh?' He shook his head. 'What are going to do with you?'

With a snap of his fingers, Sharp stood back, and Sam could feel the hands of the guards wrap around his wrists. As he was dragged across the floor like a mop, his brain began to unscramble and the last thing he saw before being hauled from the room, was an impressed smile on the face of the bearded old man, whose goons he'd just dispatched.

As he was led down the hallway, Sam didn't know if that was such a good thing.

CHAPTER TEN

A week had gone by and Singh hadn't heard a single thing.

No reports on how Sam was surviving in Pentonville, or any updates on how he'd been assimilated into prison life. While Ashton had been forthright with her demands for Singh to distance herself from Sam for the good of her career, and her own, Singh had snuck onto the intranet a few times, checking the inhouse records but coming up blank each time. She was by no means a technological wizard, but the Met Police internal web system was hardly the *Matrix*.

But every search came to nothing.

Discreetly, she'd reached out to a trusted ally who worked in the IT department, but they too had been met by nothing but disappointment.

Something didn't feel right.

Singh had broached the subject once with Ashton, who had been hamming up her personal touch with everyone in the office, ensuring the support of many when she rose to the top seat. It was as transparent as a pane of glass, and every time she offered Singh an empty smile, it made her skin crawl.

It also caused her to reflect.

Just over six months ago, Singh looked at Ashton with wide-eyed respect. A woman who had risen through the ranks, making impeccable career moves, and forging the right friendships. It was inspiring to Singh, who was also climbing through the ranks and back then, Singh would have been congratulating Ashton for playing the political game.

But things had changed.

Sam Pope's war against injustice, either side of the thin blue line, had opened her eyes.

She didn't want to throw away her career, but Singh's motivation had moved away from what style of epaulettes she wore on her shoulder. Now, it was about making a difference.

About ensuring that true justice was carried out and she wasn't going to allow her own aspirations to blur her view on right or wrong.

Not since Sam had laid it out so clearly.

Her requests to Ashton for an update regarding Sam were met with a condescending shake of the head and a warning that she should know better. The rumours about her collusion still hadn't gone away, but in the eyes of the media, she was a beacon of hope for a police force whose credibility had been fed through a wood chipper.

But she was a damn good detective.

When presented with a version of the truth that knotted her stomach, Singh couldn't help but investigate it. It was that dogged nature that made her such a valued detective, that had seen her put forward to hunting down Sam in the first place.

Which now made her a pain in the arse.

The media had been quiet, too. Ever since the despicable murder of Helal Miah, the press had given the Sam Pope story a wide birth. There was extensive coverage of the sentencing for the first couple of days, with some of the more liberal papers printing Sam's speech verbatim as some sort of rallying cry. It was a dangerous tight rope to walk, as while Sam's acts were noble in theory, they were criminal in execution.

Celebrating him could lead to imitation, and Singh doubted anyone looking to take up the mantle would have the same skills he did.

But there had been no pressure from the journalists to bring Sam's first week behind bars to the public domain and the guilt of Helal Miah's death hung heavy on her conscience. Almost all of them had been in touch, wanting an interview with the star detective who had brought the UK's most dangerous man to justice. A part of her wanted to scare them off, to tell them the truth about how Helal Miah was even caught up in a series of events that would end in his murder. Although he was brutally tortured and killed by Farukh Abdul, she was the one who had brought him into the frame.

She'd sold Miah the story.

Had put him in the firing line.

And while she didn't beat him to a pulp, nor wrap the noose that choked the life out of him around his neck, she still had blood on her hands.

It was why she was determined to keep her career going. Sam had given his freedom for her own and Helal Miah had died to bring the truth to light. The article published in his memory by his heart broken boss, had lifted the lid on the extent of Wallace's crimes.

They had honoured Miah by getting the story he'd died for out there.

Sam had honoured his death by bringing those responsible to justice.

She would honour it by not letting those sacrifices be for nothing.

But still, something didn't sit right.

She'd thought about bouncing some ideas off Pearce. Seeing him at the trial had been the one brief moment of happiness she'd endured in months and knowing that he effectively retired in the face of helping save her life had rewritten the betrayal she'd original pinned to him.

But he was out of it now.

Retired.

Dedicating his life to a new cause and one that she didn't want to disrupt. Singh had also considered going to speak to Etheridge, but the man's cowardice in the face of Sam's incarceration had caused her blood to boil. Etheridge may have been beaten and shot for the cause, but Sam had saved his life when they were soldiers.

The least Etheridge could do was be there for Sam when his life as a free man was coming to an end.

Singh sat back in her chair, rested her hands on her head, and took a deep breath. The sleeves of her neatly ironed, white shirt had been rolled up to the elbow and she stared at the phone on her desk.

The idea running through her head should have made her stomach flip, but the knot caused by Sam's sudden disappearance had held it steady. She hated the thought of what she was about to do, but what else was there?

Singh was out of ideas.

And she needed to know what the hell was going on.

With a resounding sigh, she leant forward, logged into her terminal, and brought up the police directory. After a few clicks on the keyboard, she found the number for the administration office for Pentonville Prison.

Prison Guard Matt Allison had made no secret of his attraction to her on the few times she'd visited the depressing structure, annoying her with suggestive comments as she made her way to interrogate a prisoner.

Despite her rejections, he never wavered. There was always an offer for a drink and promise of a good time.

He was either extremely confident or wildly deluded.

From Singh's experience, most men seemed to be made up of a mixture of both.

She dialled the number, and as the phone rang and then automatically put her in the queue, she gritted her teeth. A non-descript Coldplay song echoed in her ears, a depressingly apt tune as she abandoned her morals. Using her womanly charm was never a weapon that she kept in her arsenal. It went against everything she'd built for herself.

But she had to know.

Something wasn't right.

And Singh was damn sure she was going to find out what.

———

The week in solitary confinement passed a lot quicker than Sam had expected.

After literally being dragged through the prison, to the delight of the inmates, Sam had been hauled to his feet and roughly pulled down two flights of stairs to the basement which housed a dank corridor, lit only by a few bulbs that were running on empty. There were four, thick metal doors, each of which opened up to a thin, empty room. As the guards unlocked the one in the furthest corner, Sam was happy to smell the putrid smell of damp.

It meant the shock he'd received hadn't blasted away his sense of smell, but he was soon hurled into the room, followed by a few empty threats and meaningless curse words, before the door slammed shut, sealing him in his dark tomb. As he pulled himself to a seated position, the bottom panel of the metal door slid open and a stained, metal bucket was tossed into the room, clattering loudly.

Then darkness again.

The following day, Harris had come to see him, offering his apologies that Sam's first night had resulted in such a mess. Sam held his tongue, not wanting to add to the man's clear health problems by suggesting that it was a set up. Harris wasn't an idiot, and he confessed as much to Sam that he knew Sharp had a way with inducting new inmates that wasn't part of the prison policy.

But Sharp, despite being a cruel and power-hungry man, wasn't an idiot. He had already submitted the necessary reports to ensure that Sam's incarceration in solitary was acknowledged and approved, which meant Harris's hands were tied. He could try, but it would take longer than the week Sam had been assigned.

The best he could offer, was to ensure his bucket was cleared out daily and to keep the light on in the room for a few hours a day. Then, in an act of kindness that touched Sam, he handed over a copy of *War and Peace*, and told him to tuck in.

So Sam did.

After day five, Sharp had entered the room with a few of the guards, goading Sam to lash out to no avail. Sam had kept his calm, even when Sharp had snatched up the book and dumped it in the foul-smelling bucket.

All Sam did was remind Sharp that the book belonged to Harris and smiled when Sharp cursed loudly and stormed out of the room, flanked by his goons.

Moments later, the light went off.

It didn't come back on for the rest of Sam's stay.

After what Sam judged to be roughly seven days, he heard the jingling of keys and murmured words through the door, then the loud clank of the lock turning. The light that burst into the room burnt his eyes and he looked away, drawing a delighted chuckle from Sharp.

'Wakey, wakey,' Sharp said, his smugness telling Sam it was clearly rehearsed. 'Fucking hell, it stinks like shit in here.'

'I'm pretty sure it stinks like shit in every room you enter.'

Sam paid for the remark, as Sharp drove his thick, metal capped boot into his ribs. As the air rushed from his body, Sam hunched forward and wheezed.

'Get him up,' Sharp commanded, and two guards strode in and hauled Sam to his feet. It was the first time in a week he'd stepped a foot outside the small room and the lack of proper food and water hit Sam like a tidal wave. He stumbled to the side, collapsing against the wall, much to the crazed delight of Sharp.

'Not such a smart fucker now, are you?' Sharp spat, not expecting an answer. Sam didn't offer one, anyway. Sharp turned on his heel, walking proudly ahead, as the two guards chaperoned Sam behind. As they made their way up the stairs, Sharp, clearly enjoying the sound of his own voice, spoke.

'See, Sam. Despite what Harris thinks, I run this side of the prison. He's on his way out and soon, he'll be gone for good. He's the last of a dying breed. A man who thinks he can make a difference. He believes that a place like this may not change men like you, but it can at least give you a sense of peace.'

They stepped through the doors and into the main corridor where a week ago, Sam had been hauled across the floor like a bag of cement. Sharp continued.

'But me, I see this place for what it is. A cage. A place to keep the scum and make sure they spend every day regretting every fucking action they took. Now, I don't expect a man like you to change overnight. I expect you will try to hold your head up high, be this dignified soldier you make yourself out to be. And that's fine. It will be fun to beat that out of you.'

Sharp stopped in front of the double metal doors that led to the canteen. He turned to Sam with a smile.

'But you will break, Sam. And when you do, I'll be there to collect the pieces with a smile on my face.' Sharp offered him a vulgar grin, his stained teeth shooting out from his gums like crooked stalagmites. 'Now, you must be hungry, right?'

Sam sighed, arching an eyebrow in agreement.

'Yes.'

'Yes, what?'

'Yes, *deputy* warden.' Sam's emphasis on the word caused a flash of fury to betray Sharp's calm demeanor. He quickly tried to mask it, but Sam clocked it. He also noticed the time on Sharp's watch, seeing it was well past the allotted time slots for dinner. 'I take it you haven't put on a special dinner for me?'

'Oh, I haven't. No.' Sharp smirked, trying his best to be mysterious. 'But someone has.'

'Who?' Sam asked, flashing a quick glance at his surroundings, his training kicking in when an ambush seemed imminent.

'Like I said, I run *this* side of the prison.' Sharp opened the door. 'Bon appetite.'

Two hands roughly slammed into Sam's back, shunting him through the door and into the canteen. The door slammed behind Sam, and he turned to look at the room which had been plunged into the darkness. The halogen tubes he'd stared up at as he was pulled across the floor a week ago were off, but Sam couldn't see the fixtures at all. He knew where they were, he'd logged that detail away, but the darkness was so thick, he couldn't even see his hand in front of his face.

The only light in the room came from the table in the far corner where a lamp had been placed, its bulb bathing the metal table in a bright glow, illuminating the solitary plate that was covered in food. Sam's hunger and curiosity drew him towards it, walking slowly so as not to collide with any of the other furniture. As Sam approached, a waft of meat and vegetables filled his nose and he hurried his pace. Just as he adjusted to take his seat, a figure stepped out from the shadows opposite him.

The bearded man from the first night, who had watched approvingly as Sam had dismantled his two men. Without saying a word, the man stepped to the other side of the table, his advanced age showing as he lowered himself to the chair opposite. As he adjusted his sizeable gut, he looked up at Sam with a powerful glare, one that was used to demand respect and furious that Sam wasn't showing any.

'Jesus fucking Christ, would you sit down?' The man's East London accent was as thick as his beard. 'Your food's getting cold.'

Sam looked around, seeing nothing but darkness, before slowly lowering himself into the chair, not taking his eyes off the prisoner.

'Who are you?'

'I'm the 'Guvnor',' he replied proudly. 'And once you have a nice full belly, I'll explain to you just how well and truly fucked you really are.'

CHAPTER ELEVEN

It took Harry Chapman over twenty years before he was known as the Guvnor. He always saw it as paying his dues, but there was an underlying frustration that it took him that long to rise to the top of the criminal underworld that ran through London like an insidious vein.

He got his first taste of his future during his teenage years. Growing up on an estate in Stockwell on the south side of the Thames, he and his older brother, Mike, were on amicable terms with the drug runners that frequented their building. The large tower block comprised of eight concrete floors of identikit apartments and was owned by the council and filled with many people living below the poverty line during the seventies. Harry would often stare out from their seventh-floor window. The view his bedroom window afforded him, especially at night, was a cacophony of lights.

The city of London in all its majesty.

It was beyond the version he'd grown up in, and his father, who worked as a bus driver, would constantly complain about the rat race that infested the city.

Giles Chapman was an honest man, who had worked

hard to emerge from a monstrous childhood to build a quaint life for himself. Happily married for fifteen years until the untimely death of his wife, Giles had worked diligently to ensure their two sons were given the opportunities that he never had.

Looking back at it, Harry often wondered whether his father would have been proud of the man he became. Sure, he eventually rose to being the most notorious criminal in the UK, but he built an unshakable legacy that was still standing long after his incarceration.

During his teen years, Harry had towed the line. He had gone to school. He had done his homework, excelling in maths which would eventually be the greatest tool in his arsenal. By being able to read the numbers and plot ahead, Harry took the drug empire to places it had never been before.

Back then, he wanted to be an accountant. His father often spoke about the rich men he saw while having a cheeky cigarette by the side of his bus. All of them marching around Marble Arch in their fancy suits, weaving in and out of accountancy firms.

'Money is what really equals power. Not position.'

Those words always stuck with Harry, and during his rise up the criminal food chain, they echoed in his mind with every move he made. Whether it be when concluding a multi-million-pound drug deal or slicing open a snitch's throat with a box cutter, those words rang in his head.

The dream of being an accountant began to fade when Mike was approached by the local drug dealers to become a spotter, and within six months, was promoted to an actual dealer. At just seventeen years old, Mike was bringing in more money than their heart-broken father. That heartbreak was soon superseded by lung cancer and while he would regret not speaking to Mike before he passed, he'd begged Harry to follow the right path.

To keep following the numbers.

To seek out money, not reputation.

Harry had every intention of honouring his father's dying wish, but when Mike was beaten and hurled from the fifth floor of the block less than a year later, Harry's life took a turn. There was a flash point, a fork in the road where he could have carried on, allowed the trauma of losing his family to spur him on to a decent life. Or seek revenge and never look back.

The fact Mike didn't die on impact was what allowed him time to think it over. For fifteen grotesque hours, surgeons tried their best to fix his broken body. The pain must have been insufferable and as he watched them rush his shattered body into surgery, Harry had wept. Through his tear-stained hands, he thought of their time together, roughhousing in the living room. Mike had always looked after him, ensuring no one ever picked on his little brother.

Now it was Harry's turn to protect the only thing he had left of his brother. His memory.

A local dealer, a sinister man with dreadlocks named Sy, took Harry under his wing, telling Harry he felt somewhat responsible for the death. A rival dealer had targeted Sy's patch and Mike was an unfortunate victim of the game they played.

Harry smiled politely, accepted the lame apology, and worked round the clock to become Sy's number two. By the age of twenty, Harry had killed three people.

The two men responsible for killing his brother, and the man who had sent them. He was christened the 'BC', as he'd slit their throats with a rusty box cutter.

Another year later, he'd nailed Sy to a chair and set him on fire in front of the rest of his crew, taking control of the drug empire and changing the course of his future forever.

The following two decades were a whirlwind of money,

women, and drugs. The harder he crunched the numbers, the quicker he expanded, and by making smart moves with suppliers, he was able to triple his income year on year. A bigger target was painted on his chest, from both sides of the law, but the mammoth wealth he amassed not only ensured his safety, but the blind loyalty of his men.

They killed for him.

They died for him.

Harry Chapman, on the eve of his forty-second birthday, was christened The Guvnor for the first time. One of the tabloid papers coined the term and it soon stuck. By building an empire of so many levels, it was almost impossible for the police to pin anything to him. With his eye on an early retirement, he traded the gangster lifestyle for a luxurious estate in Surbiton, where he went through two messy divorces and sadly, never fathered a child.

It was his only regret of a life that had far exceeded the insurmountable odds placed against it.

Two years before his eventual capture and incarceration, The Guvnor changed the criminal underworld permanently. By combining the estates of other empires and offering a share of the spoils, he soon brought together an enterprise so powerful that even the police wanted in.

A series of buildings, known effectively as 'High Rises' were purchased and renovated, with each one offered to a crime boss. Harry's money meant the police stayed away and his contacts ensured a steady flow of product was available for the customers. Women, men, children, drugs. Whatever was desired by the paying customer was reachable and soon, The Guvnor was not only tripling his multi-million fortune, he also had every major criminal in the damn country begging to be on his staff.

'Money is what really equals power. Not position.'

No truer words had a greater man spoken.

The press would run features on the supposed Guvnor,

christening the rumoured High Rises as 'The High Street', a place where the elite could live out their most depraved fantasies but with no evidence to back it up, valuable witnesses going missing, and over half of the Met Police in his back pocket, he was untouchable.

Or so he thought.

A needless trip to the theatre with a young lady turned out to be a honey trap where he was caught on camera confessing his implicit involvement in the trafficking of women. Unfortunately for him, one of the detectives, Adrian Pearce, was an incorruptible bastard who ensured those working the case saw it through to the end.

At the age of fifty-one, Harry Chapman was sentenced to life in prison and soon found himself locked down in the most secure facility in Europe.

It wasn't too bad. His reputation and his manner soon got him a seat at the top table, with the inmates bending over backwards to work for him. The prison guards were either paid off or their families threatened.

When Harris was in attendance, Chapman towed the line. He was too old to fight back, but after a decade under his watch, he'd come to respect Harris for his dignified leadership.

Sharp, on the other hand, was a joke of a man but he had a thirst for power that Chapman could manipulate.

Once Harris retired, and it was soon coming, Sharp may be in line for the throne, but The Guvnor would be running The Grid.

And now, as he sat opposite Sam Pope, he couldn't help but smile at the hand fate had dealt him once more.

––––––

Despite the ominous warning of the large, bearded man before him, Sam ploughed into the dinner like a man possessed. Having survived off the one measly bowl of cold porridge afforded to him in solitary, the taste of vegetables was welcome. It was the first proper meal he'd had since his time spent in West Hampstead Police Station, where an affable officer had ensured he was well fed and had also brought him something to read.

Sam was under no illusion that this dinner was being provided out of the goodness of his fellow inmate's heart. As he mopped up the last remnants of gravy with his final fork of meat, Sam looked up at the man opposite and took his last mouthful. The man warmly smiled, nodded, and then relaxed back in his seat.

'Good?'

'Not bad.' Sam wiped his mouth with the back of his hand.

'I should think so. It came from my private stash.'

Sam stared at the man, who seemed aggravated by his lack of appreciation. The man cleared his throat.

'Do you know who I am?' His tone was menacing, yet clearly rehearsed.

'The cook?' Sam shrugged.

'Very funny. My name is Harry Chapman. Ring any bells?' Sam shook his head. 'Or, like I said, you can call me The Guvnor.'

'I'd rather not.' Sam extended his hand. 'I'm Sam.'

'Oh, I fucking know who you are. See, while you may have had the country shaking in its boots for the last year or so, I've been doing it for nearly four decades. And I may have been in here when you went on your little quest for justice, you still stepped on toes you really shouldn't have.'

Chapman carefully eyed Sam, the lack of fear in the man's eyes causing his fists to clench in anger. He continued.

'Now, you want to go around killing bad guys or bent coppers because your little boy got killed, that's fine by me.

As far as I'm concerned, there is nothing worse than a bent copper and most of the fuckwits running the streets these days don't know their arse from their elbow. In some ways, you were actually providing a service. But then you took down a good friend of mine, Frank Jackson.'

'He had friends?' Sam responded, knowing his flippant answers were angering Chapman. The Guvnor pursed his lips in contemplation.

'*Friend* might be a little strong. How about *acquaintance*? Frank ran a tight ship in his High Rise. He paid the right people to keep the wolves from the door and his clientele was almost as valuable as the money he made. His building was the number one location on the High Street, which you've pretty much brought crashing to the ground since you filled him with bullets.'

'So?'

'The High Street belongs to me.' Chapman slammed his hand on the metal table to emphasise his point, the impact echoing loudly throughout the dark room. 'Every building, every bag of cocaine, every disease-ridden whore. They belonged to me. I may be on this side of freedom, Sam, but believe me, I still ran that fucking show. But then you strolled in, the avenger, with a gun in his hand and nothing to lose. This isn't the wild fucking west, son, and while you didn't have anything to lose, unfortunately for you, I did.'

Chapman sat back in his chair to catch his breath and Sam noticed the beads of sweat beginning to form across the man's thinning hairline. As he pulled out a handkerchief to dab at it, a guard appeared from the darkness with a glass of water. Sam raised his eyebrows to meet the scowl of the man, who slipped seamlessly back into the void. Chapman took a sip of water and continued.

'Money is what equals power, Sam. Not position. Your attacks on the High Rise, your obliteration of the

Kovalenkos, all of it directly hit my pockets. Now in here, I can get whatever I want, whenever I want. The guards know it. The inmates know it. And I want you to know it.'

'That's very impressive,' Sam said dismissively.

'Shut your fucking mouth. As far as I see it, you've cost me millions of pounds. And the only reason I haven't had your solitary door ripped from its hinges and had you beaten to death is that it's too good for you. I would hazard a guess that you would quite like to die a martyr to the hero worshippers who see you as more than what you really are.'

'And what's that?'

'A killer.' Chapman clasped his hands together, interlocking his fingers and doing his best to calm his temper. 'Whatever reason you tell yourself, you killed those people because you liked it. I get it. I've slit enough throats in my time to get the lust for it, the power surge that rattles through every muscle when you end a man's life. But you have this irritating boy scout bullshit which means death is too good for you. So instead of dying for what you took from me, you're going to work it off.'

'You want me to wash your car?' Sam asked, but this time, Chapman smirked.

'I would suggest you take this seriously. There are a lot of desperate men in this place, Sam. A lot of them wanting the smallest crumb from my table and I'll make every single day you have left in this place a living hell. You don't have any guns in here. No plans. No backup. Like Sharp says, everyone walks their final mile in this place and up until I decide when yours has arrived, you will work for me. Is that clear?'

Sam regarded Chapman with an unnerving stare and then pushed his plate to the centre of the table and stood.

'Thanks for dinner. Oh, and although I've only been here for a week or so, I'd steer clear of quoting anything

Sharp says. You wouldn't want to get tarred with that brush.'

'Quite.' Chapman slowly lifted himself from his chair. 'Obviously, you need a little time to think about it so let me just reinforce exactly what I mean when I say I run this place.'

Chapman slowly lifted his hand into the air and then clicked his fingers. Instantly, the halogen bulbs clunked loudly, illuminating the entire cafeteria. Sam scanned the room and lined up against the walls, previously shrouded in darkness, where over ten prison guards, all of them with their metal batons in their hands.

Each with their eyes locked on Sam.

Fixing them all with an unblinking stare, Sam cracked his neck and then calmly walked back through the room towards the door, a silent dare to any of them who fancied their chances. Even before one of them provided the Guvnor with a glass of water, Sam knew they weren't alone. He also knew that the numbers were against him and if all of them called his bluff, then he was in for a hell of an uncomfortable night.

The guard nearest to the door stepped forward, meeting Sam a few paces from the exit and with a swift flick of his arm, he drew the baton up and brought it crashing down.

He stopped it less than an inch from Sam's temple.

Sam didn't flinch.

The guard scoffed nervously, his eyes darting around the room for support and then he slowly stepped to the side in embarrassment. Sam sighed and looked back over his shoulder at Chapman, who arrogantly smirked.

'Can I go now?' Sam asked with a sense of boredom.

'Of course.' Chapman motioned with his hand. 'But keep your energy up for tomorrow night, Sam. You're going to need it.'

Sam took a step, stopped, and turned back.

'What's tomorrow?'

The Guvnor, who had retaken his seat, fixed Sam with a confident gaze, stroked his bearded chin, and smiled.

'Day one.'

CHAPTER TWELVE

'Fancy another?'

Matt Allison offered his best smile, and Singh sighed inwardly. For all intents and purposes, he was a good man. Well-built and with a strong jaw, he was the identikit police officer. For over a decade, Allison had been on the beat, loving the thrill of the unknown and the adrenaline of every 999 call. But after a nasty traffic collision caused serious damage to his spine, Allison had to step away from his dream job.

He was lucky not to be paralysed, but his limited mobility meant there was no chance he could return to the streets. Not to be outdone by the cruel hands of fate, he took up a position as a prison guard at Her Majesty's Prison Pentonville in Kings Cross and from what Singh had gathered, he was well liked and respected.

He was just a little too blatant in his attraction to her.

As he went to get them both another drink, she scolded herself for her actions. Allison was a good man and in a rugged way, quite attractive, even if middle age had greyed his hair and slightly bulged his waistline. But he'd made the effort tonight, with his beard trimmed neatly and his smart shirt had clearly been brought for the occasion. The guilt Singh was feeling was that to him, this evening was a shot at potential happiness.

For her, it was a fact-finding mission.

As he returned to the table with another pint of ale and a gin and tonic, he afforded her his best smile. She returned in kind, thanked him for the drink and took a sip.

'So, what's it like being the hottest detective in town?' Allison asked, before taking a swig of his drink.

'Not as glamourous as you might think,' she responded, poking the stirrer into her drink dismissively. 'Lots of attention.'

'You must be used to that.'

She smirked, flattered slightly and that small twinge of guilt returned. The bar was packed, the Thursday night crowd in London was the same as every other night.

Out for a good time.

Swathes of local businesses had poured in, with numerous co-workers drunkenly clambering over each other with regrettable abandon. Judging by the wedding rings around some of their fingers, Singh wondered how many were possibly on the verge of making a drunken mistake. Quickly, she returned to the conversation.

'Well, funnily enough, in our line of work, attention isn't always a good thing.'

'That's true.' Allison agreed as he sipped his pint. 'Being called an ugly cunt by an inmate isn't much fun.'

Singh scoffed into her drink, her mind racing at the thought of actually enjoying herself. Judging by the effort Allison was making, he saw this as a date. Despite being the one to call and arrange the meetup, Singh had to disassociate herself from that idea.

She wanted to find out about Sam.

Somewhere in the back of her mind, the notion that he

was the reason she wouldn't allow herself to enjoy it gnawed away at her like a toothache.

But this wasn't about them, if there even was a *them*.

She still hadn't found anything relating to Sam's incarceration at Pentonville. No reports. No news articles.

Nothing but closed doors and vacant shrugs.

The most wanted man in the UK finally put behind bars, yet nobody wanted to talk about it.

'Lots on your mind?' Allison asked, his words slightly worried. Singh returned a smile.

'Long week, that's all.'

He nodded, more to reassure himself than in agreement and took an anxious sip and placed down the empty glass.

'Another?' She offered, but he held up a firm hand.

'No, this evening is on me.' He stood, nodded to her half empty glass and she shrugged her acceptance. When he returned, the confident swagger that verged on desperation had returned.

Singh seized her moment.

'Must be a media frenzy at your place at the moment, eh?' she said playfully as she finished her previous drink.

'Not really. People don't get that excited about prisons these days unless Ross Kemp is telling the world how shit they are.'

Singh giggled flirtatiously. She hated herself for doing it. She was a highly trained, highly decorated detective with over a decade on the job. Her career had seen her burst into drug dens with an assault rifle, bring down paedophile rings, and fight against Ukrainian sex traffickers.

But here she was, using her gender and the possible allure of a sexual encounter to get what she wanted.

To her, it felt like a betrayal.

Not just of this sweet man's trust, but of every value she held dear.

But she needed to get to the truth.

To do what was necessary.

It's what Sam would do.

'Oh, come on.' Singh sipped her drink. 'Not a day has gone by where the press hasn't asked me about arresting Sam Pope. Bringing in the biggest vigilante this country has ever seen. They must be swarming all over your prison like ants at a picnic.'

'I'd liken the press more to flies around pig shit.' Allison chuckled. 'But no, it's been fine.'

'Bullshit.' Singh playfully retorted. She saw a flicker of excitement in his eye and as he peered over his shoulder, she felt the muscles in her body tighten.

He was about to tell her something.

Trust her.

She felt sick with guilt.

'Thing is, we haven't seen him.' Allison shrugged. 'We were all on high alert, there was even talk about a possible assault on the prison to get to him, but nothing.'

'What do you mean?'

'I mean' – he looked around making sure no one was in earshot – 'he didn't show up.' Allison spoke in hushed tones. 'Me and the boys, we were excited, you know? I mean, he may be a criminal, but the man is a legend. He took down so many scumbags, he put us all to shame. But the day came, the trial finished, and by the evening, we all clocked off, and nothing's been said since then. Word from the skipper is to keep quiet and not talk about it.'

'Are you telling me that Sam Pope never made it Pentonville?'

'Yup.' Confidently, Allison finished his drink. 'Fuck if I know where they buried him.'

For a few seconds, the bar froze. None of the drunken

banter or tedious pop music filtered through. Singh sat, shell-shocked, her mind racing as if she'd just emerged from water, before all her senses returned, along with a sense of clarity.

'I have to go,' she said firmly, standing immediately. Concerned, Allison stood, his hands held out in surprise.

'Is everything okay?'

Singh stopped and laid a sympathetic hand on his arm. He was a good man and she could see the hurt in his eyes. She knew he would question everything he said, where he went wrong. The usual checklist people who were looking for love ran through when a date fell through.

With an apologetic smile, she answered him.

'No, Matt. I have a bad feeling that things are very far from okay.'

Before he could respond, Singh marched to the door and as the cool breeze of the spring evening hit her, she felt the air rush into her lungs and she allowed herself to breathe.

———

The security system at Ashcroft had amazed Sharp since the day he'd started. No expense had been spared and it was common knowledge that the government had contracted the very best experts to create an impenetrable system and they'd been just as generous with the staff employed to run it.

During the quiet hours, between the staggered exercise breaks and dinner time, Sharp enjoyed spending time within the security office, the numerous screens on the wall offering a visual of every corridor and cell.

Watching the inmates maintaining their hourly push up routines was mundane, but there was a perverted sense of power Sharp felt when he observed them sat on the toilet or pathetically masturbating.

Even in their most private moments, Sharp ruled over them.

Along with the misguided sense of control, he enjoyed the fear he instilled in the security operators, especially Spencer Watkins. The man had more degrees than Sharp could count, but while his brain may have been impressive, his thin, breakable frame was not and Sharp enjoyed adding a little extra impetus into every backslap he gave the man.

Small displays of his strength, along with the hours of footage of him belittling and beating the inmates, meant Watkins shrunk into himself when Sharp sat idly by his side.

Today's entertainment was Sam Pope.

Sharp glared at the screen, watching with a jealous rage at the calm man who sat quietly in his small cell with his legs crossed and his eyes closed. The idea of being locked away in this underground hellhole seemed to hold no fear to him and having reviewed the footage from his discussion with Chapman, the very real threats to his future had raised zero concern.

Sam's calmness worried Sharp, but he would never admit it. The thought that he could beat Sam into submission, break him so he bent to his will was quickly becoming a fool's errand.

After reviewing the footage of Sam's dinner with Chapman, Sharp had begun to worry about how he would be perceived by The Guvnor going forward. Sure, Harris was sat in the main chair, but Chapman was running the prison. The inmates scattered when he walked by, laughed when he told a terrible joke, or asked 'how high?' when he told them to jump.

Sharp was Chapman's safety net.

A very well-paid safety net.

With the man's limitless fortune, Chapman had offered Sharp riches and pleasures beyond the paltry salary he earned from the government, and had sent him to the few establishments Sam hadn't burnt to the ground.

With the money in his bank account and his name on the guest list, Sharp had indulged in his most depraved fantasies. Multiple women had been trapped under his meaty body, submitting to his grotesque demands while he stuffed as much cocaine up as his nose as he could. He could do whatever he wanted with them and he would often laugh when he tossed whatever money he deemed their worth, as they cried over what he'd put them through.

Well, the ones who were still conscious.

All he had to do to keep the gravy train running was facilitate Chapman's life behind bars.

Sharp allowed him to bring in as much contraband through the guards as he desired, would set his guards on whoever Chapman pointed at and gave him the keys to his own cell.

It was a small price to pay for the doors Chapman had opened and in the back of Sharp's mind, the idea of ending The Guvnor's rule when he took the top job had crossed his mind once or twice. Until then, Sharp was more than happy watching his bank account grow and his desires fulfilled.

Watkins was aware of Sharp's deal with Chapman, but a very clear threat to his family kept him quiet. A meek man, Watkins took his job seriously and he baffled Sharp with his technical talk. He was foolishly asked how secure the doors were, but as soon as Watkins began mentioning algorithms and self-changing identifiers, he glazed over, called him a nerd, and slapped him hard across the shoulder blades.

All Sharp knew was the prison was as secure as Fort

Knox, but instead of being locked down by sadistic guards, it was controlled by Watkins and his team of bookworms.

Sam's lack of fear was boring him, and he glanced at his watch. It was almost time to take Sam for his dinner, which drew a smile across his face.

Almost time to let the man know what he was in for.

With a large sigh, he sat forward in his chair, gazed around the room – which had the feel of an airport control hanger – and nudged Watkins with his meaty elbow.

'Go on. Zap him.'

Sharp grinned, showing his coffee-stained teeth. Watkins shook his head.

'Every use of the tag system has to be logged and reasoned with. While you might find it fun, deputy warden, there are only so many flagrant uses I can cover when we get audited.'

'You are such a fucking wet blanket.' Sharp stood and slapped Watkins across the back, ensuring he leant into it. The whimper of pain drew a smile. 'Lighten the fuck up.'

Watkins mumbled something under his breath and Sharp thought about calling him out on it. It would make him feel good, but ultimately, it would just be treading old ground. The man was scared shitless, and that's all that mattered. Reaching forward and hitting the 'lockdown' button, which would zap every pathetic member of the prison population, would have been fun but Sharp relented.

He had something better for his evening's entertainment.

Without offering a goodbye, Sharp stormed from the office, nodded to his subordinate who stood guard in the hallway and they made their way to the underground levels of the structure. As they ventured through the corridors, Sharp made a mental note of which cells were open, as the staggered dinner had just begun.

No one of any real bother. Most of the prisoners were resigned to their fate and, with the opportunity of garnering drugs, cigarettes, or porn from Chapman, they towed the line.

There were no problems.

Except one.

Sharp stopped at Sam's cell and his colleague went through the usual rigmarole of slamming his baton against the door and demanding Sam face the far wall. Watkins, hidden away in his control room, activated the door, and the guard hauled it open.

Sharp hid his fury as Sam hadn't moved. Still sat on his bed, he arched his head up, met Sharp's angered glare with a dismissive roll of the eyes and spoke.

'Can I help you, deputy?'

A cruel grin spread across Sharp's face. Sam's insolence was only going to make this evening even sweeter.

'Let's go, boy scout.' Sharp kicked the bed with his steel capped boot. 'It's showtime.'

CHAPTER THIRTEEN

Sam had followed Sharp obediently as he left the room, ignoring the cocky smirk of the prison guard accompanying them. After the lame attempt of intimidation after his dinner date with Chapman, Sam was under no illusion who was truly running The Grid.

Throughout the day, there had been this lingering sense that he was in trouble. A few snide remarks from the guards, the near silence that greeted his emergence during the exercise hour. It all told Sam that whatever Chapman had planned for *day one* had spread through Ashcroft like wildfire. It didn't bother him.

This was never supposed to be a relaxing holiday.

As he followed Sharp to the cafeteria, a few other guards offered him a sympathetic shake of the head, as if apologising for his loss.

The doors opened and as Sharp strode in, a hush fell across the canteen.

It wasn't for him.

All eyes were on Sam.

'Eat up.' Sharp smugly grinned at Sam. 'You're going to need your strength.'

Sam ignored Sharp, striding past him to the metal counter where he was greeted with another uninspired selection of meat and vegetables. With his stomach rumbling, Sam took a tray and turned to face the room. Everyone who had been looking at him quickly bowed their heads, returning to their tasteless meal or equally tasteless conversation. In the far corner, as expected, Chapman sat. Either side of him sat his henchmen, Glen and Ravi, both of whom were staring daggers at Sam through their heavily bruised faces.

Sam couldn't help himself, and he gave them a polite nod. Instantly, Ravi slammed his fist on the table in anger and made to stand up before Chapman reached out and yanked him back down by his heavily tattooed forearm. It was a pathetic attempt at intimidation and Sam dropped his tray in front of the closest vacant seat and sat down to eat.

All conversations stopped and Sam looked at his fellow inmates, who refused to make eye contact. Beyond them, by the door, Sharp watched, arms crossed and a cocky grin across his face. As Sam lifted a forkful of barely cooked carrots to his mouth, he imagined the satisfaction he would have in wiping it off his face.

His train of thought was halted by the inmate to his right.

'Yo, Sam, right?'

Sam put his fork down and glanced up. The man offered a strong handshake, his black skin coated in faint tattoos similar to Ravi. He was well built, with his hair shaved close to the scalp in contrast to the scruffy beard that framed his strong jaw.

'Yup,' Sam replied carefully.

'Leon.' He pushed his hand closer. 'Nice to meet you.'

Sam took the handshake.

'Not sure it should be.' Sam shrugged. 'I'm not too popular around here.'

'Nah, I get that. Lotta these guys got guys you put in the ground, you get me?' He flashed Sam a grin, revealing a solid gold tooth among his pearly whites. 'Me, I ain't really got no ties so as far as I'm concerned, you killin' rapists and sex trafficking mother fuckers is more like doin' this country a service.'

Sam chuckled. Of all the places he expected to find a charming conversation, over a tepid meal inside a maximum-security prison wasn't top of the list. Leon flashed a few concerned glances towards Chapman's table, immediately looking away as Ravi met his eyes.

'You ready?' Leon asked, not looking up from his meal.

'For what?'

Before Leon could respond, a hand grabbed the back of Leon's head and slammed him face down into his dinner. The thud was sickening and the howl from Leon told Sam his nose had been broken. Sam instantly stood, grabbed the prison guard's wrist and twisted it, bringing the man to his knees and a sharp cry of pain to echo out.

'Let him go.' Sharp's voice boomed and Sam turned to face the deputy warden, who had his hand resting on the handgun strapped to his waist. Sam relented, roughly releasing the guard's arm, who scurried back a few steps to Sharp.

'That piece of shit nearly broke my fucking wrist.' He barked, shooting Sam a venomous look.

'I'm sure you can wank with the other hand,' Sharp said, seemingly expecting a laugh that never arrived.

'That was uncalled for,' Sam stated, pointing at Leon who was sat upright, his hands pressed to his broken nose, the blood filtering through the gaps in his fingers.

'I didn't want old motor mouth here to ruin the

surprise,' Sharp responded. He moved his hand from his sidearm and slapped Leon around the back of the head. 'So keep your fucking mouth shut.'

After a few more moments, Sharp and the guard made their way to the door, calling time on everyone's meal. Sam offered Leon a hand up, but the consequences of association saw him reject it. Sam understood, but found it hard to muster guilt.

However friendly Leon was, he was in Ashcroft for the same reason as Sam and every other man in identical T-shirts.

They were dangerous criminals.

As everyone filtered to the door, Sam watched the crowd parting as Chapman and his goons exited. As Sam went to leave, Sharp stopped him for a split second, allowing the prison guard to drive his left fist straight into Sam's stomach. Sam hunched over, gasping for the air that had been driven from his body and the guard theatrically shook his hand.

'I can do more than just wank with this hand, you piece of shit.'

It was a cheap shot, but Sam straightened up, took a few deep breaths and fixed the guard with a stare that stopped him in his tracks. Sharp shoved Sam to the door and as they approached the turn to Sam's cell, Sharp instead pulled open the door to the stairwell.

'Where are we going?'

'Let's take a walk,' Sharp said, patting his firearm to insinuate the outcome if Sam refused.

'You're not going to give me another one of your speeches, are you?' Sam asked dryly, following Sharp as he marched down the stairs, followed by the other guard.

'I'm getting sick and tired of your smart mouth.' Sharp said as he ascended to the underground floor, where Sam had spent his first week in solitary. 'But Chapman, he has made it clear that putting a bullet in your head is off the table.'

'Does he always tell you what to do?'

Sharp stopped on the last step, snapping his neck back, his eyes filled with rage.

'No one tells me what to do. Let me make it fucking clear to you, I only let him think he runs this place because I get paid. If I wanted to, I could end him and his little crew like that.' Sharp snapped his fingers. 'But having him around means my bank account grows and we get to have evenings like tonight.'

Sam didn't question any further, following Sharp out of the stairwell and into the grimly lit corridors of the lowest floor of The Grid. In the distance, Sam could hear the echo of a crowd, the wild cheers of a blood-crazed audience. Sharp strode towards the noise, stopping at the slightly ajar metal door. With a sick grin, he shoved it open and stood to the side, ushering Sam towards it.

'Welcome to 'Fight Night', you little prick.' Sharp spat. 'Guess who's top billing for tonight?'

Sam stepped over the threshold and into an attack of his senses. The boisterous noise echoed loudly around the large, empty storeroom, with almost all the prison's capacity circling the room. The smell of sweat and blood filled his nose and he looked over the hyper crowd to the clearing in the middle where two inmates, stripped to the waist, were beating the hell out of each other. The chants of the baiting crowd told Sam that there were stakes attached and sure enough, in the far corner, Chapman was sat alongside the weasely Glen, taking bets. With a disbelieving shake of his head, he turned back to Sharp, who beamed with an unearned sense of achievement.

'You allow this?' Sam asked in disgust.

'Gotta give the people what they want.'

'This is barbaric.'

'Coming from a man who's killed countless people, you're a fine one to talk. Now get the fuck inside.'

Sharp placed his hand on the grip of his firearm to accentuate his point and Sam shook his head but obliged. As he stepped through the rocking crowd, a few eyes landed on him and he felt the excitement levels rise. As he stepped towards the front, he could see one of the men mounting the other, driving his broken fist into the man's bloodied face. Judging by the limpness of his defence, the man was out cold, and each blow was taking him closer to death.

Sam looked around the room.

The inmates were cheering him on.

The guards, lining the room, watched on with sickening glee.

Chapman was counting the money.

'Fuck this,' Sam muttered to himself and stepped into the middle of the room. To the dismay of the audience, he shoved both hands under the victor's arms and hauled him off. Crazed from the fight, the inmate tried to lash out, but Sam twisted the hair under the man's armpit, and he howled in pain. With one swift movement, he hurled him into the crowd, ending the fight to a slew of expletives.

Chapman's voice boomed out.

'Quiet!' An instant hush filled the room and Chapman extended his hand to Sam. 'Let's give a warm welcome to our main event.'

Sam shot a few glances to the other inmates, who were practically salivating. He turned back to Chapman, shaking his head.

'This isn't my fight.'

'I'm sorry, son. But you don't have much of a choice. Everyone fights.'

'And you? Are you going to step in here?'

Chapman sat back down, pressed his fingers together, and smiled.

'I have a representative.'

A worried whisper spread like a disease through the room, immediately out-heard by the scraping of metal on the cold, concrete floor. A few inmates near Chapman parted and Ravi stepped through, his shirtless torso rippling with ink-covered muscles. His broken nose, purple and swollen, sat between two eyes that bore through Sam like a pneumatic drill. Around his wrist was a thick, metal cuff, linked to a long, rusty chain. Without breaking his stare, he reeled the twenty-foot chain up, until he held an identical cuff in his hand. With the intention clear, and to the delight of the onlookers, he tossed it across the fight pit to Sam.

'Put it on.' Chapman demanded coldly. Before Sam could answer, he followed Chapman's gaze as he looked towards Sharp, who nodded. The implication was clear, and Sam doubted that it was an empty threat. To host an evening such as this, there would be someone with their finger on the button, ready to electrify the entire prison at the first hint of unrest.

For Sam, there was only one way out of the situation. As much as it pained him, all other paths had been closed off.

He had to fight.

With a resounding sigh, he pulled his T-shirt up over his head, the silence that greeted his body wasn't unexpected. Despite carrying half the bulk of Ravi, Sam was in peak physical condition. His lean muscles were well rounded, and his chest was as broad as it was thick.

It was the scars that stopped them dead.

Remnants of the explosion all those years ago that had rendered him MIA in a small town in Afghanistan, peppered the right side of his body. There were scars in his shoulder and his stomach, fresh bullet wounds he'd experienced in the heat of his war on organised crime. A long, painful scar ran down his spine, the stitches only recently removed from the near fatal attack suffered at the hands of the Hangman of Baghdad.

And the two, white, round scars on his chest, from where Wallace had tried to kill him all those years ago.

He didn't bear the same tattoos as Ravi, but his scars held more meaning.

A permanent index of the war he'd raged.

Slowly, he bent down and lifted the cuff, looking once more to Sharp, then to Ravi, and then to Chapman.

'Last chance.' Sam spoke calmly, the other inmates watching in pent up euphoria. Ravi stepped forward a few paces and cracked his neck, his answer clear. Slam snapped the cuff around his left wrist. 'Fine.'

Instantly, Ravi hauled his left arm back, tugging Sam towards him as he himself stepped forward. A roar exploded from the room, the thirst for blood reaching fever pitch as Sam adjusted his feet and took hold of the chain with his right hand. Ravi swung a ferocious right hook, but Sam ducked it, looping the chain over the man's bulging forearm and hooked it in tight. In one fluid motion, he snapped the chain tight, slid his shoulder under the man's elbow, and then pushed himself up while pulling the chain down.

The snap of Ravi's bone cracked like a fortune cookie, and the sickening sound echoed off the walls and stunned the room into silence. Ravi roared in agony, his broken arm gushing blood from the bone protruding through the skin. A red mist ascended in his eyes and he foolishly swung his chained arm towards Sam.

Sam knew he'd already won.

He sidestepped the intended blow easily, the pain and

quickly escalating blood loss affecting Ravi's balance and before Ravi could stumble forwards, Sam wrapped his arm around the man's thick neck. In one swift movement, he drove Ravi's body backwards, while drilling a knee expertly into the base of his spine.

Ravi dropped to his knees, his back jarred out of position, and as he tried helplessly to tend to his destroyed arm, Sam looped the chain twice around his throat and pulled it tight. Sharp had seen enough, and he stomped through the crowd, his hand to his hip, ready to take Sam out.

But Chapman stood, held out his hand to stop him and then he planted his eyes firmly on Sam. Returning the gaze, Sam yanked the chain, arching Ravi back and gently resting the back of his head on his knee. With the man fighting for breath, and just one quick snap away from a broken neck, Ravi looked at Chapman with the desperation of a rat caught in a trap.

'Do it,' Chapman barked, almost with glee.

The crowd cheered loudly, their thirst for death sickening Sam to his stomach. With a final glance to Sharp, who was trying his best to hide the fear in his eyes at Sam's brutal dismantling of Ravi, Sam then loosened his grip of the chain, placed his boot on Ravi's back, and pushed him forward. The hulking fighter fell onto his front, blood pumping from his arm as he whimpered in agony. Sam held Chapman's furious stare, unblinking as the crowd began cheering.

Seething at Sam's victory and subsequent defiance, Chapman angrily nodded at Sharp and two seconds later, Sam felt another surge of electricity race through his body, paralysing him and sending him jerking to the hard ground.

As the pain jolted his body, he could feel the cuff being removed from his wrist and his body being dragged through a joyous crowd, with the odd boot slamming into his ribs as he went. As he was hauled down the darkened corridor towards the solitary confinement cells, he afforded himself a wry smile, before he was hurled into one of the narrow, sparse rooms and as the metal door slammed with a mighty thud, he was enveloped by darkness.

CHAPTER FOURTEEN

FOUR YEARS AGO...

'Here you go, pig.'

A bowl of vegetable scrapings was tossed carelessly into Mac's cage, spilling across the piss stained floor. Hunched in a ball, he slowly extended a quivering, skeletal arm out to retrieve it. His hand shook, his filthy hands scarred from where the Taliban soldiers had removed his fingernails.

It had been a long time since he'd felt any pain.

Seven years in captivity and Mac still had no idea where he was.

The Taliban camp was sizeable, with at least fifty recruits being put through their paces on a daily basis by the dozen or so soldiers who ran the show. During the first few months of captivity, Mac had focused on learning their names, focusing on their identities as a way to fight through the pain. The medic they had within the camp had tended to the significant burns that dominated the left side of his body, but that was the only hospitality he'd experienced since his ordeal began.

As the months ticked by, Mac had become resigned to his fate.

The notion of rescue soon dissipated completely and his idea of collecting valuable intel died.

There was no rescue.

No hope.

Within the first few weeks of his incarceration, he'd been whipped mercilessly in front of the new recruits, his back slashed until it looked like a beaten leather sofa. The blood loss had caused him to pass out, and when he awoke, he was face down in the cage that would become his home.

Every few months, he was hauled from his cell, a broken and frail shadow of the soldier he once was and used as an educational tool to the brain-washed men who had joined the cause.

They beat him, to not only show them who was in charge but also to bring their war against the western world to reality. The soldiers running the camp would never go to war. They would never be called upon to detonate a bomb in a busy city.

They were there to groom the next generation to do their bidding.

Therefore, Mac was the target for their pent-up hatred and they made sure he felt it to his very core.

They would urinate through the bars of his cage, splattering him and the floor of his cell with warm piss, laughing as they did. They provided him little food or sanitation, ordering a young recruit to clear out the excrement he unloaded in the corner only once a month.

When the soldiers got bored, they would take a hammer and spread his fingers across the ground. Then, as fast as they could, they would slam the hammer in the gaps between and when they finally missed, and they always did, they would crush his bone with a sickening thud.

He would howl in pain.

They would laugh maniacally.

Then another soldier would have their turn.

Mac had also been raped. On three occasions he'd been roughly pulled from the cell, beaten until he could barely move, and then sodomised by a soldier. Despite their strict insistence that they were *serving their god, they were willing to defy him in order to assert their dominance.*

To show Mac that they were his masters and he was nothing more than an animal in their eyes.

There had been times when he'd tried to end it all, mustering up the energy to slam his head as hard as he could against the harsh, stone wall of his cell until he split his skull open.

But he was always nursed back to health.

They would rather he be kept as a pet than bury him in the ground.

Through it all, he remembered Sam's words. It had been eight years ago, but he could recall them as if they'd spoken yesterday.

'I promise I will do everything to keep you alive.'

Sam had failed to keep his promise.

He had left him here, to be tortured. To be killed.

The anger had toiled away in Mac for years, and he hoped Sam had survived the blast so he could one day have the pleasure of putting a bullet in his skull.

Mac was no longer a soldier.

He was no longer a person.

As he reached out and slid a rotten piece of carrot into his mouth, he heard a large explosion from outside the base, the impact rocking the cell and causing a few stones to scatter across the floor. Panicked cries echoed in the distance, followed by the unmistakable barrage of gunfire. The senior soldiers rushed to the door, barking orders in their native tongues as they reached for their rifles. Two of them stayed back, a clear sense of panic between them as another explosion shook the room.

Mac pushed his wiry frame upward, lifting himself to his knees.

Gunfire echoed directly outside the room, followed by a spray of bullets thudding against the door. The final two captors stood, rifles aimed, although their hands shook.

The door slid open.

They fired wildly, not noticing the flashbang that had been rolled in and everything went white. Mac's hearing dropped to a high-pitched squeal but as his eyes adjusted to the room again, he saw a burly general march in, flanked by two rifle wielding soldiers. The man in charge stepped over the dead body of one of the captors to the other, who, riddled with bullets, was praying to God.

The man ignored it, casually lifting the Glock in his hand and pulling the trigger. The captor's skull exploded, much to Mac's delight. That quickly turned to horror as a rifle was thrust into his face.

'General, we have a captive here.'

The soldier called across the room, and the murderous General marched over, peering through the bars at the pathetic, beaten human before him.

'State your name, son?'

Mac couldn't believe it. It was years since he'd heard an English word that hadn't been an insult in broken English, or had been treated like a person. A tear formed in his eye as he searched his brain rapidly, trying to recall an identity that had long since been swept away.

'P-p-private Matthew McLaughlin, sir.'

The man smiled warmly.

'My name is General Ervin Wallace. You are safe now, soldier.'

———

Mac sat at the laptop which lay open on the small desk that his small room could accommodate. After he'd returned to the UK alongside a terrified Josh Maxwell, he'd calmly strangled his driver and left his corpse in the back of his truck. The entire journey had been fraught, with Josh mourning the murder of his brother and despite his pathetic pleas for his life, Mac couldn't afford to leave a loose end.

There would be a time for him to face the consequences of his actions, but not until he'd put Sam through as much pain as humanly possible.

Ever since he'd been liberated by Wallace, he'd researched all he could about the life Sam went on to lead.

He had married the wonderful woman who'd shown Mac such kindness and even fathered a son. While Jamie Pope's demise was unfortunate, Mac felt no sympathy. Having spent seven years in a Taliban prison cell, any semblance of humanity had left him.

Wallace had seen that and had allowed Mac to channel it towards his bidding.

With no empathy coursing through his veins, Mac was a perfect killing machine and whatever names were sent to him through the Blackridge network, he eliminated them ruthlessly and without question.

Men.

Women.

Children.

They were just names on a screen.

But Sam would mean something. Killing him would grant Mac peace for the trials he went through. Once Sam had begged him for death, he would gladly go to jail or to the afterlife, safe in the knowledge that he'd restored the balance.

Set things even.

After killing and robbing Josh Maxwell, Mac had made his way to London by train and then found the nearest Internet café near Waterloo Station. Despite the usual quizzical looks his charred face drew, he found a quiet seat in the far corner of the room and was able to log onto the private servers of an online RPG called *Warrior's Call*.

Video games had never appealed to Mac, his rough upbringing saw him spend his time out on the streets as opposed to stowing away in a bedroom, fighting monsters in the vain attempt to raise his online credibility. But Blackridge had provided their Ghosts with a log in and a playable character, purely as a failsafe if they went off the grid.

Mac had hoped the server was still running, despite the

dissolution of the organisation in the wake of Wallace's death.

The General had saved his life, given him a purpose, and whenever he thought about his passing, it only added fuel to the vengeful fire burning within him.

The server was still active, although the small chat box in the top right showed only two active users.

Ignoring the colourful imagery of the game, Mac typed in his passcode and waited.

Whoever else was logged in kept him waiting, but after five minutes, they responded.

'Welcome back to the server. Please state your quest?'

Mac rolled his eyes. He was sure that whoever was on the other end of the keyboard was a snotty, computer nerd who enjoyed pretending he was a mythical creature. The irony was, he was a mythical creature to Mac, as they would never meet. The operatives who controlled the logistics and tech side of Blackridge were kept out of sight, locked away in dark terminals, plotting the elimination of targets.

While Mac may have been the one pulling the trigger, the one's pushing out the orders were just as complicit in the bloodshed.

Mac responded with the pre-rehearsed lingo he'd committed to his memory.

'Retribution quest. Need nearest loot box.'

Again, he cursed himself as he typed but the phrase was designed not to flag up on any potential searches. Blackridge may have had close ties to the government, but their business wasn't strictly legal. Wallace had garnered enough power to operate throughout the world, smiling and nodding in the official meetings and dealing with legitimate threats off the books.

Mac rubbed his chin with impatience as the nerd

began their response, the small notification that they were typing felt like a personal mocking.

'TS,0.3KM,F1,L32,C4881'

Mac smiled. The response would flag as nothing more than a gaming coordinate, but to him, it was a map. Having dialled into the IP of his computer, the genius on the other end of the chat had quickly ascertained his location. The train station a third of a kilometre away, first floor, locker thirty-two. The four digit combination code would grant him access, where he would find a 'survival pack', a safety net that Blackridge had set up in almost every town or city within which they operated. The fact that this one was located within Waterloo Station, a short walk up the road, brought a smile to his face.

It would contain a black satchel, with a pack of fresh underwear, toothbrush, ten thousand pounds in cash, and a loaded handgun.

Enough tools to drop off the radar.

But Mac was preparing for the exact opposite, and he patted the inside of his jacket, feeling the solid steel of the SIG Sauer P226 he'd used to put a bullet through Eric Maxwell's head.

The very same gun he'd nearly killed Sam with.

Another message popped up, drawing his attention.

'Is there anything else I can provide before you embark on your quest?'

There was no coming back from what Mac had planned, and with Wallace dead, there seemed little need to protect the integrity of the web server.

Blackridge was over, and while the operative on the other end of the web chat was valiantly trying to ensure support for the assets who were now being hunted by the government, it would only be a matter of time before it all came crashing to the ground.

A fitting way to end, considering the four-storey

plummet that its founder had taken at the hands of Sam Pope.

With his plan of vengeance starting to take place, Mac allowed a wry smile to creep across his scarred face.

'Expert needed.'

He waited patiently. The icon flashed his response was incoming.

'Expert need for what purpose?'

Mac leant forward; his eyes bright with malice.

'Explosives.'

CHAPTER FIFTEEN

Since the moment her first request for an update on Sam Pope had been rebuffed, Singh had felt something was wrong. As one of the finest detectives in the Met, a gut feeling was usually the catalyst for solving a case. It was what made her, and many fine detectives before, so good at their jobs. The ability to process information, but immediately question its validity had helped her put a number of criminals behind bars.

While her dealings with Sam over the past six months had seen her question a number of things, from her trust of her superiors to the very badge she stood for, one she never questioned was her gut.

Something was wrong.

She knew it.

A residual guilt still lingered in her mind the following morning. Matt Allison had been the perfect gentleman, charming in some ways and although under different circumstances their union would have been just as unlikely, she felt bad for stringing him along. Not only was it cruel to offer him hope of progressing his clear attraction to her, but it also undermined her stern stance that her gender had no effect on her ability to solve a case.

Using the potential allure of sex to garner information made her feel sick to her stomach and when she'd arrived back at her flat later that night, she had a stiff whisky and went to bed. A night of restless sleep followed, and she found herself at the coffee machine at half five the following morning, yearning for the caffeine boost as much as the truth.

By eight o'clock, she was at her desk in the New Scotland Yard building, gazing out of the windows over the glorious River Thames. A few boats were slowly passing through and she cast her gaze out to the wider city.

A city in chaos.

To its inhabitants, it was a booming city, filled with shops, businesses, and bars, the epicentre of the British economy. Whatever street you walked down, there was always a buzz of activity, with tourists, shoppers, and workers weaving in and out of each other's way like a strange dance.

To those walking the streets, it was a place of wonder.

To those protecting the very same streets, it was haunting.

Before her life intertwined with Sam's, Singh had already seen the worst of humanity. She'd worked diligently on Project Yewtree, hunting down the necessary evidence to ensure that when they hauled the vile paedophiles off the streets, they stayed off them,

She'd burst into drug dens, armed and flanked by her team, engaging in gunfights with drug lords.

She'd shot people.

Critically injured them.

But she'd never killed.

Since then Sam Pope had consumed her career. As soon as she'd been assigned as the head of the task force, he'd taken a permanent residence in her mind. But as the hunt drew out, and the lines began to blur, he'd consumed her thoughts for other reasons.

The pain he'd been through.

The war he'd raged to save innocent children.

The sacrifices he made to bring down one of the most notorious global terrorists.

The risks he took to save her life.

That kiss.

She could feel her fingers tightening around the coffee cup, only for her thoughts to be disturbed by a familiar voice.

'Singh. You're here early this morning.'

It wasn't so much a question as a statement of fact, but Singh could hear the surprise in Deputy Commissioner Ashton's voice. Turning away from the grey sky that hung over the capital like a grim warning, Singh offered her superior a smile.

'Just wanted to get ahead of a few things, that's all.'

'Good to hear.' Ashton nodded curtly, removing her hat and revealing her greying blonde hair, which was tied back in her usual bun. As she marched towards her office, Singh placed down her coffee mug and followed, whipping her blazer off the back of her chair and sliding it over her crisp white shirt. As Ashton circled her desk, she looked up with surprise as Singh knocked on the door and effectively let herself in.

'Can I have a quick word, ma'am?'

'Quickly.' Ashton sighed, half rolling her eyes as she made to look busy, shuffling some papers on her desk. 'I have a meeting with the Home Secretary in thirty minutes.'

'Fun,' Singh replied dryly, regretting it as soon as Ashton shot her a furious glance.

'What do you want, Singh?' Ashton took her seat as Singh approached the desk.

'Ma'am, I think something has happened to Sam Pope.'

'You are right. Something has happened to him,' Ashton replied, without looking up from her papers.

'Ma'am?'

'Justice.' Ashton looked up smugly. 'The man committed countless crimes, killed numerous people including a senior government official, and engaged in a gun fight with our own men. Now he is behind bars and you would do well, Singh, to leave it at that. Dragging up the past will only impede your future.'

Ashton returned her eyes to her paperwork, signalling the end of the conversation. It was a silent request that Singh ignored.

'Ma'am, I have reason to believe that Sam Pope's transfer to HMS Pentonville either went array or didn't happen. Is there any way we can look at the transfer logs and…'

'Singh, your job is to catch the criminals. One that you're very good at,' Ashton said, rubbing her temple in frustration. 'But in the interest of keeping this relationship amicable, I can tell you in the strictest of confidence that moments before Sam's incarceration, I received approval from Commissioner Stout on my request to have Sam moved to somewhere more befitting his crimes.'

Singh clutched the back of the chair opposite Ashton's desk until her knuckles whitened.

'What do you mean?'

'I mean I made good on my promise. I told him I was going to bury him in the deepest, darkest hole I could find. I didn't expect Stout to sign off on it, but with his impending departure I guess he thought it was a fitting conclusion to a job well done.'

Very rarely was Singh lost for words, but the revelation that Sam had been swept off the radar hit her like a freight train. A cocktail of fury and fear shook inside her and she took a long, deep breath. Ashton peered up from her desk, a wry smile across her face.

'Is that all, detective?'

Singh opened her eyes, regarded Ashton with a look of clear frustration and nodded.

'Yes, ma'am.'

As she angrily wrenched open the door to the office, Ashton sat back in her chair, victorious.

'As I said, I consider this entire ordeal over. Is that understood?'

Singh slammed the door, ignoring her senior officer's question and she headed straight for the stairwell, her body clambering for a hit of fresh air and the chance to clear her thoughts. As Singh stepped out into the brisk wind, a gentle splattering of drizzle greeted her. Outside one of the entrances, a few officers were chatting over a cigarette. She walked across the Embankment, looking out across the river once again, regarding the dull, grey city that transformed overnight into a magnificent skyline.

Sam was gone.

He had forfeited his freedom for her and now he was locked away in a place worse than prison. She owed it to him to find out where, to ensure he was okay, and possibly have the decision reversed.

But if Deputy Commissioner Ashton wasn't willing to talk, then Singh knew there was only one more step up the rung she needed to climb to find the truth.

———

When the door to his cell opened the following morning, Sam wasn't surprised to see Warden Harris. With his hands on his hips and an apologetic smile, the Warden looked like he'd had a rough morning. With his crippling disease increasingly dominating his body, Harris was facing a very real possibility of stepping down from his role.

Either that or he would be pushed.

Sam had enjoyed the peaceful night in solitary. Despite the lack of bed or anything remotely resembling a human touch, he'd regulated his heart rate after the electric shock and soon found himself drifting off into a dreamless sleep.

Most nights, he was haunted by heartbreaking images of his son, his innocent smile beaming towards him. But ever since he'd buried the ghosts of his past and found out the truth about Project Hailstorm, he found he was sleeping easier.

What worried Sam most, was the less he dreamt of Jamie, the further from that life he ventured.

Harris shuffled in, trying his best to hide his discomfort, his left foot barely leaving the ground as he entered the cell, the light from the corridor illuminating his path.

'You don't look so good?' Harris offered.

'I could say the same thing.'

Harris chuckled and extended his hand, which Sam took. Sam hauled himself up on his own, not wanting the warden to exert any more effort than was needed.

'Let me guess. You were misbehaving again?' Harris asked dryly, not believing his own words.

'If you call being chained to and forced to fight a violent inmate for the entertainment of the prison, then yeah. I was misbehaving.'

'Christ,' Harris uttered, to himself more than anyone. He shot a glance over his shoulder, where Sharp stood calmly in the corridor. 'Not this again?'

'Oh, I'm not surprised it's happened before.'

'Would you be surprised if I told you that we had an issue with our security camera feed last night? For a few hours, we lost all transmission from every camera within the facility.'

Sam shook his head, looking beyond the distraught warden to Sharp, who fixed him with a mean glare.

'Computer's, eh?' Sam shrugged. 'I'm sure Sharp knows what happened?'

Harris turned to face Sharp once again, who stepped forward to attention.

'Sir, Pope lashed out at an inmate and shattered his arm. I thought an electric shock was a more than justified approach to restraining him.' Sharp raised his eyebrow. 'After all, he did tell us he was dangerous.'

Harris furiously squeezed the bridge of his nose and then walked out of the cell. Sharp smirked at Sam, motioned for him to follow and the three of them headed towards the stairwell. After a few steps, Sharp shoved Sam in the back, drawing a heavy sigh from Harris, who stopped.

'Sharp, please wait for me in my office.'

'Sir?' Sharp protested.

'Get out of my sight.' Harris's change in tone caught Sam by surprise. Behind the deteriorating body, the fire that had seen him entrusted with the most dangerous prison in the UK still remained. 'I'll deal with you shortly.'

Sharp held his tongue, shot Sam a look as if it was his fault and then stomped towards the stairwell like a petulant kid. Sam watched him leave before turning back to the Warden.

'You do realise he thinks he runs this place?'

'The higher ups see him as a model employee. Tough on the prisoners, but no offence, our guest list is hardly the pride of the country.'

Harris leant forward, pressing his hand against the wall and he gritted his teeth in agony. Struggling to steady himself, Sam reached out to provide some stability.

'You okay, sir?'

Sam's kindness took Harris by surprise and he uncomfortably nodded.

'I'm fine. Thank you. My body just can't keep doing this.' Harris straightened up. 'For what it's worth, Sam, I don't think you belong here.'

'I've done a lot of bad things, sir,' Sam said ruefully. 'No matter why I did them, I still broke the law. I put a lot of people in the ground. I don't regret doing it, but I don't blame the government for putting me here.'

'Well, if it's any consolation, I've asked them to investigate why your transfer was so last minute. Usually, these things take a few weeks to process.'

Sam shrugged.

'I guess somebody wanted me in here.'

Harris stood up straight and then motioned for them to continue. As they approached the door, Sam held it open for Harris, who was once again perplexed by the man's integrity.

He was a soldier. Not a criminal.

As they stepped onto the prison floor, they were greeted by two guards, both of whom Sam recognised from the baiting crowd and both of whom were sheepishly looking at the floor. They were to accompany him back to his cell but before they did, Harris rested a comforting hand on Sam's shoulder.

'Until I find out how it happened, do me a favour?' Harris leant in, speaking quietly to alienate the guards. 'Just do whatever you can to survive.'

Sam nodded and the warden patted him, before hobbling in the opposite direction, heading towards the lift. Sam knew Harris's reprimand would fall on Sharp's deaf ears and most likely, the repercussions would fall squarely at his cell door. After a few hours resting on his bed, he was called to stand, before being escorted to the canteen for the evening meal. The entire room fell silent as he stepped in, a wave of fear washing across the inmates after Sam's quick and ferocious victory over Ravi.

Sam ignored it, walking calmly to pick up his tray of food before scanning the room for a seat. With Harris's plea for survival echoing in his mind, Sam took a deep breath and strode across the room. He felt the tension rise in the room, quickly followed by a few terrified murmurs as he approached Chapman's table.

Sat with a giant grin on his face, Chapman ushered Sam to take a seat. With Ravi in the infirmary, Glen sat silently beside his boss, refusing to meet Sam's glare.

Sam dropped the tray on the table, the clang of metal echoing through the canteen. Everyone went back to their meals, a new sense of terror running through them. Slowly, Sam dropped onto the chair opposite Chapman and through gritted teeth, realised what he had to do.

'You win,' Sam said quietly.

Chapman leant forward, reached across the table, and took a potato from Sam's plate.

'I always do.'

In a needless show of power, he crushed the potato in his hand, before wiping it on Glen's sleeve. Sam lowered his head, focusing on his meal.

He hated himself for doing it, but Harris was right. Sam needed to survive his stay in prison and to do what was necessary, he needed to gain Chapman's trust.

CHAPTER SIXTEEN

That evening, Sharp had watched with glee as Harris had gingerly lowered himself into the back of his car. The driver knew the routine and rolled to a stop at each gate before taking the immobilised warden back to his house.

Harris's health was in steep decline and it was unlikely he would be back for a few days. A twinge of guilt sat uncomfortably in Sharp's gut, his actions clearly adding to the warden's stress, but he would soon forget about it the next time he visited Kayla and paid her to fulfil his darkest desire.

As he bounded out of the office, he mused upon how he could reassert his dominance over Sam.

Breaking the imperious soldier down would be his crowning victory and once he'd proven to the prison that even a man as untouchable as Sam Pope feared him, they would all do the same.

The power he would wield would be unstoppable.

As he made his way back through the prison, a guard informed him of the events at dinner. Stammering his words through fear of repercussion, Sharp could feel his hand shake at the news.

Moments later, a guard informed him that Chapman had requested his presence at his cell.

On his way, Sharp stopped in the bathroom, locked the door, and thumped the glass mirror until it cracked. Despite everything he'd done, he was still not in control.

Harris, for the time being, sat in the office.

Chapman still sat on the throne.

Sharp quickly collected himself, straightened his shirt, and tried his best to control the seething fury that was jack-knifing through his body. There were no guards standing outside the cell, usually on hand to answer any of Chapman's requests like a highly trained, armed butler.

It was just Sharp and Chapman.

To try to gain a measure of control of the situation, Sharp didn't knock. He stepped through the door, catching Chapman by surprise. Sat at his small side table, Chapman lowered his head, peering over his reading glasses and sighed. He placed a bookmark into the novel he was reading and turned to face the deputy warden.

'Sharp. Do come in.'

'What the hell is going on?' Sharp demanded, abandoning the calm approach he'd practiced on his journey.

'I've just got to a really good bit, actually.' Chapman flippantly responded, motioning to his book.

'Not your fucking book, old man. What the hell is the deal with Pope?'

Chapman exuded menace. Every small mannerism had been carefully crafted over decades of being one of the most powerful criminals the country had ever seen. With a calm that forebode the imminent danger Sharp was in, he slowly removed his glasses, folded them, and then rested them on the book. With his only weakness being his age, Chapman groaned slightly as he stood. He was an inch shorter than Sharp, and father time had relaxed most of his body.

But he stood straight.

His eyes were fixed on Sharp.

They both knew who was in charge in the room.

'With Ravi out of commission and the considerable damage he has done to my empire, I offered Sam a more amicable way to wipe the slate clean. Or, worded slightly differently, I don't have to tell you a fucking thing.'

Chapman's hand shot forward, like a cobra snapping at its prey, and he tightly gripped Sharp by the throat. Shocked, Sharp stumbled backwards and Chapman pinned him to the wall, his fingers digging deeply into the deputy warden's throat. A trickle of blood emerged from the pressure of Chapman's nails against his windpipe.

'Listen here, Sharp.' Chapman spoke slowly. 'This is my fucking prison. So, when I tell you right now, that Sam Pope is off limits, what do you say?'

Gasping for breath, Sharp struggled to speak. Through short intakes of air, he spluttered his response.

'Off limits.'

Chapman relinquished the hold and then gently patted the side of Sharp's red face.

'There's a good boy.' Chapman turned and stepped back to his seat. 'Now fuck off, will you? Like I said, I've just got to a good bit.'

Sharp stayed pressed against the wall for a few moments, gathering his breath and calming his anger. The thought of grabbing the back of the old man's head and slamming it against the brick wall until it was nothing but paste crossed his mind.

But he would certainly find himself dead within days.

Realising where the true power sat, Sharp straightened his shirt, marched out of the room, and headed towards the guard quarters, hoping beyond hope that one of his men would speak out of turn so he could offload the fury encaged within.

Sam felt sick to his stomach.

It had been two days since he'd taken his seat at The Guvnor's table. By effectively kissing the ring, he'd allowed the entire prison to see that he was not above corruption. Every inmate had targeted Sam upon his arrival at The Grid, many of them eager to tear the criminal killer apart. While some of them had accepted their incarceration and had dedicated themselves to a quiet, peaceful existence behind the fortified walls, there were still a number of exceedingly dangerous criminals vying for his blood.

Because he wasn't one of them.

But now, having hitched his wagon to Harry Chapman, he'd shown them all that he was no better than they were.

Chapman had maintained his calm, but Sam was certain he couldn't have been happier. For a man who wielded such power, on this side and the other, having broken the unbreakable and forced him to bend to his whim would have been his greatest triumph.

Chapman had the control.

Always had. Always would.

The first day, Sam's cell door was opened at nine o'clock in the morning and to his surprise, there was no guard to greet him with a snide comment or an errant baton to the stomach. Afforded the freedom on the prison floor, Sam was guided by uncomfortable guards to Chapman, who had been allocated two cells. One was his personal quarters, which was strictly off limits to everyone, including the guards. Such a statement made Sam scoff in disbelief, but when the occupant had the power and resources to eradicate your family from the face of the earth, you towed the line.

Chapman, however, didn't take the violent route. The

guards were handsomely rewarded for their obedience and Chapman lived a comfortable existence within Ashcroft. The cell which Sam entered was decked out like a small office, with Chapman sat in a leather chair next to a side table. A storage cupboard was pushed into the corner to the side of the door and a bench ran along the opposite wall. It was a tight squeeze, but Sam appreciated the leather cushion that met his rear as he sat down. Glen didn't seem too keen on his arrival and seemed even less impressed when Sam turned down his offer of a cigarette.

'It's fine.' Chapman encouraged. 'You work for me, now.'

The implication was clear.

Now that Sam had bent the knee, the guards would no longer focus their attentions on him.

Chapman had nonchalantly told him that Sharp *would no longer be a problem.*

Sam wished he'd been a fly on the wall when that conversation happened, but he just shrugged and sat quietly while Chapman went about his business. Throughout the morning, The Guvnor took a number of phone calls on his mobile phone, as if he were sat in a London office as opposed to a maximum-security prison. As he barked out orders to his men on the outside, he ended every call by telling Glen and Sam how incompetent criminals were these days.

Although he didn't disagree, Sam didn't say anything. He hadn't agreed to Chapman's demands to enjoy light banter about the inner workings of a criminal empire.

It was out of necessity.

Just after eleven, a prison guard arrived with three mugs of tea and Sam couldn't help but smile at the pathetic team in charge of the prison. Harris was in no fit state to change anything, but Sam wondered just how much the warden knew about Chapman's set up. Despite his disgust that the men put in charge of the criminals were bending over for Chapman, the tea was a wonderful treat.

Sat on a leather chair with a cup of tea was a world away from lying on the cold floor of solitary confinement. The comforts didn't outweigh the fact he had to spend time with Chapman or inhale a continuous stream of second-hand smoke.

There was little in the way of conversation and Chapman returned to reading his novel while Glen shuffled a pack of cards. Catching Sam eyeing the stack of books atop the cupboard, Chapman encouraged Sam to help himself. The small pleasure of reading was welcomed, and he sat down with a copy of *I Am Pilgrim*, a thick book that Sam had never heard of. After a few pages, he was engrossed.

A well-prepared lunch was brought to the cell, and Sam understood why every inmate was falling over themselves to find their way into Chapman's good books. The usual lunchtime meal was a bowl of porridge of questionable quality and temperature, which made biting into the cheese baguette something of a luxury.

Don't get drawn in, Sam told himself, as he polished off the sandwich and followed Chapman and Glen to the outside courtyard for a private exercise session. Chapman and his confident took a seat in the shade, while Sam took advantage of a vacant weight bench to work out. Slowly, more prisoners ventured into the opening, their hour would be monitored strictly.

Throughout the hour, Chapman kept his eyes on the inmates, intermittently telling Sam to stare at a certain inmate as a thinly veiled threat. He didn't like it, but Sam followed orders.

He was a weapon at Chapman's disposal, and after his dismantling of Chapman's previous heavy, Sam knew he was feared by the rest of Ashcroft's population, on both sides of the cell door.

The rest of the day was spent reading the book, with Sam finding himself engrossed. Despite falling deeper into the story, he kept his ears tuned to Chapman whenever he took a call.

Glen sat quietly, working his way through another packet of cigarettes as he thumbed his way through a pointless game on a cheap, throwaway phone that Chapman had provided. A few inmates were brought to Chapman, offering up whatever valuables they had or favours they could offer in exchange for a phone call or a fix. Once agreed, Glen would fetch their request from the cupboard and send them scurrying.

After a relatively quiet meal, Sam spent the rest of his evening lying on his cell bed, devouring his book and appreciating the lack of interruptions. The one time he saw Sharp, stood stoically in the corner of the canteen, the deputy warden refused to make eye contact with him.

The following day was much the same, with a morning spent reading in Chapman's cell, listening as he barked orders and threats into his phone, while demanding a fresh coffee from the guard who went scurrying away like a bumbling waiter.

After another delicious lunch, Sam found himself with the freedom of the exercise section of the courtyard and despite the snide comments from Glen, he put himself through his paces. The stiffness in his shoulder had all but gone and although his back gave him the odd flicker of pain, he found himself feeling revitalised after a good workout.

As the other prisoners filtered out into the courtyard for their own hour of fresh air, Sam slowly made his way back to Chapman's side, ready for another peaceful afternoon of reading. As he sat down beside Chapman, dabbing at his sweaty brow with a rag, Sam noticed Glen had disappeared.

'Where's Glen?'

'Working,' Chapman replied coldly, his eyes fixated ahead. Sam followed the gaze and saw Glen calmly talking to a clearly terrified inmate. The man, a chubby, balding man in his mid-fifties, was pleading with Glen but the cruel smirk on Glen's face told Sam it wasn't going to work. Resound to his fate, the prisoner slowly followed Glen back towards the bench where Sam and Chapman sat, his head lowered in defeat. As he approached, Chapman snapped into action.

'Jimmy.' He spoke in a condescending tone. 'You knew this was going to happen, didn't you?'

'Please, just give me another week.' Jimmy was shaking with fear, trying his best to maintain his composure. 'I'm good for it.'

'But you're not, are you? Look at me when I'm talking to you.'

Jimmy did as he was told, and Sam shuffled uncomfortably in his seat. A group of inmates were watching on with interest. The guards had all turned away.

'Please…' Jimmy's voice trailed off.

'Three bets over the last six months, none of which you've been able to pay. You know the rules.'

Chapman motioned to Glen, who launched forward, wrapping his arm around Jimmy's throat locking him in place. Glen thrust a knee into the back of Jimmy's legs, dropping him to his knees before slamming the man's hand down on the bench, locking it in place with a firm grasp of his wrist. An audible wave of excitement weaved through the watching crowd and Sam shook his head.

'Now…I'll go easy on you. Just the one.'

Chapman held up a finger on his left hand, but with his right, he theatrically slid the blade up on his box cutter.

Jimmy squealed in terror, but a sharp knee to the spine stopped his squirming. Chapman then turned to Sam, offering him the box cutter.

'Take his pinky.'

Sam stared at Chapman in disbelief, his instinct to take the man down overshadowed by the dire situation he was in. He needed to gain Chapman's trust, to be part of the gang and a refusal to fall in line would undercut the reputation he'd already established with the other prisoners.

It would also see him struck from the group and undoubtedly be put back in Sharp's firing line.

Do what you can to survive.

Harris's words echoed in his mind and reluctantly, Sam took the blade, offered the terrified man an apologetic look and in one swift movement, sliced through the man's bone. He screamed in agony before passing out, the myriad of pain and shock rendering him unconscious. The guards swiftly moved in, hoisting the prone inmate away for medical attention.

A terrified silence swept across the courtyard, only interrupted by the click of Glen's lighter as he partook in a celebratory smoke.

With his hands covered in blood, Sam handed the cutter back to an approving Chapman, swallowing his own nausea at the barbaric act. Reminding himself that the man he'd disfigured was a violent criminal, Sam stared at the blood on his hands and wondered how long he would be to keep this up.

CHAPTER SEVENTEEN

Getting a meeting with Police Commissioner Michael Stout was one of life's hardest tasks. As head of one of the world's leading police institutions, the man was constantly on the move. A number of his scheduled appointments were more political than anything else, as a man of his power and status needed to be seen in the right rooms with the right people. Despite a glistening career that had spanned almost three decades, he was not entrusted with his own words. Reporting directly to the Home Secretary, every public speech was carefully crafted by a team of highly literate professionals, all to ensure that the public message was clear and concise.

It was a high-pressure role that Singh had no desire to fill.

The fact Ashton would soon be sitting in the seat filled her with a sense of dread, but considering the political game she relished, Singh had to admit she would be a good fit.

There was enough steel in Ashton to take the inevitable criticism of the public, but after her shocking revelation the day before about Sam's transfer, there was also a perverse side that Singh knew a position of that magnitude needed.

Ashton played her own games, focused on what she wanted, and she did so seemingly within the confines of the rules.

But Singh needed to know exactly what Ashton had put in motion.

After spending the entire day calling Commissioner Stout's PA, requesting an urgent meeting, she'd finally managed to attain a five minute window at the end of the day, just before he was due in a cabinet meeting at Westminster.

Stout's office took over a quarter of the top floor of New Scotland Yard, the views from the window offering a tremendous view of the city he protected. Sat in the PA's office, Singh thumbed through her phone, trying her best to research government facilities but they were either general articles or off limits.

Although her status as the Met's shining star had granted her an audience with Stout, she still had access permissions in line with her paygrade.

On the other side of the lavishly decorated room, Stout's PA, Marie, was frantically typing away on her keyboard, all the while juggling phone call after phone call. Singh chuckled at the thought that she was as busy as the commissioner himself. She'd arrived fifteen minutes before her allotted time, agreeing to wait patiently as Stout was currently in a budget meeting. The thought of overseeing the organisation finances was just another reason why Singh never wanted to climb that high.

As the clock affixed to the wall ticked past her appointment time, she fidgeted on her chair, drawing a wry smile from Marie.

'These meetings tend to overrun, I'm afraid.'

Singh nodded politely, doing her best to hide her agitation. Another minute fell from her small window of opportunity and just as she was about to remonstrate with Marie about the commissioner's time keeping, the door flew open. A bespectacled man carrying a laptop and a few folders bounded out towards the stairs looking as if he'd just been tied to a chair and beaten. Commissioner Stout followed swiftly, sliding his arms into his jacket as he closed the door behind him.

He didn't even notice Singh.

'Marie, ask Mohit to bring the car around.'

Without thanking her, he strode towards the door and Singh leapt from her chair.

'Commissioner Stout?'

He turned, clearly in a hurry.

'Detective Inspector. Wonderful to see you as always.' Singh nodded and she saw the confusion on her his face. 'Can I help you?'

'I have an appointment with you, sir.'

'Well, we'll have to take it on the road. Walk with me.'

Without waiting for her response, he pushed open the door and left the office with Singh scurrying behind. As he descended the steps at a pace that made a mockery of his advancing years, all the officers he passed stopped and saluted. A man of the people, he acknowledged every one of them, much to Singh's annoyance.

'Sir, I need to speak to you about Sam Pope.'

'Yes, quite. A fantastic piece of work there, Detective. I did ask for Deputy Commissioner Ashton to pass on my praise.'

'Thank you, sir. But I'm not here to pander my ego.'

Stout chuckled out loud, appreciating the straight talking of a prominent detective with a reputation for her bullish nature. He stepped off the bottom step and headed towards the door where a large, Mercedes C class was waiting.

157

'Anyway, you can put that matter to bed now. Sam Pope is behind bars thanks to your sterling work.'

'But, sir, I need to follow up my investigation with him but I can't get access to him.'

With the automatic door to the building opening before him, Stout stopped and turned to her. A gust of wind flew through the reception, a sprinkling of rain on its coat-tails. He raised an eyebrow at her.

'Singh, if you need access to the prisoner, you need to go through the necessary channels.'

'That's the thing, sir. I need to know which prison you transferred him to.'

Stout laughed, shaking his head.

'I signed the papers to lock him away in Pentonville,' Stout said, clueless. 'I was told you were at the trial?'

'You didn't sign any others?'

Stout regarded her with a fleck of irritation in his eye.

'Is there a problem here, Singh?'

It was clear to Singh that the commissioner had no idea what had happened. Whatever transfer papers had been signed by the commissioner hadn't come from his office. Which meant that either Ashton had forged them, or someone wanted Sam locked away from the world.

After a few seconds of contemplation, Stout's tone stiffened.

'Detective, I asked if there was a problem?'

'No, sir. No problem.'

Stout nodded his head firmly, pulled his coat tight, and stepped out into the spring shower, darting to the back door of the car which was held open for him by the driver. As the car pulled away, Singh watched with her hands on her hips, wondering what the hell was going on.

———

As they sat for dinner that evening, the entire canteen was silent. There were no hushed conversations or empty threats exchanged between the inmates. Even the guards, usually keen to assert their authority, were uncharacteristically subdued. It was if Sam's act of debt collection and solidification as Chapman's muscle had ushered in a new reign of fear.

Sam sat quietly, picking at the mash potato on his plate, his appetite long evaporated.

Chapman was basking in his achievement. Having Sam under his command had once again elevated his control over the facility and he made no effort to hide the grin across his face.

When the door opened midway through the meal and Ravi hobbled in, there wasn't even a murmur. With his arm covered in a cast, Chapman's henchman glared at Sam, but took his seat alongside him at the table. Sam shrugged, pushed his plate away, and headed back to his cell, hoping that an evening reading would take his mind off the situation.

It didn't help, despite two hours of staring at the pages.

He had promised his son he would read more and as a way to cope with the grief of losing him, Sam had absorbed many books during his absence.

Lucy would have been proud, knowing that Sam was keeping a promise to their son. The fact he'd broken his other and had killed numerous criminals only underlined how correct she was to leave him.

During the few weeks before his transfer, he heard that she'd given birth to a baby girl. Happily remarried to a man named Jason, Sam always felt his heart break whenever he thought of her.

Although she'd moved on, she'd never recovered from what had happened to their son.

To their life together.

They had been wildly in love from the moment they'd crossed paths in a club, with Sam enthralled by the combination of her wit and her beauty.

They built a wonderful life together, living in a quaint house in Ruislip just outside of London and when they welcomed Jamie into their lives, Sam felt complete. He had been discharged from the army after the horrors of Project Hailstorm and had a real future worth fighting for.

But by failing to protect their son, he'd lost everything.

Now, as he sat in his tiny cell, in a prison only those in a privileged position knew about, he wondered how she rebounded from the devastation in a way so drastically different to him.

It was a loaded question; one which Sam already knew the answer to.

He was a born killer.

But through it all, Sam had always carried a sense of nobility. Whether he was staring through the scope of his sniper rifle in the middle of a tour, or wiping out a criminal empire, it was always for the greater good. Now, as he recounted Jimmy's howls of anguish, he tried to trace back to where he finally crossed the line that kept him from the other inhabitants of Ashcroft.

Before his thoughts could lead him any further down the depressing rabbit hole, a metal baton clattered against his cell door, breaking his train of thought. Moments later, the door opened, and a guard poked his head in.

'Guvnor wants to see you.'

Sam sighed.

He was being beckoned. Like a lap dog.

Sam lifted himself from the bed, nodded his thanks to a nervous guard, and then walked through the empty corridor. As he headed towards Chapman's makeshift office, he could feel the envious eyes of the other inmates peering through the small peephole of their cells.

Approaching the door, Sam could hear Chapman on the phone.

'If he doesn't want to cook, offer him more money. That prick may be a smart-arse, but he makes the purest fucking meth in the country.' Sam waited just outside of the door as Chapman continued his conversation. 'I don't give a fuck, Dom. Get him onside or put a bullet in your own fucking skull.'

Chapman tossed the phone down on the desk, giving Sam his cue to enter. As he stepped into the doorway, Chapman was leant forward, elbows on the tables, and massaging his temples in anger.

'Everything okay?'

'Sam.' Chapman snapped out of it, looking somewhat embarrassed by losing his cool. 'Come in.'

Sam stepped in anxiously. Without Glen hankered down in the corner, surrounded by a cloud of cancerous smoke, the cell looked a little bigger. Although he wondered how they would all fit inside now Ravi had returned and something told Sam that Ravi wouldn't be too keen sitting on the floor. As he lowered himself onto the leather cushion of the bench, Chapman reached under the desk and pulled out a bottle of whisky. He shook it proudly at Sam, then retrieved two mugs from the shelf above.

'I thought we could have ourselves a little drink,' Chapman said, pouring two generous helpings and handing one to Sam. 'To a job well done.'

Reluctantly, Sam clinked his mug and took a sip. Never one for a whisky, Sam was surprised how nice the burning sensation was as it slid down his throat. In a place where luxury was prohibited, being afforded one certainly added to the flavour.

'You wanted to see me?'

'I thought it would be a good idea to get to know each

other a little better. What do you think?' Chapman smirked.

'I've heard better ideas.'

'That's the spirit.' Chapman chuckled and took a sip. 'Your dry sense of humour will keep you sane in here a lot longer than snorting any of my shit up your nose, I'll tell you that for nothing.'

'Then why do it?' Sam asked, coughing slightly at the extreme heft of the drink. 'Why give them the option?'

'Because I can. Because I run this fucking place. I know you have this moral code that paints you like a martyr, but the harsh reality is this place needs someone like me. I keep the inmates in line a shite sight better than the guards do and the poor fuckers in their cells get to block out the horrible truth of their existence.'

'And you? What do you get out of it?'

'Jesus. Fucking twenty questions. I get what I always have. Power. They can put me in this place, throw away the fucking key, and I still have every fucker in here dancing on command. Guards, inmates…hell, even the legendary Sam Pope.' Chapman finished his drink and poured another, reaching over and topping up Sam's mug. 'So, answer me this, Sam. How the fuck did you end up in here, anyway?'

Sam baulked at the question, taking his time to find the right words. There was something unnerving about Chapman, a strong sense of intimidation underpinning his charm. Sam could see how a man like him could rise to the top of the underworld.

'Same reason we all did, right? I broke the law.'

'Don't give me that shit.' Chapman's words carried a slight inebriation. 'You're the hero of the country. You were taking down drug dens, killing foreign pimps. Hell, they even said you exposed a global terrorism unit.'

'Guilty.' Sam smiled. 'Hence why I'm in here. It doesn't matter why we do the things we do. Eventually, we all have to face the consequences of our actions, this side or the other.'

'Wow. That's some deep thinking.' Chapman shook his head and then looked at Sam with a pitiful frown. 'I guess we're not that different after all.'

'Oh, we are very different.'

'Are we?' Chapman topped up his drink. 'I read all about you in the papers when you were on trial. They were fascinated by you. Some of them pegged you as a crazed soldier, unable to step away from the war and blah blah blah. Others said you were doing it because your son was killed, and the law did nothing.'

Sam shifted uncomfortably on his seat, staring at his drink. Chapman continued.

'I'm sorry that happened to your boy. When I was younger, my brother, Mike, was killed by a local drug dealer. Being a scummy family from an East End estate, the police did nothing. Chalked it off as just the rats eating each other. There was no justice for Mike, so I made damn sure the fucker responsible got what was coming to him. The rest, as they say, is history.'

Before Sam could respond, Chapman quickly glanced at his phone, dropped it on the desk, and stood.

'Need to take a piss.'

He patted Sam on the shoulder as he hobbled through the door to his own, private cell and as Sam heard the crashing of urine in the water, he reached across, snatching the phone before the screen locked. Quickly, he flicked to the call history, found the last call and memorised the number instantly. Carefully, he locked the phone, placed it back on the desk and sat back, sipping his drink as Chapman returned.

'That's better.' He dropped back into his chair and lifted his mug. 'To our partnership.'

Sam joined in, raised his own and then polished off the

last of his whisky. He placed the mug onto Chapman's desk and stood, smiling.

'Thanks, boss.' Sam shuddered at the term. 'I appreciate the drink.'

'Plenty more where that came from.'

As Sam made for the door, he stopped at the threshold, and turned back to an interested Chapman.

'One more thing. I noticed Glen had a phone. I was wondering if…'

'Top drawer.' A slightly light-headed Chapman pointed sloppily at the cupboard. 'They only have ten or so calls in them but help yourself. Although, not sure Domino's delivers at this time.'

Sam genuinely chuckled and opened the cupboard, rooting through a few iPods, porn mags, and other contraband until he pulled out a crummy looking phone. It was an unknown make, but Sam wasn't looking for quality.

He just needed to make a call.

Sam held the box up, Chapman nodded, and Sam thanked him and headed back to his cell. As soon as he did, he slid the phone from the box, booted it up and waited.

One bar of signal.

It was enough.

Sam dialled a number and held the phone to his ear; the call was answered on the third dial.

'Hello?'

Sam had never been more grateful to hear Etheridge's voice.

'Paul. It's me.' Sam spoke quietly. 'I got it. Do you have a pen ready?'

CHAPTER EIGHTEEN

TWO YEARS AGO...

Mac had never felt so valued.

After being rescued by Wallace two years prior, the General made it his personal mission to nurse Mac back to health. Having spent seven years in captivity, he was dangerously malnourished and although the burns and scars that tattooed his body would never disappear, Wallace went out of his way to nurse the mental trauma he'd experienced.

Insisting Mac stay in a government treatment facility, where he was tended to by the very best doctors and nurses, he soon found himself gaining weight, recovering some of his composure, and soon enough, was able to begin weight training. After a year of physical and psychological rebuilding, Mac felt like a new man.

A man with an extreme amount of hate bubbling inside.

With his focus on revenge, Mac wanted to know where he could find Sam so he could make him pay for his treachery.

But Wallace had different plans.

Through a series of deep discussions, Wallace had told Mac he had so much more to offer the world besides being angry at it. While what he'd experienced had been monstrous, the world was full of people willing to do the same thing to millions more. Blackridge, Wallace's covert anti-terrorism unit, were spread across the globe, fighting the good fight to keep the world safe.

Mac had already proven he was a skilled marksman and despite his fractured mindset, could be a valuable asset.

All Mac had thought about during the beatings and the years spent in his cage was getting his hands on Sam.

Wallace was offering him so much more.

The General told Mac that killing Sam wouldn't change what happened. That when he finally did, he would discover how hollow he was now he didn't have that fury to hold on to. But, once Mac had served his country, like the true soldier he was, Wallace promised he would put Mac and Sam in the same room together and let Mac have his vengeance.

Sceptical of once again becoming a soldier, Mac deliberated for a few weeks. It was only when Wallace drove him to a secure location just outside of Solihull that Mac changed his mind.

As the car approached the large, derelict concrete structure, Mac turned to Wallace in the driver's seat. His heart fluttered with panic as memories of being confined in a Taliban base rushed back to him.

'What is this?'

'Relax, Mac,' Wallace said calmly as he pulled the car to a stop outside the door. 'I have something for you.'

Despite his reservations, Mac trusted the General implicitly and exited the car. Wallace marched to the front door where he was immediately greeted by a tough looking woman, who stood to attention. Decked out in the same black polo shirt and trousers as Mac, it was clear this was a Blackridge facility. That information calmed Mac slightly, but as they meandered through a few rooms and descended a staircase, he could feel his nerves rising to the surface.

'Sir?' Mac's words were fraught with fear. Wallace stopped on the second step, turned, and fixed the young soldier with a warm smile. Slowly, he extended his hand.

'Trust me, Mac. I won't leave you behind.'

Mac took a long intake of air and then took the General's hand, following him down the steps until they came across a large, metal door. Outside was another Blackridge operative, a large black man with a bandage wrapped around his knuckles. He too, stood to attention as Wallace approached, which the General kindly dismissed.

'How is he?'

'He was being a bit mouthy.' The operative motioned with his bandaged hand. 'I had to quiet him down.'

'Very good.' Wallace shot a glance to Mac, then back to the operative. 'Why don't you take a fifteen-minute break?'

'Yes, sir.'

The man answered instantly, nodding his goodbye to both men and then disappeared up the staircase. Before Mac could ask what was going on, Wallace hauled open the large metal door, his bulky frame making it look easy.

'After you.' Wallace gestured for Mac to enter and hesitantly, he did. The room was dark and empty, the walls thick reinforced with thick, soundproof panels. The concrete floor was spattered with historic bloodstains. A single light dropped from the ceiling, offering a circular glow around the man who sat, strapped to a chair beneath. With blood trickling from his eyebrow across his swollen eye, the man had clearly taken a beating.

Mac stopped in his tracks and Wallace stepped forward, approaching the man who begged for his freedom in Arabic, tears streaming down his face and collecting in his bloodstained beard.

'This, Mac, is Ahmed Bin Salma. A Taliban general who my team flew into the UK this morning. As you can see, he isn't exactly as powerful as he once thought.' The man spoke and Wallace clipped him across the face with the back of his hand. 'Shut up.'

'Sir?' Mac stepped forward cautiously.

'This man was in charge of the Taliban recruitment camp that held you hostage for seven years. Unfortunately for him, he wasn't there when we stormed the base. Which means now, he is in a lot of trouble.' Wallace gestured to a small table that was shrouded in shadow on the far side of the room. 'He's all yours, Mac. When I tell

167

you that I'll let you take back what people have taken from you, I mean it. I'll be outside.'

Wallace slapped Mac on the shoulder and squeezed it, before stomping back towards the door which closed behind him. Mac stood still for a few moments, contemplating the promise the General had made. Here before him, unable to escape, was the man who made his life a living hell for over half a decade.

Everything Wallace was offering was real.

The chance to make a difference.

An opportunity to channel his anguish into something real.

The promise of revenge.

A cruel smile grew across Mac's charred face and he walked casually over to the table. Without pausing to choose, he lifted the claw hammer, felt its weight in his grip, and then stepped into the illuminated ring where the man sat. The fear that grew in his eyes when he recognised Mac, knowing full well the torture he'd put the man through. With a whimper of acceptance of his fate, the man took a long, deep breath.

Mac swung the hammer, the connection sending a vibration through his arm as it cracked the man's skull.

The impact of the blow sent the man sideways, tipping the chair and he fell on the floor, his breathing intensifying as he tried to handle the pain.

With blood pouring from the man's skull, Mac crouched over the top of him and as he let out a guttural roar of pure rage, he brought the hammer down on the man's skull again and again and again until he was hitting nothing but brain soaked concrete.

———

Mac sat on the uncomfortable bed of his hostel room and took a deep breath. Remembering the thrill of exacting his revenge on the man responsible for his torture only reaffirmed his desire to bring a similar fate upon Sam.

Ahmed Bin Salma may have been the man who sanctioned his living hell.

It was Sam who had left him to it.

He stood and walked to the misty mirror that hung crooked on the wall. Shirtless, he examined the horrible burns that had scarred his body for life, reliving the agony as the missile struck the ground, blowing him into oblivion.

All the scars his body wore were reminders.

General Wallace's death had hit Mac hard. Furious that he wasn't given another chance to bring Sam to his knees, Mac had taken the time to recuperate from being run over but he never stopped pining for another opportunity. He would have killed Sam outright, but Wallace needed information from Sam, which he clearly didn't get.

The tabloids and news channels held little regard with Mac, who often found the presenters more interested in their appearance of reputation than the news itself. But when the story broke about Blackridge, it hit him hard.

Being one of Wallace's Ghosts had given Mac a renewed sense of purpose, with countless targets eradicated by his hand. It had pulled him back from the brink, turned him into the soldier he always knew he could be.

Losing Wallace was the worst part of it.

Despite the wild claims of terrorism, Mac had trusted in the General more than anyone else. After having his trust obliterated by Sam's abandonment and the subsequent years of horror, Wallace had wrapped an arm around him.

Turned him into something worthwhile.

Wallace had cared.

But once again, it was Sam Pope who was the cause of his pain. Once again, Mac had been chewed up and spat out, left to rot by a man who pretended to give a damn. Sam could hide behind the grief of losing his son, but Mac knew there was something rotten inside Sam. The man was a survivor, but he didn't care about the cost.

That was about to change.

After his exchanges with the anonymous Blackridge operative, Mac ensured his phone was on for the duration of the next twenty-four hours. Sure enough, a delivery was arranged to the front desk of the hostel which Mac intercepted before anyone had the chance to investigate it. He had fought too long and hard for his revenge to allow a nosy receptionist to potentially bring it all down.

With the package carefully sat in the cheap wardrobe in the corner of his room, he set about the next stage of his plan.

He needed the country to hand over Sam Pope.

That would be easy enough and with a little research, he knew he would find something.

The hardest part was the third stage.

Giving Sam a reason to beg.

Mac ran his hand across the limited stubble that spurted around the scar tissue on his chin as a horrible feeling of regret manifested in the bottom of his stomach.

He knew exactly how he would do it.

He searched for any part of himself that would regret what he was about to do.

He found nothing.

———

There is nothing worse than knowing a crime has been committed but having no pieces to the puzzle. It was one of the lectures Singh had related to most when studying to become a detective, and now, having long since reached the rank of DI, it was rearing its head again.

No evidence meant there was nothing she could do.

Not within the structure of the legal system, anyway.

A part of her wanted to follow Sam's lead by pushing the law to the side and doing what was necessary to get to the truth. But there were too many eyes on her. Ashton was keeping tabs on her movements, ready to throw her to sharks if she messed up or jump in and promote their relationship should Singh succeed.

Now, having mentioned it to the Commissioner, she was sure he would at least pass an interested glance in whatever she did next.

Singh had left the office that evening with her mind scattered. As she took the Jubilee Line back towards Canons Park, she knew she was battling two separate, but equally overwhelming, feelings.

The fury that someone had tampered with Sam's transfer, along with the worry for his safety.

Ashton knew where Sam was, but wasn't going to share that information. Singh opened her fridge and stared at the bottle of wine sat inside the door. Her drinking was beginning to dance dangerously along the line of becoming a problem and she slammed the fridge shut, turned, and popped a pod into her Tassimo coffee machine instead.

She needed a clear head.

Finding Sam was going to be harder than she ever imagined. As the coffee spluttered into the mug, she retrieved her laptop from her study and sat it on the kitchen counter, staring blankly at the search bar. There was little chance of her finding anything from Google.

If Sam was being kept hidden somewhere, she doubted the facility would have its own website.

Singh sipped her coffee and after an hour of staring at the screen, she slammed the laptop shut.

She needed a good night sleep.

Staring at the screen wasn't going to do her any good and the chances of the answer just falling into her lap were non-existent.

As she reluctantly headed towards her bedroom, she heard the faint buzz of her mobile phone and darted across her plush flat, fumbling with her jacket that had been slung over the back of a chair.

She retrieved the phone mid-ring, not recognising the number, and hesitantly answered the call.

'DI Singh,' she said firmly.

'Amara. How are you?'

'Paul?' Singh sounded shocked. She hadn't spoken to Etheridge since the day of the trial, where her anger at his non-attendance had built a friction between them.

'The one and only.' Etheridge sounded his usual, jovial self.

'Paul, I need to talk to you.' Singh began, knowing she was taking the first few steps on a road that would lead to self-ruin.

'What a coincidence. I need to talk to you, too.'

'Really? Is it about Sam?'

'Sort of.' Etheridge paused. 'Tell me, how do you feel about taking down the biggest criminal in the country?'

CHAPTER NINETEEN

It took every ounce of Singh's negotiation skills to get Ashton to agree to the raid.

As always, Ashton wanted to know all the details, demanding to know where the anonymous tip came from and to satisfy her own ego, why it didn't go to her? Singh knew how to play the game, leaning on the work Ashton had done to push Singh front and centre which seemed to placate the Deputy Commissioner.

Ashton agreed to the raid and as they both stood against the police car, they watched as an Armed Response Unit infiltrated the JB Meat Co. factory, located in a remote business park on the outskirts of Aldershot, Hampshire.

Singh watched intently, remembering the days when she rode with that crew: vests, and helmets on, rifle by her side. It had been as exhilarating as it had been terrifying but bursting into a drug den and facing open fire had toughened her up.

Built her into the tenacious woman she was today.

It wasn't her tenacity that had brought them to this location. Etheridge had told her he'd traced a phone signal that had received a call from Harry Chapman to the location, which he'd investigated. The large, metal structure was a clear meat packing factory, but Etheridge had scoured through the building plans and financial reports with a fine-tooth comb and something didn't add up. How he got those records, Singh didn't ask but there were definitely grounds to investigate.

'You better be right about this.' Ashton warned, looking straight ahead as she spoke. The brisk, spring morning brought with it a chill and Singh began to feel the effects of no sleep. A few coffees had kept her going and the forty-mile drive with the window open had kept her eyes open.

But now, with the chances of this all being a mistake, she began to feel completely exhausted.

Through the crackle of the radios, they heard the ARU command people to drop their weapons and then a loud crack of gunfire.

Singh and Ashton looked at each other and then marched forward, moving between the other squad cars that were parked in front of the building. Waiting by the door for further instruction, Singh felt her hands twitch with excitement.

Etheridge had been right.

Moments later, the captain of the ARU emerged, informing them that the gunfire was a warning shot and the workers within the lab had immediately surrendered.

'You found drugs?' Ashton barked, and Singh detected a hint of annoyance in her voice.

'I'll say. It's like an Amazon warehouse full of the stuff.' The captain turned to Singh and nodded. 'Good call, Singh.'

Singh smiled, not only at the compliment but by the horrible shade of green Ashton turned.

The rest of the morning played out as expected. As the

early morning employees began to arrive, they were held back by a police cordon, all of them agitated at not being told why they couldn't get through. That in turn, brought interest from the passing public and sure enough, the press followed.

By eight thirty, the national news was broadcasting the sensational story of a drugs bust in a meat packing plant and how the Metropolitan Police had, years after his incarceration, finally felled the mighty drug empire of Harry Chapman.

It was sensational stuff and Singh knew she was too exhausted to face the media. Having been the one to bring Sam to justice, this was only going to launch her further into the public eye, a place she despised.

Whether it was lucky or not, she knew someone who would jump at the opportunity.

Singh turned her focus back to the ongoing raid, watching with amazement at the vast supplies of drugs that were seized from the property. Behind the front of the meat packing plant, there were two well concealed drug labs, their work disguised by the overpowering stench of raw meat. The 'cooks' were brought out in cuffs, all of them resigned to their fate of a lifetime behind bars.

It had been a hell of a morning, piled on top of a day filled with confusion and Singh needed to get her head down. Ashton begrudgingly congratulated her on another incredible piece of work, but her mood increased when Singh asked her to cover the media duties.

Ashton was never one to shy away from the spotlight, not when she could align the bust with her own agenda.

Singh made her way to her car, dropped into the driver's seat, and reversed out. Driving carefully through a small gaggle of reporters, clambering over each other for a quote like a horde of zombies on the hunt for fresh meat, she hit the open road and put her foot down.

Etheridge had just handed her one of the biggest wins of her career on a platter, but she couldn't muster a smile.

Not because she was so tired.

Because she still didn't have a clue what the hell was going on.

Singh headed back towards London, knowing that the relentless call of sleep needed attending to before she spoke to Etheridge himself.

———

With the cameras flashing as she took her seat behind the desk, Ashton couldn't help but smile. The Metropolitan Police logo was proudly displayed on the board behind her and she gently flattened her immaculate tunic as she took her seat.

As Deputy Commissioner of the organisation, she was a well known and for the most part, well-respected figure among the press, with many of them already correctly predicting she'd be the next incumbent of the top job.

Ashton wasn't going to correct them should they make such a claim, especially as Commissioner Stout had already told her the wheels were in motion.

As she looked out at the eager journalists, all of them fiddling with their phones, laptops, and notepads, she took a brief moment to reflect on her success.

Sam Pope was behind bars.

They had just shut down the biggest drug operation in the history of the UK, a feat that nobody had been able to in over three decades.

All of it under her command.

It would take something spectacular to stop her ascension now.

With an understandable degree of confidence, she pointed at a journalist to begin the questions.

'Thank you, ma'am,' the young journalist began. 'First, congratulations on an incredible day for the Metropolitan Police. Can I ask, how did the information about the location of the laboratory come about?'

Ashton offered a warm smile, a well-rehearsed move that made her a pro at her job.

'Thank you, John. We received an anonymous tip in the early hours of the morning. While we are investigating the source from where it came, I never doubted its legitimacy. Once we were able to secure the warrants to search the premises, we ensured that due care was taken to ensure a successful raid.'

Her response was met with a flurry of activity, with fingers clicking across keypads and pens scratching notebooks. Despite not actually answering the question in-depth, Ashton knew she had them in the palm of her hand. She waited a few more moments, before pointing towards a bespectacled woman in the second row.

'Yes?'

'Thanks, ma'am. Original estimates place the value of the drug empire that you've brought down to be in the millions, some even saying over a hundred million. Is this the case and if so, is this the most lucrative bust the Metropolitan Police has ever had?'

'Well, until we have the full facts and figures, we won't know for sure, but considering the lab is linked to the biggest drug ring within the UK, we estimate the value at the highest end of the scale. Without a doubt, this is a glorious day for our country, as by working diligently, we can reduce the amount of drugs and money illegally running through it.'

As Ashton smiled warmly, she took another question.

'Ma'am, are the reports linking this drug factory to the notorious Harry Chapman true? And a follow up question if I may, if this is the case, how was he able to operate and control an entire operation when he has been incarcerated for over a decade?'

Ashton shuffled uncomfortably, a slight sneer of agitation creeping across her well-trained smile.

'Crime will never go away,' she said dramatically. 'As we are aware, there are people who dedicate their lives to it and taking Chapman off the streets was a momentous achievement for this organisation. But crime doesn't stop with him and the fact that now, despite the length of time, we've cut off the supply line that created his empire, we should be celebrating a job well done as opposed to questioning it.'

The reporter shook his head slightly and flustered, Ashton turned to another sea of raised hands. She nodded and awaited the question.

'Ma'am, since the trial of Sam Pope concluded, there has been no update on his condition, nor any official word from yourselves or HMS Pentonville. Are you able to update us on Sam Pope's condition?'

Ashton's eyes flickered with a furious envy. Insulted that the press were still focused on Sam as opposed to her, she snapped her response.

'As far as I'm concerned, Sam Pope is no longer an issue that the press or the public need to worry about.'

'But ma'am, considering the public interest in Sam's trial, and the split belief among them that he was a hero, do you not think that they deserve to know?'

Ashton slammed her hands down on the table, a gasp echoing from the watching reporters. The Deputy Commissioner was renowned for her composure and seeing a clear act of annoyance would be worth a few lines itself. Embarrassed, Ashton readjusted her cravat, cleared her throat, and leant forward to the mic.

'The Sam Pope situation has been concluded, as has this press conference. Thank you for your questions.'

Ashton stood, bringing an abrupt and regrettable conclusion to the proceedings. As the reporters called out in the hope of a final question, Ashton marched towards the door, trying her best to keep her cool. Once she'd made her way through the small PR team who offered her praise, she entered her office and slammed the door shut.

As she sat her desk, she took a few deep breaths. As far as she was concerned, Sam Pope was a non-issue and the sooner the country forgot about his pathetic mission the better. Reaching for the bottle of Scotch in her locked cabinet, she poured herself a celebratory drink and toasted to her own future, knowing that as long as she kept a lid on Sam's incarceration, she'd soon be sat where she belonged.

———

Four hours sleep was more than enough for Singh to recharge her batteries and she awoke on top of her covers, still dressed in her shirt and trousers. The previous few days had been exhausting and she pushed herself off the bed, stripped off, and stepped into her shower.

As the water crashed over her, she felt her energy levels return. For ten minutes, she let the water pour over her, running her hands through her thick, black hair and gave herself a few moments to think. With another high-profile success against her name, she was well aware that doors would open for her. Despite their personal animosity, Ashton would soon be the most powerful person in the Met and Singh was her golden goose.

She should have been thrilled, but the thought of being used by the woman as a political tool turned her stomach.

But that wasn't the real reason for her unease.

Singh stepped out of the shower, dried herself off, and dressed herself in jeans and a hooded jumper before heading towards her increasingly valuable coffee machine.

The caffeine hit her like a bolt of lightning, and she checked the time. It had just gone one o'clock and she turned on the TV, watching as Ashton settled down behind the desk, a victorious grin across her face. With interest, she watched as Ashton fielded the questions, impressed with the command and ease that the Deputy Commissioner handled the room.

Singh couldn't help but smile at the clear irritation Ashton felt at being questioned about Sam and watching her lose her cool at a journalist's insistence was a welcome treat.

But Ashton wasn't the only one irritated by the Sam Pope situation and taking it as a cue, Singh made her way to her car and headed towards Farnham, determined to get the answers that her very sanity rested upon.

The drive around the M25 was relatively easy, only hitting traffic near Heathrow airport and as Singh turned off at the junction leading towards her destination, she took a moment to appreciate the beautiful countryside. The vast, sprawling green fields were the personification of freedom and she worried about Sam.

Where was he?

How was he?

She would soon find out.

With a sprinkle of rain dotting her windscreen, she pulled up in front of Etheridge's house and she stepped out, approaching the locked gate with purpose. Despite the records showing that he'd sold the house and was living in Tenerife, she knew otherwise and she scaled the gate impressively, her daily workouts giving her surprising upper body strength.

Not caring if she'd been seen or not, she approached the front door which Etheridge pulled open with a smile on his face.

'Amara,' he said joyfully. 'Lovely to see you.'

'We need to talk,' Singh said firmly, marching past Etheridge, who ushered her in like a maître d'. Singh stepped into the hallway, once again impressed by its size. Her modest two-bedroom flat could fit in the living room, especially as Etheridge no longer had any furniture. With his prominent limp, Etheridge led her to the kitchen, and she was reminded of the pain that the man had gone through.

He had given himself to Sam's cause as much as she had.

The kitchen was just as derelict as the front room, with nothing hanging from the walls and the large, marble work tops empty apart from a cheap kettle and toaster. Etheridge pulled open the fridge with a strong arm and pulled out two bottles of beer, opened them on the fridge mounted opener and handed her one.

Hesitantly, she took it, her brain warning her of her weakness.

'It's good to see you,' Etheridge began, taking a sip. 'I felt bad about how things were left when we last spoke…'

'I need to know what the hell is going on,' Singh blurted, putting her untouched drink down on the side and walking to the back door, peering out over the garden. 'Sam is missing, and I feel like I'm going insane talking about it. No one has the answers and then suddenly out of nowhere, you call me with the tip of the century—'

'You're welcome by the way,' Etheridge interrupted with a wry smile. Singh turned to him, her eyes watering with concern.

'I just don't know what's going on.'

Etheridge placed his drink down and took two steps towards the detective and placed a caring hand on her shoulder.

He offered her a warm smile.

'Like I said before, Amara. There is always a plan.'

CHAPTER TWENTY

THREE WEEKS AGO...

'What choice do I have?'

Sam stood in Etheridge's office, the walls lined with screens offering a selection of security footage, spreadsheets, and nondescript coding. Moments before, Sam had discovered the horrifying truth of his past. Project Hailstorm had hung over him like a dark cloud and his mind had tried to piece together the fragments of the fateful night when he'd nearly been killed.

Shot twice and left for dead in the wastelands of Afghanistan, Sam had soon discovered that the bullets were from Wallace's gun. His commanding officer had left him to die as Sam had stumbled upon the truth. Their target was not a known terrorist, but in fact a young man trying to protect his family. A man who had discovered the reality of Wallace's operation and in doing so, had marked himself for death.

The files they'd trawled through painted a bleak picture.

Project Hailstorm had been brought together by Wallace, recruiting the very best soldiers to eliminate what Sam thought were wanted criminals.

They were never briefed.

They were given a name and a location, and they would eliminate the target.

In effect, they'd been a hit squad, spilling the blood of anyone who dared step in the way of Wallace's domination.

Blackridge had been the afterbirth, born out of Wallace's decision to shut down the project and Sam was shipped back to the UK on death's door. Lucy had lovingly stayed by his side and they'd started a family, one which had cruelly been ripped away from them.

But after dealing with the truth and accepting the blood on his hands, Sam turned back to the task at hand. He was in possession of a USB stick that incriminated Wallace and every other high-ranking official who had links to the project. Carl Marsden, Sam's mentor and friend, had been killed for it.

He had been willing to die for it.

Sam wasn't going to let that be for nothing.

He had to fight for something.

Etheridge took a sip of his coffee and let out a deep sigh.

'Going after Wallace, not much of a choice.'

Sam grunted, the stakes had been changed. Moments before, they'd received a call from Wallace himself, boasting about how he'd abducted DI Amara Singh and he now held the winning hand. He demanded Sam hand over the files and himself, otherwise the young detective would die.

Both Etheridge and Sam knew it wasn't a bluff, nor was it the truth.

There was no way Singh would be left alive.

Wallace would bury her with Sam and there would be no enquiry. The man wielded unprecedented power and the only option they had was to fight back. Sam had stormed out of the house, barking orders at Etheridge to feed him the information he needed to locate his guns and to cut Wallace's motorcade off. Etheridge had managed to pull Sam back into the house to discuss strategy.

Sam was a fighter.

But Etheridge, while not as skilled with a gun, had the brain to formulate a plan.

They had five hours until Wallace's motorcade would pass London Bridge, which gave Etheridge minutes to relay his thinking to Sam. With the sand falling in their hourglass, Etheridge had begged Sam for five minutes to run him through it.

Now, relaying the consequences to him, Etheridge was impressed with how little fear it held to him.

'And you can make this happen?' Sam asked, turning away from the whiteboard where Etheridge had collated his information. 'Isn't Ashcroft the most secure prison in the world?'

'It might be, but there is something you should know.'

'What's that?'

Etheridge smiled.

'I built their system for them.'

Sam's eyes lit up.

While he'd been recuperating in Italy after his attack from the mysterious man in black, Etheridge had gotten to work. Sam had been impressed by his newfound focus, stripping away his body fat and giving up his life of luxury. By building an intricate web of lies, Etheridge had convinced the world he'd retired to Tenerife, selling off his company and living a comfortable life under the exotic sun.

But he hadn't.

He had been working.

After Sam had taken down the High Rises and raged war with the Kovalenkos, Etheridge dug deeper into the records. After quickly finding a link between them, he followed the trail back to Harry Chapman, the notorious crime boss who had been arrested over a decade ago. Now situated behind the secure walls of Ashcroft, he was untouchable. With his resources limitless, Chapman had assumed control of the facility, paying off the guards and still running his empire from the inside.

The only piece of information not on the board was the one bit that would bring it all down.

The final domino that would send it crumbling.

His drug lab.

Despite Etheridge's skills, there had been no hint of a location, not enough for him to take to the police. There were numerous possible locations, which Sam could investigate himself.

But taking down Wallace meant it was a one-way mission and they'd spoken about the outcome being Sam being carted away in cuffs.

Sam knew it was the only outcome and if he could save Singh's life, if she was still alive, then he could clear her name and also be put on the road to Chapman.

Two birds with one stone.

'You do know that once you're in there, I can't literally open doors for you,' Etheridge warned. 'It would raise alarm bells and they would shut it down and you'll be in there forever.'

'I know,' Sam said, not wavering his eyes from the board.

'Ashcroft has the worst of the worst in its roster and a lot of them don't like you.' Etheridge hobbled across the room and stood next to his friend. 'You'll have to do everything you can to survive.'

Sam offered him a rare smile.

'That's what I do.'

'Okay then. Getting the transfer there won't be difficult. Forging documents is child's play.'

Etheridge limped back towards his chair, dropping into the fine leather and taking the pressure off his damaged knee.

'You know, you would make one hell of a criminal.'

'We are criminals, Sam.' Etheridge chuckled. 'Now you need to get going if you're going to do this.'

Sam nodded firmly, threw his arms through the sleeves of his jacket again and headed for the door. Before he left, he turned to Etheridge.

'And once I get you that location, then what?'

Etheridge offered him a concerned look.

'I'll do my best to get you out.'

———

Singh listened, open-mouthed as Etheridge concluded his story. Processing their elaborate plan had sent her mind into a spiral and she wasn't sure how she felt. There were several emotions all vying for dominance.

The confusion that such a plan could be hatched.

Relief that she knew where Sam was and for all intents and purposes, was alive and well.

The outrage that Etheridge and Sam had infiltrated a government prison and the number of laws they'd broken to do it.

Etheridge sat quietly, looking up at the whiteboard that was still covered with the information he'd present to Sam. When putting the information together, he did so with a heavy heart, knowing that despite his genius intellect, he wouldn't be the one putting his body on the line. To bring down Chapman's empire, Sam would need to willingly walk into hell and keep himself alive.

Judging from the fierce scowl on Singh's face, she felt similar.

'This is wrong.' Singh finally spat. 'You should be locked up for this, you know that?'

'I do.'

'You forged the signature of the fucking Commissioner of the Metropolitan Police. You've hacked into a maximum-security prison. Jesus, Paul. What were you thinking?'

'The same things you were,' Etheridge snapped back. 'You could have arrested Sam when he met you at Liverpool Street Station, but you didn't. Because you feel the same damn way I do. Hell, the same way Pearce felt as well.'

Singh shook her head, her tongue pressed against her lip.

'And what's that then?'

'You believe what Sam does is necessary.'

The words hit Singh like a dart and she knew she

couldn't argue. She turned in disgust, more at herself for her agreement. Sam was necessary. At least once a day she scolded herself for how she dismissed Aaron Hill when he first came to her, begging for help in the hopeless search for his daughter. If she'd put as much effort into finding Jasmine as she had into finding Sam, maybe she would have brought her home too.

But it was unlikely.

Sam was willing to do what the police weren't.

He was willing to go to war.

Singh stood, picked up her beer, and devoured half of it in one mouthful. Etheridge pulled himself to his feet, too, steadied himself and then walked over to the fridge beneath his desk. As he opened another drink, he looked at Singh and offered her an apologetic smile.

'Sam was willing to trade himself for your life. Either that or willing to go to jail. He knows that one day everything he's done will come back on him. I know it, too. But right now, this country needs Sam out on the streets, fighting back against the people the police don't go near. You might not like it, Singh. But Sam is as necessary as the goddamn badge you have in your pocket.'

Singh sipped her beer, shaking her head. A tear had begun to form in her eye, and she wiped it with the sleeve of her hoody. Staring at the bottle, she spoke.

'I've always prided myself on never being afraid.' She chuckled to herself. 'I fought back against an oppressive system to become one of its best detectives. I did a lot of good but when I had the chance to bring Sam in, it was my meal ticket. Hell, I remember how much I hated him when he handcuffed me to your goddamn patio door. But the farther along we chased, the farther down the rabbit hole I went, I saw the truth and that was what scared me. For the first time, in a long time, I was actually afraid.'

'That you would die?' Etheridge asked, taking a step towards her.

'No. That Sam would.'

Like a supportive parent, Etheridge reached out and gently patted her shoulder. Although his marriage had dissolved not long after Sam had engaged in a shootout in his house, Etheridge was still a hopeless romantic at heart. He wasn't blind to the blossoming feelings between Singh and Sam and he felt sorrow for how cruelly fate had led them together.

There was no chance of happiness for them.

They both knew it.

But Singh's anger at their plan hadn't been rooted in a firm stance against breaking the law. It was out of her genuine fear for Sam and his survival in a locked down building swarming with men who would want him dead. All Etheridge could do was reassure her that they had it under control.

'Look, I know you care about Sam. We both know that if anyone can survive this, he can. The man is immortal.' Singh smiled and Etheridge continued, 'The second I get the go ahead from him, I'll be at that computer, guiding him out. Okay?'

Singh nodded, but then furrowed her brow in confusion.

'The *go ahead*? Hasn't he already sent you the location?'

'Yup. But you know Sam…he has a certain finality with how he operates.'

Singh screwed her face, battling the morality of Sam's actions. Although he was targeting dangerous criminals, she could never condone the idea of him killing. They had already shut down Chapman's operation, meaning he would spend the rest of his life in his cell, knowing his stranglehold of power had been lifted.

But Sam wouldn't think about that.

He'd think about all the lives the man had ruined. All the families devastated by the drugs he'd peddled, the vast number of careers ended by taking back handed payments.

Sam would total it all up and hold him accountable for every single action.

Cutting through the tension in the room, Etheridge's mobile buzzed. Singh darted over with concern as he looked at the screen.

'It's go time,' Etheridge said.

'What does that mean?' Singh demanded. Etheridge looked up at her, trying to mask his worry with a smile.

'It means we don't have much time. Tell me, Amara... how quickly could you drive to Sussex?'

Within seconds, Singh was bounding down the stairs of the loft conversion, running as fast as her legs could carry her. Etheridge remotely opened the gate and she powered through the rain to her car, knowing that every moment could be Sam's last.

CHAPTER TWENTY-ONE

It didn't take long for the news to spread through the Grid. Chapman's fury exploded the moment he was told, his loyal employees calling him just before they were arrested. With a rage that sent shivers down the spines of the guards and inmates, Chapman had screamed until he was hoarse, telling his men to sort it.

It was a hopeless request and sure enough, through the murmurings of the guards, it was confirmed that Chapman's drug empire had been found and subsequently shut down. Millions of pounds worth of drugs and cash seized by the police and an immeasurable impact on his clients. With it, went his stranglehold over those in charge and the biggest topic on anyone's lips was how it would affect his control of Ashcroft.

Sam, still granted the freedom being part of Chapman's gang allowed him, made his way to Chapman's cell as soon as he heard the anguished roars of failure. As he entered, Chapman was sat at his desk, his head in his wrinkled hands, the weight of his loss hanging heavy. Sat on the bench behind, Glen peered up at Sam with distrust, his beady eyes scanning Sam for any sense of betrayal.

Stoically stood with his back against the far wall was Ravi, his one good arm outstretched, his mighty hand rested on his boss's shoulder.

'What the fuck happened?' Sam demanded, acting as annoyed as Chapman.

'The fuckers took it all.' Chapman spat into the desk. 'They found the location. For thirty fucking years I kept that place off the map. It wouldn't even flag up on a fucking radar!'

'Fuck,' Sam exclaimed, convinced of his acting.

'Fuck indeed.' Ravi stepped forward. 'Seems a bit suspicious that you join us and suddenly the boss gets fucked over.'

'Yeah.' Glen stood, cowering behind Ravi's imposing frame. Sam shook his head.

'What's the matter? You still pissed off after I wiped the floor with you in front of everyone?'

'Fuck you!' Ravi stepped forward.

'Enough!' Chapman yelled, slamming his fists on his table, shaking every item on it. He turned in his chair and glared at all three men. 'There is a bigger fucking problem here than whose dick is bigger. Without that lab ticking over, I'll lose everything. Once the fuckers who run this place realise I don't have the power or money to keep them at bay, they will come for all of us like a pack of hungry wolves.'

'They wouldn't dare touch us,' Ravi responded, his eyes still locked on Sam, who stood a few feet from the door. The room was no bigger than his own cell, and with all four of them occupying it, he knew the space would make it difficult.

'Yeah,' Glen chimed in again, and Sam rolled his eyes.

'What can we do?' Sam asked, turning his attention to Chapman who looked deep in thought.

'It will take them a while to close off all avenues of my

enterprise.' He stroked his beard as he spoke. 'We need to get a call out to a few of my guys. Get them to send a message that money never could.'

'Meaning?'

'I don't know. Fuck up their family. Kill a wife.' Chapman shrugged nonchalantly. 'I don't give a shit. If I'm going to be locked up in here for the rest of my life, I'm going to make damn sure I run this place.'

Sam's hand twitched. Seeing Chapman crumble at the same time as his empire brought a certain satisfaction, but the idea that his plan could impact an innocent family caused his fists to clench.

He needed to end this now.

'Boss, what we need to do is find out how they found it.' Ravi suggested, finally taking his eyes off Sam. Chapman had picked up the box cutter from his desk, and balancing it under one finger, let the blade spin on the desk.

'Oh, I'll find out all right. But until then, I'm going to make sure every fucker in this place knows I'm still in charge.'

Sam peaked over his shoulder. The corridor was clear. The guards had rightly stayed away, knowing they would most likely feel the wrath of Chapman. It meant that the four men were alone, but Sam knew Sharp would be waiting like a coiled spring the moment anything happened. Casually, Sam turned and pulled the door closed, knowing it wouldn't lock until the computerised mechanism was activated.

It's what he was counting on.

'What the fuck are you doing?' Chapman demanded. All eyes were on Sam.

'I thought it would make sense to not advertise what's going on to the rest of the prison,' Sam replied calmly. 'Like you said, they'll start circling.'

The three men looked at Sam with suspicion, until Chapman turned back to the desk, pushing the box cutter to the side and lifting his phone.

'I'll call around, see if I can find out how this happened. You boys beat the fucking truth out of every piece of shit in this place. If they have nothing to say, then at least it will be a reminder to them of who's in charge.'

Ravi and Glen nodded, with the larger man pushing past Sam and heading towards the door. Sam slid his hand into his pocket, running his thumb over the keypad of the burner phone Chapman had given him. The text was simple, the word *NOW* ready to send and Etheridge's number tapped in. As his thumb arrived at the enter key, he pushed it.

A few seconds later, the lock of the door thudded into place, catching the other three men off guard. Not to be deterred, Ravi slammed his mobile arm into it a few times, trying his best to take it off his hinges.

Sam pulled the phone from his pocket and tossed it on the table.

'I'll save you the hassle, boss,' Sam said, steadying his feet, ensuring a solid base. 'I did it.'

Chapman looked blankly at the phone, trying his best to recount the memory of giving it to Sam. A hazy recollection formed in his mind and his eyes widened with surprise.

'But how the hell…'

'It doesn't matter. It's over.'

Chapman stared at Sam in disbelief and then, after a few moments, he slowly reached for the box cutter.

'Oh, it's over you piece of shit.' He spat through gritted teeth. 'This place will bow to me when I take that head off your shoulders.'

'Yeah,' Glen helpfully added. 'You dumb fuck, you're locked in here with us.'

Sam smiled. His fists clenched.

'Wrong. It's the other way round.'

Sam swivelled on his right foot and drove a right hand straight into Glen's jaw, knocking him off balance and sending him careening into the brick wall. In one swift movement, he drove his elbow into the side of Chapman's face, driving him onto his knees and slamming his ribs against the table, the box cutter falling onto the wooden desk. Before Sam could plant his foot back down, Ravi charged, the impact of his truck-like body sending Sam slamming into the wall. To lighten the collision, Sam lifted his knee, steering it into Glen's crotch. Ravi looped his good arm around Sam's neck and wrenched back as hard as he could, crushing down on his windpipe and almost lifting him off his feet. Struggling for air, Sam pushed back with both feet, the two men traversing the small floorspace and Ravi slammed into the door. His grip didn't budge as he wrenched at Sam's head, Sam frantically rammed the point of his elbow into the cast.

He felt the material cracking and with one final swipe, his elbow broke through, slamming into the surgically repaired bone and knocking it out of alignment. Ravi howled in agony, loosened his grip and Sam slammed his head off the metal cupboard in the corner of the room.

Spluttering, Sam turned to the room, watching as the elderly Chapman reached for the box cutter. Sam kicked the chair forward, the metal scraping the floor and colliding with the man's ribs. Before Chapman could get his breath back, Sam lifted the box cutter, held Chapman's hand in place, and slammed the blade through the back of it.

It ripped through the skin and cartilage and penetrated the desk underneath.

The roar of anguish was guttural, swiftly drowned out by the pounding on the locked door. Sam shot a glance towards the glass, where Sharp's furious face was puffing steam onto the window. Behind him, his guards were grouping, all of them ready to rip Sam apart.

That was a problem he would face shortly.

The pathetic Glen had finally stood, still movingly gingerly after the shot to his genitals and he threw a right hook at Sam, which he easily dodged. Sam's hand shot out, hooked the arm, and he twisted it, the tendons ripping. In one fluid motion he slammed Glen towards the bench, his head hitting the edge of the seat and his teeth broke against the hard metal.

Sam then stomped, breaking his neck and killing him instantly.

Ravi woozily jumped into action, catching Sam with a vicious left hook that sent blood spraying from his lip, but the follow-up swipe gave Sam an opening. Ravi wasn't a southpaw, and Sam blocked the incoming blow with his forearm, drove a stiff knee into the man's solid abs, and hunched him over. Then, with all his might, Sam ran and slammed Ravi head first into the unforgiving steel of the door, the top of his cranium denting the metal with a sickening thud.

The large man slumped the ground, motionless, a streak of blood trailing from the dent to his skull.

Sam took a moment, shot Sharp a look through the glass, and then turned to Chapman.

Cries of *TAG HIM!* bellowed from Sharp, but Etheridge had done his job. Sam's tag was decommissioned and there was no way to stop him.

Sam sat on the edge of the table, doing his best to avoid the blood that was pooling around Chapman's hand as the old gangster twitched in pain. With his final reserves of energy, Chapman swung wildly at Sam, who blocked the feeble swipe and then rocked Chapman with a right hand.

Accepting his defeat, Chapman stopped his attack and looked up at Sam.

'Why the fuck are you doing this?'

Sam leant in close, his words laced with menace.

'Because your business has cost people more than you have gained. Not just the people you've killed but the people who you infected. The lives you ruined with the High Rises. The young girls you sanctioned with the Kovalenkos. All the families rocked by drug abuse or the fear you instilled. You ruined this country, all for money. But what makes this personal, is due to the people who worked for you, the death of my best friend is on your hands.'

With one swift tug, Sam wrenched the box cutter from Chapman's hand, causing him to howl and turn, his back resting against the table. As with most criminals, when stripped of their power, Chapman began to beg.

'I can make this right.'

'Look at me,' Sam demanded. Chapman did, his watery eyes wide with fear. 'I did this to you.'

Sam's wrist flashed past Chapman so quickly, he didn't realise what had happened. Only when the skin of his throat began to tear open and a waterfall of blood spilled down his front did he grasp at the wound with both hands, falling to his side as he frantically tried to hang onto his life.

He wouldn't.

Sam tossed the bloodied box cutter onto the table, and stood, turning his attention to the door where Sharp angrily screamed that he was a dead man. To his left, Glen's broken body lay, only the whites of his eyes showing. Infront of the door, the hulking frame of Ravi was lying, his blood still painting the steel like cheap graffiti.

And before him, Chapman gurgled and then stopped moving.

Sharp stared in disbelief.

Chapman had walked his final mile.

Behind him, there were over fifteen guards, all of them ready to unload on Sam and beat him to death. Sharp would ensure it would be brutal.

Retrieving his phone from the desk, Sam stepped towards the door, cracked his neck, and began to type.

———

Etheridge had purposefully not brought up Chapman's cell camera onto his screen. He had full faith that Sam would succeed, but he didn't want to witness the gory details.

He wasn't a fighter.

With a click of a button he'd locked the cell door and then disabled the tags of the four occupants.

The rest would be on Sam.

Etheridge had one screen trained on the corridor outside the cell, the clear CCTV footage showing him the steel door and the surrounding area. After a few moments of anxious nail biting, he saw a guard approach. And then another.

Soon, there were seventeen guards, all of them stood in a semi-circle as their boss slammed his fist on the door. There was no audio, but from the clear agitation of the man, he assumed Sam had done exactly as intended.

The phone on his desk buzzed, and Etheridge scooped it up immediately. He opened the text message.

NOW.

Laughing at Sam's precise messages, he turned back to the screens. He couldn't imagine what his friend had been through, nor the brutality with which he finished it. But they were far from out of it just yet and Etheridge brought up the schematics of the Grid and frantically hammered his keyboard.

His override code was immaculate, and he took control of the entire facility.

Etheridge glanced up at the screen, sent Sam a silent *good luck*, and then pressed the button.

He watched as the guards startled in disbelief as throughout the entire building, the mechanical locks of the cell doors flew open.

Etheridge sat back in his chair and watched as the inmates began to emerge from their cells like rats from the sewer.

'Time to move, Sam,' he said out loud, and with the guards beginning to fend off a wave of furious and violent prisoners, Etheridge unlocked Chapman's cell door, and Sam stepped out into the mayhem.

CHAPTER TWENTY-TWO

As soon as Harris was informed of the drug bust, he shuffled to his wardrobe to retrieve his uniform. To the dismay of his wife, Anna, he was heading into work on one of his mandated rest days and as he struggled to pull his shirt sleeve over his arm, she began to cry.

'You need to give this up, Geoff.' She wept. 'It's not doing you any good.'

Harris sighed.

'Something major has happened that needs my attention.'

'Your health needs your attention,' Anna responded, shaking her head. 'I hate seeing you like this.'

Harris grunted and yanked at the sleeve with frustration. His declining mobility was a sickening slap in the face from the cruel hands of fate. After twenty revered years of service in the armed forces, and an immaculate reputation as a police Warden, Harris had never been one to take his foot off the gas. But life had a funny way of revealing your mortality and it pained him to be a burden on his wife.

Anna took a breath, stood, and marched from the doorway to his side. Tentatively, she pulled the sleeve over his arm and then went about buttoning the shirt. Towering over her, Harris leant forward, and gently kissed her forehead.

'I love you.'

She smiled warmly.

'Then stay here. With me.'

Anna finished buttoning his shirt and turned to the wardrobe, lifting his immaculately polished shoes from the rack that sat beneath a rail of identical, crisply ironed shirts. Harris tucked in his shirt and despite his protests, allowed Anna to tie his laces. Feeling so helpless was the biggest struggle of his multiple sclerosis, as his immune system was mistakenly attacking his brain and nervous system. His balance had been deteriorating for a while and he could barely make it through the day without feeling exhausted.

Anna was right.

He needed to give it up.

But not today.

Anna helped him to the car which had pulled up outside their plush cottage, thirteen miles away from Ashcroft and she held him closely. They kissed once more, and he eased himself into the back seat and the car sped towards the prison. On the journey, he called Sharp count-less times, his rage increasing with each call that didn't connect. As they approached the first gate, Harris cursed the numerous safety measures designed to keep people out.

He needed to get in and restore order.

As they cleared the final door, he was shocked to be met by Spencer Watkins, his face pale with fear.

'Jesus, Spencer. What's wrong?' Harris's voice was laced with concern and as he struggled from the backseat, Watkins gave him a guiding arm.

'I don't know what happened, sir…'

'What? What is it?'

'No matter what I did, I lost control. Like someone else was controlling the panel and...'

'Breathe, Watkins,' Harris said calmly, resting a comforting arm on the young man's shoulder. It was also a useful support.

'I tried, sir. I really tried.'

'Take a moment and tell me what happened?'

Harris felt a flutter of irritation in his gut. After the news of Chapman's empire falling, he needed to get inside the prison and ensure that the notorious inmate was still behaving as expected. Sure, the veteran gangster rode his luck at times, but for the most part, he was respectful of Harris. While the warden expected some sort of retaliation against his staff, he was confident he could talk some sense into the man. Watkin's was clearly afraid, but Harris had no time for his dithering.

'Jesus Christ, son. Spit it out.'

Watkins looked up at the wiry Warden, his eyes watering.

'The doors, sir. All the doors opened.'

Harris's jaw dropped. Not once in the years that he'd run the prison had he been faced with a riot. The prisoners mostly stayed within the rules, understanding the finality of their situation and many opting for an easy existence. A few inmates had died, others had lashed out at guards. But for the most part, the prison was a peaceful place.

But given the freedom of the prison, they would revert back to what they were.

The most dangerous criminals in the country.

Harris quickly moved to the boot of the car, the driver flicking the switch so it automatically opened. With his left leg dragging across the gravel, Harris steadied himself and then reached into the compartment. He pulled out a bulletproof vest, slid it over his head, and pushed his arms through.

Then, for the first time since he was put in control of Ashcroft, he picked up his handgun.

The Glock 19 felt heavy in his hand, a long-lost friend from a life he used to have. He slid it into the holster attached to his belt and turned to Watkins.

'Get in the car and ask the driver to take you to the nearest police station.'

'But, sir…'

'Go,' Harris demanded, and Watkins obliged, ducking into the car which lifted a cloud of dust as it sped back through the open gates.

Harris watched the cloud begin to settle and then turned and faced the entrance to Ashcroft and took a deep breath. With one hand on his handgun, he shuffled towards the door, fearful of what was on the other side.

———

As soon as the first inmates emerged from their cells, Sam could see the fear spread among the guards like a disease. With the shackles of their cells relinquished, the inmates ventured into the corridor and it took only a matter of seconds for a panicked guard to pull the trigger in their direction.

An inmate yelled out in pain from the gunshot and like a tidal wave crashing over them, the guards soon found themselves set upon by the inmates. The vicious criminals, subjected to the violent and oppressive rule of Sharp's men, launched at them with reckless abandon, dragging the guards to the ground and brutally beating them with fists and feet.

Gunshots echoed around the corridor, with the remaining guards throwing caution to the wind, abandoning protocol, and doing whatever they could to survive.

Sharp was screaming at a group of inmates to stay

back, as three of them approached. Leon, the prisoner who had been assaulted for talking to Sam stepped forward and Sharp whipped out his weapon, pulled the trigger, and sent the top of the man's head exploding backwards. The body collapsed into a pool of blood and brain and Sharp waved the gun at the other two.

Sam took his moment.

Launching forward from his cell, he shoulder tackled Sharp in the ribs, knocking the hefty deputy warden off balance. As he sprawled across the floor of the war zone, the two prisoners set upon Sharp and Sam began to veer his way through the mayhem, with Sharp's anguished cries echoing behind him. To his left, he saw three inmates stomping on a guard, who was motionless, his face covered in blood. In front of him, two of the inmates were settling a blood feud and as one pinned the other to the ground, he began slamming his head against the solid, concrete floor.

Sam intervened, wrenching the inmate off his motionless opponent, and slammed him into the door frame, knocking him unconscious.

Halfway towards the door to the stairwell, Sam was confronted by a guard, clearly in his element, who pointed his blood-soaked baton at Sam. With his right eye swollen and blood dripping from his lips, he charged at Sam, swinging wildly. Sam weaved underneath, the metal missing the top of his skull by millimetres, and Sam drove an elbow into the back of the man's skull. The guard was unconscious before he hit the ground.

Sam's eyes focused on the door to the stairs once more. Etheridge had explained that the upper two floors operated on a looser security system, meaning once Sam had navigated his way to them, he could lock the prison down. Sam had been worried about the safety of the guards, but having spent two weeks in their hospitality, he felt little remorse for their fate.

They were as bad as the inmates.

A few steps away from the door, Sam felt a sharp pain in his left shoulder blade, followed by the burning sensation of a blade searing through his back muscles. The blade slashed down, slicing his skin open and as he stumbled forward, he turned, just as a blood-soaked Ravi launched at him, the box cutter tightly grasped in his only working hand.

Sam managed to get a hand up to stop the attack, the blade slicing across his hand and sending a spray of blood across the floor. His hand burnt and the pain caused his vision to blur, but Sam adjusted his feet and steadied himself. In a blind rage, the hulking man charged at Sam, demanding blood for his betrayal.

Sam managed to push the blade to the side, but Ravi's superior bulk collided with him and they both fell backwards, with the tattooed henchman landing on top of him. Despite the shattered bone in his arm, Ravi fought through the pain, raining down on Sam with thunderous blows, splitting his eyebrow open. As Ravi's colossal hands clamped over Sam's face, Sam could feel the man's thumbs pressing against his eye sockets. Reaching out his hands in hope, Sam's fingers found the box cutter and he drove the blade into Ravi's stomach and twisted it. Ravi released his grip and Sam drove his knee into the man's spine, pushing him to the side and stumbled to his feet. As he did, he felt the hard metal of a baton crash against the base of his spine and Sam dropped to his knees, just as the attacking guard drove it down again towards his skull.

Sam leant back and the guard lost his balance, driving the baton against the concrete, the impact sending a shock up his arm and he lost his grip. Sam stood, caught the man with a hard left hook, before hurling him back into the baiting crowd, the inmates wrenching the guard to the ground for a potentially fatal pummelling.

Sam turned back to Ravi, who was holding his stomach together with his unbroken arm. Sam took two steps forward and then drove the box cutter into the soft patch of skin underneath Ravi's chin, before slicing downwards, cutting open the man's throat vertically. With his eyes wide with shock, Ravi collapsed onto the floor, the blood gushing from the wound and his life left him immediately.

Sam tossed the box cutter into one of the empty cells and clenched his fist, trying his best to stem the flow of blood that was pumping through the deep gash that ran across his palm. Ignoring the pain, he slammed open the door to the stairwell with his shoulder. A bullet ricocheted off the door, missing Sam by inches and as he glanced in the direction of the shooter, he saw a blood soaked Sharp holding the gun.

The deputy warden was missing some teeth and one of his eyelids was stuck shut with blood, the eyeball torn out by a violent inmate looking for retribution.

Sam barged the door open again and once again, evaded a bullet that shattered the glass window in the middle of the door. Making his way up the stairs two at a time, Sam stopped as he approached the door to the main floor and leant against the wall.

His hand was thick with blood, and he could feel another trail trickling down his back. With his vision still blurred from Ravi's attempted blinding, Sam breathed a sigh of relief when he heard the echo of the lock clicking into place at the bottom of the stairs. Moments later, a chorus of painful shrieks burst out through the prison as Etheridge sent a shock through every tag besides Sam's, ending the riot. There had been a number of casualties, but Sam found it hard to sympathise.

The guards and the inmates had been performing a dangerous dance that would eventually end in bloodshed.

Sam had just sped up the process.

With considerable pain, he pulled open the door, only to be met by the barrel of a gun.

'Stop,' Harris commanded, both hands expertly gripping the gun, his eye carefully looking down the sight. 'Don't move.'

Sam held up his hands, keeping the left one closed to stop the blood from pouring out. Harris took a step to the side and motioned for Sam to move. Sam obliged, taking careful steps into the corridor. Harris regarded Sam with a look of bewilderment.

'What the hell happened?' Harris demanded.

'I took down Chapman and his entire operation,' Sam said truthfully, finding no reason to lie to the Warden.

'You've undone everything I've worked to achieve here.' The warden's words were fraught with pain.

'No, sir.' Sam shook his head, the blood flicking from the gash on his eyebrow. 'Sharp has been running the place with Chapman like his personal torture chamber. He's been paid to let Chapman run free.'

'Don't listen to him, sir.'

Sharp stepped through the doors to the corridor, his gun gripped by blood-soaked fingers and pointed directly at Sam's temple. Stood between both men, Sam had nowhere to go.

'Sharp. Jesus, what the hell happened to you?' Harris couldn't believe the state of his deputy, whose uniform was tattered and coated in the blood of numerous inmates. His one good eye venomously trained on Sam.

'This man killed Chapman and several other inmates,' Sharp spat, blood spilling to the ground with every word. 'I don't know how he did it, but he set everyone free and now most of my men are dead.'

'Your men were as bad as those you were paid to police,' Sam responded, his eyes still looking at Harris.

'You might be on this side of the cell, Sharp, but you belong in there with rest of us.'

'Fuck you,' Sharp spat, his finger twitching on the trigger.

'Sharp, put the gun down,' Harris demanded; his own gun still trained on Sam.

'This piece of shit needs to be put in the ground.'

'Sir, check Sharp's bank account. Chapman has been paying him for years.'

'Shut your goddamn mouth!' Sharp spat.

'Sharp, lower your weapon. That is an order.'

'I'm sick of your fucking orders…' Sharp turned the gun on Harris, and a gunshot echoed in the corridor. Sam shut his eyes, expecting the feel the metal bullet lodge in his body before everything ended.

After a second, with no damage to his body, he slowly opened them.

Harris stood before him, slowly lowering his gun, his face a picture of composure. Sam spun around, looking down at the ground where Sharp lay, breathing heavily as the air escaped from the bullet hole in his chest. Sam looked back to the Warden in shock.

'You need to leave,' Harris said calmly, his eyes fixed on his deputy whose eye had rolled back into his skull.

Sharp was dead.

'Sir?' Sam said, taking a step towards him.

'You don't belong here, Sam. Whatever you are, you are not like these men.' He gestured to Sharp. 'This place isn't long for this world and wherever you end up, you're not a criminal. You're a soldier.'

'Thank you, sir,' Sam said, his words stammering slightly. 'Will you be okay?'

'I'm overdue my retirement. I just need to clean up this mess.'

Sam extended his hand to the Warden, who took it

firmly. Sam turned and marched towards the exit of the building, which Etheridge ensured was open. With every step, he craved the freedom of the outside world and as he barged open the door with his shoulder, the fresh air hit him like a bucket of cold water.

Sam took a deep breath and hunched forward, resting his hands on his knees.

He had made it through.

Had survived.

With the guards that manned the gates and watch towers summoned inside by the riot, Sam took a second to breath in the quiet.

The freedom.

Overwhelmed by the moment, Sam had failed to notice the car parked a few feet away. The familiar voice drew a smile from his beaten face.

'You look like hell.'

Sam stood and opened his arms as Singh took a few steps forward and embraced him. Moments later, she helped him to the back of the car, fired up the engine, and sped back through the gates Etheridge had disabled and within minutes, Sam was asleep, his head pressed against the door, the blood from his eyebrow smearing the plush interior as they headed back to London.

CHAPTER TWENTY-THREE

Mac had sat in the car for over an hour.

On the drive over to Maidenhead he'd thought it would be easy. For so long, he'd dreamt of the day when he would get even with Sam. When he was rotting in that cage, he prayed not for his own survival, but for Sam's. The chances were, Sam had been obliterated by the missile that had rocked Mac, as he knew Sam was chasing behind him. The blast had smashed into the ground behind Mac as he ran for his life, so logic had dictated to him that Sam had perished.

His captors never found his body.

Mac had been left alone.

But every day he wished for Sam's survival instead of his own death, the notion of finally looking the man in the eyes had kept him alive.

But now, as he sat in the car he'd stolen from a multi-storey car park beside Waterloo Station, he hesitated.

This part of the plan was always going to be difficult, but Mac was surprised he had any compassion left. Wallace had ensured it had stayed hidden, if it even existed and for every target Mac had mercilessly killed, he'd been certain any emotion, besides the seething rage that burnt within him, had been extinguished.

But he was wrong.

The Ford Fiesta he'd stolen was an easy drive, equipped with the mod cons that littered every new model. Mac had been careful to ensure the car he took had an inbuilt satnav, and he tapped in the address, following the robotic voice as it guided him through the heavy London traffic and onto the M4, which he followed until he crossed over into Berkshire. As he ventured through Slough, Mac wasn't particularly impressed by the industrial looking town, hardly meeting the aesthetic of the rural countryside he expected. Passing through towards Maidenhead, the scenery changed, offering wonderfully kept fields and charming streets. Had he travelled farther, he would have been in the historic town of Windsor, where the royal castle was situated and was a beacon for tourists along with those looking for a fun, yet expensive day out.

As Mac turned passed the Braywick Football and Rugby complex, he pulled into a quiet road, following the blue line on the screen towards the dot that nestled within a cul-de-sac at the end of the road.

He crawled to a stop.

You have reached your destination.

'Not yet,' Mac uttered, the gravity of his plan unsettling him slightly.

An hour later, he was still sat, staring at the beautiful house in the left corner of the curved road. It was beyond anything he would ever have owned himself, had he been given the option of a normal life. The detached house was immaculate, the white stone covered with ivy around the bottom two windows. It was big enough to hold four bedrooms and Mac could understand the idea of moving to such a lovely street to raise a family.

Kids where never on his radar, but he'd often dreamt

of having a young son when he was lying on the floor of his cage, drifting in and out of consciousness, teaching him how to ride a bike.

But in war, there were always casualties, and sadly, as Mac looked at the house, those words rang true.

With a deep breath, Mac wrestled with the notion of turning the car around and continuing with the rest of his plan. The country would still be demanded to hand Sam over to him and there was still a lot of satisfaction to be had by killing him slowly.

It was the least the country owed him.

But he wanted Sam to hurt. To be as destroyed as he was, to the point where nothing could put him back together.

Before he could make his mind up, the door to the house opened and he saw her.

Lucy.

Mac's mind flashed back to a decade ago, when he'd sat in the garden of Sam's house, breaking bread with the wonderful woman, sharing stories and laughter. It was the closest he'd felt to being accepted and back then, he'd considered Sam a brother.

Lucy, his remarkable wife, had been as enchanting as she was beautiful and the two of them together had planted a seed in Mac's mind of the future he wanted.

But that was long gone, scorched by the cruel flames that had scarred him for life.

Wallace had told Mac about the pain Sam had been through, the devastating loss of his son and the subsequent divorce. Mac had no sympathy for the man; that pain wasn't enough.

Not when there was still someone left on the face of the earth who he cared about.

Looking tired and with her blonde hair tied back in a ponytail, Mac watched as Lucy walked through the front

211

gate and around to the alleyway between the houses, a black bag clutched in her firm grip.

Mac left the car.

As she returned to the gate, she didn't even notice the man approaching.

'Lucy.'

She turned, instantly struck by the horrific scarring that wrapped around his face. After a few moments, realisation hit her, and her eyes widen in shock.

'Mac?' She raised her hand to her mouth. 'I thought you were…'

'Dead.' He forced a smile. 'Surprise.'

'Oh my God.' Lucy shuffled nervously. 'If you're looking for Sam, I'm afraid we separated a few years back.'

'I know. I'm here for you.'

'Excuse me?' Lucy took a step towards the gate.

'I need you to come with me.'

Mac shot a glance to the gate, raising his only eyebrow at the now terrified woman, clearly indicating he would block her path. Lucy shook and folded her arms across her chest.

'Mac, I have a three-week-old baby in the house. I have to go back inside.'

'Please don't make this difficult.'

Mac slid a hand to the back of his jeans and revealed the gun. Lucy's face drained of colour and a tear slid down her immaculate face.

'Mac, please.'

'Is your husband in the house?' Mac demanded.

'Yes.'

'Then your baby will be fine.' Mac gestured for her to move away from the gate with the gun. 'If you do exactly as I say, then I promise you, I'll do my best to bring you home to them.'

Lucy shot a final glance towards the house. Sam had

spent years grieving for the loss of his friend, carrying the guilt of his death on his shoulders. Seemingly back from the dead, with a clear sense of menace behind his every word, Lucy worried for the safety of her new family. Her husband, Nick and their young daughter, Abbie, were at the forefront of her mind.

She needed to keep them safe.

Without the chance to say goodbye, Mac ushered her towards the car, opened the passenger seat and she obediently got in. With the gun still in his hand, Mac fired up the engine, pulled out of the cul-de-sac, and headed back towards London. His heart was racing, and he hated himself for the fear he'd instilled in her.

Knowing what was in the boot of the car, along with the terror he would put her in a few hours' time, he did his best to focus on his hatred for Sam.

It was all about Sam.

That, and Mac's insatiable need for vengeance.

With tears streaming down her face, Lucy looked in the side mirror, watching the sun set behind her home, wondering if she would ever see her family again.

———

After a much-needed gulp of Scotch, Ashton refilled her glass and slumped back in her chair. Staring at the brown liquid inside the crystal glass, she knew she wouldn't find any answers in the bottom of a bottle.

How the hell did this happen?

Earlier that day, she'd been stood in front of the press, controlling a wonderful narrative around her hard-working team and top detective, cracking an uncrackable case and bringing to an end a decades long reign of terror from one of the country's most notorious criminals.

It should have been a celebratory drink, but there was nothing but remorse.

Word had reached her of the outbreak at Ashcroft and instantly her stomach had flipped. Knowing that Sam was somewhere beneath its impenetrable walls, she'd nervously wondered what had caused it. Her highly regarded position made her privy to the whispered conversations, with the senior figures and government officials wanting to keep the entire story off the record.

The country didn't know much of Ashcroft's existence.

They certainly couldn't know of its implosion.

Joining a conference call which included Commissioner Stout, along with the Home Secretary, Ashton had her worst fears confirmed.

Sam Pope had escaped.

Instantly, the conversation had turned to her, with a number of officials demanding answers as to why he was even there in the first place. When Stout spoke of his need to 'look into it', it became very clear that the blessing she thought he'd given was forged.

Throughout her decorated career, Ashton had proven her impeccable judgement, climbing the ladder by knowing where all the pieces on the chess board were.

At that moment, she realised that a different game was being played altogether.

The call abruptly ended with the Home Secretary demanding the situation be brought under control, not even bothering to explain the consequences of failure. Ashton knew, poured herself a drink and threw it back in one. The Scotch burnt her throat, but she poured another, just as the door to her office was thrown open and the irate Police Commissioner stormed in. Stout was renowned for the sense of calm he brought to the job, but the fury in his eyes and the folder in his hand meant that whoever had crossed his path on his journey to her office would have been terrified.

Without even offering a greeting, Stout slapped the folder down in front of Ashton and pressed his hands to hips.

'What the hell is this?'

Ashton leant forward and flipped open the folder, scanning the document.

'It's Sam's transfer papers to Ashcroft, sir.'

'I know that.' Stout leant forward and poked at the bottom of the page. 'This. I did not sign this document.'

'But I received this the day of the trial and assumed you had done me a favour.'

'A favour?' Stout shook his head, wrestling to control the volume of his voice. 'There are strict protocols around prison transfers, especially Ashcroft. It takes weeks. You know this, Ruth, so tell me, how could this have happened?'

Ashton could feel her world crumbling around her. Everything she'd worked for was teetering on the edge. As with all people in positions of power, Ashton had made enemies along the way, taking necessary steps for the good of her career. But she racked her brains for who could have done such a thing. A transfer request to a secret prison would only pass through certain hands, all of which belonged to people with more sense than to forge a signature.

A horrible feeling set in her stomach that she'd been set up, but with no way to prove it, she had to stay quiet. Stout squeezed the bridge of his nose in anger and took a deep breath.

'Ruth, I'm going to ask you a question and I need the truth.' He looked at her and she nodded her understanding. 'Did you forge this signature?'

The question hit Ashton like a slap to the face and her restraint vanished.

'Of course not. Do you think I'm stupid enough to do such a thing?'

'You understand how this looks, right?' Stout cut in, angered by her tone. 'Your obsession with putting Sam away was getting borderline worrying and now I'm presented with this. It doesn't look good.'

'I didn't do it,' Ashton stated. 'I'm insulted you would even question me.'

'Well, I have questions, Ruth. Fucking thousands of them. But the bigger one, beyond who signed my name to that form, is where the hell is Sam Pope now?'

Stout slammed his hands down on the desk, leaning forward with authority. In the weeks since bringing Sam to justice and being told of her ascension to Stout's position, Ashton had felt untouchable. Her confidence had spilled over the fine line to arrogance and she found herself speechless at his question.

She didn't know where Sam was.

Had no clue what was going on or any idea of what to do next.

For the first time in years, Ashton felt out of her depth and what hit her hardest was Stout knew it too. With a resounding sigh, Stout straightened up, recomposed, and stared at her.

'You need to fix this, Ruth. For both our sakes.'

'Yes, sir. I promise you I will…'

Stout held up his hand, cutting her off. Shaking his head, he shot her an unimpressed glare.

'Save it. You're on thin ice, Ruth.' Stout turned on his heel and headed to the door. 'Fix this or start writing your damn resignation.'

The door slammed shut behind him, rocking the room slightly and Ashton slumped in her chair. Her dream was slowly dissipating before her and she reached out, lifted the glass and gulped the entire glass of Scotch in one.

Somehow, despite everything she'd accomplished, Sam Pope was still the bane of her existence.

Wiping the residual drops of Scotch from her thin lips, Ashton lifted the phone and demanded to be put through to DI Singh immediately.

Ashton needed answers.

Her career depended on it.

CHAPTER TWENTY-FOUR

'Quit being a pussy.'

Sam laughed at Etheridge's comment, but then drew his teeth together and hissed in pain. Sat on a stool with his elbows pressed against the marble worktop, Sam was being patched up. His blood-soaked T-shirt had been thrown away and Etheridge was stood behind him, his latex gloved hands carefully threading a needle and stitched through his skin. Etheridge was not a medic, but he was an intelligent man and with the hospitals not an option, had offered to crudely stitch the wounds inflicted by Ravi to stem the bleeding.

Sam reached out with his bandaged hand and took a swig of his beer, hoping the alcohol would numb the pain. Etheridge had already performed a similar job on the slice down across his palm. It had stopped the bleeding, but even after a few paracetamol, Sam could still feel the fresh-ness of the pain. Considering what he'd put his body through in the last year or so, having his friend stitch his skin together wasn't too bad.

After Singh had collected him from the prison, she'd brought him back to Etheridge's house as quickly as she could. Before she'd left, she'd turned off her mobile phone and as she followed Etheridge's directions to the remote location of Ashcroft, she'd tossed it from the window at over eighty miles an hour.

The last thing she needed was for Ashton to trace her signal.

It wouldn't only lead them to Sam, but would bring the hammer down on a career which was starting to veer dangerously close to the point of no return.

As Etheridge pulled the thread tight, Sam grunted in pain and Singh shook her head.

'This is insane.'

'It's necessary,' Etheridge responded, not breaking his concentration.

'I'm fine.' Sam assured her with a smile.

'No, not this. I mean everything.' Singh stood and paced the room. 'When is it going to stop?'

Etheridge cut the thread and took a step back to admire his handiwork. The thread was neat enough, but the soreness around the wound told Etheridge that Sam would be in a bit of discomfort for a while. As he scanned over the other scars that decorated Sam's broad, muscular back, Etheridge assumed Sam would be fine with a bit of discomfort. Pulling the latex gloves off and dumping them in the carrier bag, along with numerous blood-soaked cotton balls, Etheridge patted Sam on the shoulder and stepped back.

Sam stood, stretching his back and unconvincingly rolling his shoulder, the pain striking like he'd be lashed with a whip and he turned to face Singh, who still waited for her answer.

Taking a final swig of beer before putting the empty bottle in the bag, Sam sighed.

'It doesn't stop.'

'It has to.'

'It can't.' Sam's voice rose. 'There are people out there, Singh, who think they're untouchable. People who do unspeakable things without a second thought to the damage they cause. I wish I could put my faith in the police, I really do, but when I've seen your superiors rubbing shoulders with the people I've put in the ground, I can't. Someone has to fight back.'

Singh looked offended, struggling to stop her eyes from watering. Etheridge, not wanting to involve himself in their quarrel, took his beer from the kitchen counter and stepped out into the cool spring evening, ignoring the light drizzle that was coating his garden.

'Why does that have to be you?' Singh demanded.

'Because I can. You wouldn't understand.'

Sam took a few steps around the island in the centre of the kitchen, heading for the door. Singh stepped out, blocking his path.

'I know that you lost someone close to you, Sam, but killing criminals isn't going to bring your son back.'

'Don't.' Sam held up his hand, his words heavy with pain. 'You have no idea what this fight has done for me. It has saved me.'

'That's the thing, Sam. It hasn't.' A tear fell down Singh's cheek. 'You're still in pain. No matter how many people you save or people you kill, you're still hurting. All you're doing, is digging a bigger and bigger hole for yourself. You might do some good along the way, but not for yourself. If you spend all your time trying to save everyone, when will you have time to put yourself back together.'

Singh slowly reached out her hand and gently placed it on Sam's cheek. He closed his eyes, her words hitting him like a punch to the gut. The gash above his eyebrow had been taped shut. He placed his hand on top of hers and held it for a few seconds.

A moment of intimacy his life couldn't accommodate.

'I'm sorry.'

Sam gently pulled her hand away from his cheek and stepped around her, heading for the hallway. After the tribulations of Ashcroft, Sam needed a long, hot shower to wash away the blood and pain. Singh took a deep breath, recomposed, and then turned after him.

'I can't protect you anymore, Sam,' she said with authority. 'Both of you. You forged official documentation which had led to a number of deaths. I can give you both a day to get gone, but that's as far as I can go. I'm sorry.'

She shrugged, indicating that she didn't have any other option. Sam stopped on the bottom step and fixed her with a warm smile.

'Thank you, Amara. For everything.'

With her heart breaking, she forced herself to return likewise.

'You saved my life, Sam. Twice. It's the least I can do.'

The two of them shared a few seconds of quiet, wondering what life would had been like had it taken a different path. Sam nodded, confirming to her that he felt the same way and with considerable effort, he heaved himself up the stairs towards the bathroom. Singh watched him go, each step he took away from her was like a hammer to her heart. Dabbing at her eyes, she lifted her jacket from the coat hook and headed to the front door.

'Leaving so soon?' Etheridge asked, appearing in the kitchen doorway.

'I assume you heard all that?'

'I did.' Etheridge stepped into the hallway and approached the coat rack. 'You said we had until tomorrow, right?'

'I'm sorry, it's the best I can do.'

'That means this evening, we can forget about the horrible reality of the situation?' Etheridge smiled at her, lifting his own jacket from the hook and putting hers back.

'I don't understand.'

'If we only have one night left before we have to go, prob-ably not worth wasting it, eh?' Etheridge flashed a glance up the stairs, where the hum of the power shower echoed lightly. 'I need to run an errand. Keep an eye on him.'

Etheridge winked and Singh felt her knees wobble. Etheridge opened the front door and stepped out into the rain, mumbling something about the best Chinese take-away in the country. But Singh wasn't listening.

After taking a few deep breaths, she began to climb the stairs.

———

As the water crashed down over his short, brown hair, Sam closed his eyes. Having been afforded a meek, three-minute shower in Ashcroft every other day, the high pressure water felt amazing against his skin. As the droplets collided with his shoulder, he felt a burning sensation coming from his fresh stitches, but Sam ignored the pain.

With his head down and hands pressed against the expensive, herringbone tiles that adorned the bathroom wall, Sam took a moment to clear his thoughts.

Despite his persistence to the fight, Sam had been afraid.

Locked away in a secret prison, there had been every chance the plan wouldn't have worked. Not because of Etheridge, who had proven beyond any shadow of a doubt that he was as integral to Sam's fight as he himself was, but because of the danger he'd willingly put himself in.

There was no way of knowing how sadistic Deputy Warden Sharp was and Sam knew that walking out of that prison, alive and with his mission completed, was against the odds.

But somehow he'd done it.

He had survived.

But Singh's words hung heavy in his mind.

Could he step away from his life now?

Sam had always justified his fight as one of necessity, that his quest started with innocent people dying at the hands of a power hungry criminal and a corrupt police organisation. Since then, he'd taken down sex traffickers and gone to war with a global terrorism unit, helmed by a man who had ruined his life.

Turned him into a weapon.

A weapon that Sam himself had turned back on those that deserved it.

But now, with the chance to disappear and to start somewhere else, could he step away?

Before he could contemplate any further, he heard the bathroom door opening and then quickly closing. Sam stayed in position, allowing the water to pound against his broken body. Through the muffled downpour, he heard the slight noise of clothes falling on the floor and then the door to the vast shower cubicle opening.

Singh stepped in, her hand gently sliding up Sam's spine, carefully navigating the scars he'd received in the fight to save her life. With considerable effort, Sam pushed himself from the tiles and turned, struck by the incredible beauty of her naked body.

No words were spoken.

They weren't needed.

Singh stepped forward, rested her hand against his solid stomach, and brought herself to him, their lips locking as the water crashed around them.

Months of unspoken feelings and knowing nods, along with death defying moments exploded and in the shower cubicle, with their bodies wrapped around each other, Sam

223

and Singh disappeared into each other, knowing they would never get the opportunity to again.

————

With the sun disappearing behind the London skyline, Mac had driven carefully back into the capital, ensuring the doors were locked. He had no intention of hurting Lucy and had tried his best to calm the woman, who had cried since the moment they'd departed her street.

Undoubtedly concerned for her newborn child, Mac had forced himself to focus on the mission.

This wasn't about her, or the kindness she'd shown him in years gone by.

This was about Sam.

The man who had left him to a fate worse than death.

The city was thick with traffic, every road gridlocked as an army of red busses and black cabs tried their best to weave through the narrow streets. On the parallel pavement, tourists and shoppers overran the shops, all of them scurrying around like it was their last day on earth. Mac remembered his trip to visit Sam many years ago, finding the experience overwhelming.

For those who were never brought up within London itself, the city was an intimidating place and as another pedestrian took a chance and darted through the traffic, Mac could understand why.

'This city,' he mumbled under his breath. Lucy didn't respond, she just clasped her hands together and sobbed. At a snail's pace, they made their way to Euston Road and as they drove past Great Portland Street Hospital, he could see on the satnav the blue dot marking the end of their journey.

He didn't need the screen to tell him he'd arrived.

University College Hospital London, known as UCLH,

towered high over the street, a magnificent structure of four floors, all of them lined with green windows. Opposite, Warren Street Station was a hub of activity, and Mac managed to navigate the hazardous one way system to bring the car to a stop on the street nearby. The double yellow lines indicated it was a no-parking area but with no intention of returning to the car, Mac stepped out with defiance. He hurried to the boot, opened it, and retrieved the bag, carefully looping the strap over the shoulder of his black jacket.

A few passers-by baulked at the scarring that ran down the side of his face, but with London such a vibrant place, most people didn't even acknowledge him.

Besides, Mac humorously mused, he was walking into a hospital. Most people would think that was normal for a man of his appearance.

Mac opened the passenger door and squatted down, his eyes fixed on Lucy and his hand still tightly holding the gun. Lucy leant away in fear.

'Come with me. Stay silent.' He warned. 'If you want to see your daughter again, do as I say.'

With tears streaming down her exquisite cheekbones, Lucy nodded and stepped out, the brisk wind and rain catching her off guard and she wrapped her arms around her body. Together, they marched back to the front of the hospital and ascended the six, wide steps that lead to the revolving main entrance.

The hospital was unlike anything Mac had ever seen, with a magnificent, triangular sculpture hanging over the entrance. As soon as they stepped in, the magnitude of the building hit them both. An expansive waiting area bled into a coffee shop and numerous corridors channelled off into a maze. The waiting area was almost full, with people of all ages and races scattered across the chairs, the inbuilt human nature to not sit next to a stranger clearly evident.

Nurses, doctors, orderlies, and cleaners scurried from door to door, disappearing into the labyrinth with a respectable calm.

No one had batted an eyelid at the two of them and Mac led Lucy to the large map on the wall, offering a layout of the hospital.

The Teenage and Young Adult ward was on the third floor.

The hospital was renowned for its treatments for cancer, working with a charity to help fund the necessary research to try to battle against one of life's greatest enemies.

The specialist centre for the younger generation going through their own, painful hell was three floors up and as Mac pulled Lucy towards the lift, he felt a strong sense of guilt for using them as the target.

He had been through hell.

There was only one other person in the world he would wish it upon.

They entered the lift, with another visitor politely offering for them to enter first. Mac thanked the man, but as he tried to follow them in, Mac shoved him to the ground, sending the man sprawling causing a few people to turn their heads. The lift doors closed, with the shocked man cursing in their direction, but Mac didn't care.

He unzipped the bag and pulled out its contents, causing Lucy to heave in panic. Mac turned to her, unmoved by her fear.

'Put this on.'

Moments later, they stepped out onto the third floor and followed the signs to the entrance of the ward. Mac had shed his coat, draping it over Lucy's shoulders to conceal her and as they were buzzed through the door, Mac stepped into action.

'Ladies and gentlemen, remain calm.' All eyes fixed

upon the scarred soldier as he strode into the middle of the corridor. Nurses and doctors poked their heads out from their patient rooms, many of them scowling at the interruption. 'If you do as I say, we will get through this.'

As a doctor strode out of the nearest room towards them, Mac reached to the back of his jeans and pulled out his gun. A shriek of panic echoed around the ward and Mac fired a bullet into the air, bringing it all to an abrupt silence.

'Lucy. Take off the coat.'

Weeping and shaking, Lucy obliged and as she did, the fear levels audibly rose. Strapped to her chest was a vest, lined with over ten blocks of C4 explosives, all of them wired to a metal control panel in the centre of the vest. The deadly bomb was linked to a switch which Mac confidently held up in his hand. Sobs of fear echoed throughout the ward and Mac demanded their attention. Turning to the receptionist, a young lady who was clutching the crucifix around her neck, he smiled.

'Call reception. Have them evacuate the rest of the hospital. Tell them that this will all be over if the police can do one thing.'

The young lady took a deep breath, realising the safety of hundreds of people were at stake. Her Irish accent quivered as she spoke, betraying her show of bravery.

'What do they need to do?'

Mac's face contorted in a hateful sneer. His words rocked Lucy.

'Bring me Sam Pope.'

CHAPTER TWENTY-FIVE

A taste of normality would do neither of them any good.

After they'd finished making love, Singh had helped Sam to wash the fresh wounds on his body. The scars were a rich tapestry depicting the life he lived and she knew then that there was never going to be a *them*.

Sam was built for war.

He would never walk away from it.

After Singh had dried herself with one of the rich, cotton towels and left, Sam had turned off the shower and wrapped a towel around his waist. Wiping the steam from the mirror, he stared at himself, examining the cut that sliced through his eyebrow. It would leave a scar and he shrugged at the thought. It would just be another to add to the collection.

Scouring through Etheridge's cabinet he found a razor and replaced the blade, before gliding it across his soapy face. Sam was very rarely clean shaven, but after a few weeks without any comforts, he appreciated the feel of the blade as it sliced through the thick bristles that had sprouted across his strong jaw.

They had run a pair of clippers over his brown hair

before he entered The Grid and he didn't stay long enough for the mandatory monthly trim. Thankfully, they'd shaved the sides shorter than the top, so while his hair wasn't exactly stylish, it was neat. Flecks of grey had begun to pepper the hair around his ears, and he realised he was less than a year away from his fortieth birthday.

Apparently, life began then.

Sam was just fortunate to have made it to today.

Before he dried himself, he took a moment, contemplating the notion of a different path. There was a clear connection between himself and Singh, one that was beyond the physical. Despite the passionate sex they'd just had, they were kindred spirits, wrapped around each other like coiled snakes.

The only problem was, they were both poisonous and the chances of them fatally wounding the other was too high.

They both believed in a fair world.

They just stood on opposite sides of the line that cut through it.

Sam shook his head, knowing that he had one evening to enjoy before their paths would split, most likely forever.

As he stepped out of the bathroom, the fantastic aroma of food drew him down the stairs where Etheridge had decorated the kitchen counter with a selection of plastic boxes, each containing an assortment of Chinese food.

Sam stepped into the room, drawing a warm smile from Singh, along with a cheeky wink from Etheridge.

'Nice shower?' Etheridge asked, flashing a glance at the wet hair that cascaded down to Singh's shoulder.

'Don't,' Sam responded, failing to hide the smirk that cracked on his lips. Singh chuckled and soon, all three of them were laughing.

'Dig in, buddy,' Etheridge said. 'I bet you can't wait.'

'I don't know. The poorly cooked meat and veg of Ashcroft will take some beating.'

'I still can't believe you put yourself through that,' Singh said, tipping a spoonful of noodles onto her plate.

'Me neither,' Sam said as he piled as much as he could onto his place, snapped his chopsticks open and begun to shovel the food in. The glorious tastes exploded in his mouth and he wolfed down the entire plate, much to the joy of Etheridge. No one spoke for five minutes, with each of them enjoying the flavoursome meal, as well as each other's company. While the atmosphere was pleasant, there was a heartbreaking undercurrent as they knew it would be the only time this would be possible. Sensing the tension rising, Etheridge cracked open three beers, passed one each to Sam and Singh, and raised his bottle.

'To our survival.'

All three of them raised their drinks and took a sip. Sam dropped his chopsticks on the sauce smeared plate and exhaled. A slight bit of indigestion hit and he excused himself from the kitchen, needing a hit of the brisk, evening air. As he stepped out onto the patio, Etheridge noticed Singh's longing glance at his friend.

'You know it can't happen, right?'

'I know.' Singh sighed. 'It was probably a mistake to go there.'

'Not at all.' Etheridge shook his head. 'The world needs as much love and affection as it can get. But there is no way he'll turn his back on his fight. It's in his blood. In his bones. It's who he is.'

'I've thought about it, you know?' Singh turned to Etheridge, trying hard not to show her pain. 'Ever since Sam saved those girls last year. I thought about throwing it all away, joining him in his fight. I know what he does is wrong, but I believe in the reasons he does it. Ever since then, I've just felt...'

'Restricted?' Etheridge offered and Singh nodded. 'Me too. After you saved my life and they repaired my knee, I gave up everything. Sold the business. Divorced Kayleigh. None of that mattered anymore. It's what Sam does to you. He infects you with his mission until you can't see another purpose. But, Singh, even if you tried to do that, there is no happy ending there. Not because he doesn't care. But because there is only one place his path is leading him.'

At that moment, Singh felt her heart break. Throughout her life, she'd dedicated herself to her job. To rise through the ranks of the Metropolitan Police, to experience every part of the job, and then build the career she wanted. At no point, despite her strict Hindu parents' wishes, had she ever considered settling down. Her sister, Priya, had given them the grandchildren they craved and settled down to a life of luxury, married to a successful lawyer.

But as she glanced at Sam, who stood looking out at the darkness, she saw her only desire for that life.

As Etheridge's phone buzzed, Singh sighed, finished her beer and decided it would be best not to spend the night.

The quicker she cut the cord, the quicker she could heal.

The look on Etheridge's face as he scanned his phone told her to wait and as his eyes widened, she called out to him.

'What is it?'

'Shit.' Etheridge shot a worried glance in Sam's direction. Sam, hearing the fear in the room, turned back in.

'What's going on?' Sam asked, looking to Singh, who shrugged. Etheridge didn't answer but rushed up the stairs as fast as his damaged leg could take him. The two of them followed and as they entered his control station, he pulled up the live feed from the BBC news website onto the screen.

A reporter stood in front of UCLH in Euston, with the rain pouring down. Wrapped in a thick jacket and her hair blowing, she spoke sternly into the camera.

'The situation is a terrifying one for those inside the hospital and their friends and family. The terrorist has allowed the rest of the hospital to be evacuated but has kept the entire Teenage and Young Adult ward inside. With twenty-three patients, eight nurses, two doctors, and a receptionist trapped, the terrorist appears to have also brought in his own hostage. The following image was lifted from the security cameras only a few minutes ago.'

The image appeared on the screen, a grainy, grey image showing the back of a well-built man, who appeared to be holding a device in his hand. The reporter continued.

'The terrorist has made only one demand, which has baffled the police who are trying, as we speak, to negotiate a peaceful outcome. The terrorist has requested that police bring Sam Pope, the recently incarcerated vigilante, to him otherwise he will detonate the bomb. We will have more information as we get it.'

Singh flashed a look at Etheridge, realising that they were the only two people who knew of Sam's location. But Etheridge knew getting Sam to deal with the situation wasn't going to be a problem.

Not when he saw the fury in Sam's eyes as he scanned the grey, security image that Etheridge had taken a screen grab of and expanded on a wall mounted monitor.

On her knees, cowering beside the terrorist, was Lucy.

With a bomb strapped to her chest.

Sam was out the door within seconds.

———

With the road blocked off by the flashing blue lights of several police cars, Ashton watched as her driver was waved through the barricade, pondering her next move.

How the hell did things fall apart so quickly?

Her driver pulled the car up to a safe distance from the hospital, where she was immediately greeted by Sergeant Tom Reynolds, a fiercely loyal man who would have been her choice to manage the situation had it been hers to make.

But it hadn't.

That became clear as Commissioner Stout marched across the mayhem of the police cordon, weaving between officers who were trying their best to comfort the evacuated patients, while their nurses attended to them in the cold, bitter evening. As he approached, Ashton could tell his mood hadn't improved from earlier.

It had clearly worsened.

'We have a situation here, Ruth.' Stout spoke quietly, ushering her away from the earshot of the surrounding officers and public. There was no press nearby, as they were all lined across the cordon line, all of them relaying the exact same story in their never-ending quest for ratings.

'Do we know who he is?'

'Not a clue,' Stout said firmly, drawing his fleeced jacket tight to shield from the cold. 'But we know what he wants.'

'What's that?'

'Sam Pope.'

Ashton burst out laughing, drawing a few interested looks from the nearby watchers and Stout scowled.

'Deputy Commissioner, this is no time for laughter.' He reprimanded her as quietly as he could. 'He is threatening to kill dozens of innocent people.'

'So what, he expects us to just march Sam Pope in there for him? Why does he want him?'

'We don't know,' Stout said, scanning the street in horror.

'Possible collusion?' Ashton offered, taking the chance to undermine Sam's perceived hero status.

'Doubtful. It doesn't fit the brief.'

'Sir, with all due respect, Sam Pope is a violent, dangerous criminal. Experience tells me that birds of a feather flock together.'

'Your experience hasn't helped so far,' Stout spat, crushing Ashton beneath his words. 'Is there any update on Sam's location?'

Ashton shook her head, the raindrops flicking from the small bowler hat she wore as part of her uniform.

'No, sir. Nor do we have any contact with DI Singh.'

Stout shook away the final comment due to its irrelevance, and as a car pulled up, his attention was stolen from Ashton, who fumed at her dismissal.

'The negotiator has just arrived,' Stout explained. 'Hopefully, he can get through to this man and we can shut this down. In the meantime, Ruth, find Sam Pope. And do it now!'

The emphasis on the final word may as well have been the final nail in her coffin. Ashton was furious that after everything she'd done to bring him to justice, Sam Pope would still cost her everything she'd worked so tirelessly for. She watched as Stout met the negotiator at the car, the man clearly overwhelmed by the gravity of the situation and the seniority with which he was welcomed. As Stout explained the situation and the negotiator, a middle-aged man with glasses and thinning hair, Ashton looked up at the hospital, expecting to see the third floor explode in a colossal display of fire and glass any second.

It made her sick to her stomach and Ashton knew she had no cards left to play.

Singh hammered down the M3 as fast as she could, weaving in and out of the light traffic that was trundling towards the nation's capital city. It was a drive she'd made a few times in the past few months and she knew this one would be for the final time.

The silence in the car was unbearable.

Singh didn't regret having sex with Sam, and she knew he didn't either. The tension was based on the truth that they knew it could go no further, that they'd sampled a life they yearned for but could never attain. Singh wanted to talk about it, to make peace with Sam before they walked away from the notion, but she knew it would do no good.

Sam's mind was elsewhere.

Surprisingly, Singh felt no jealousy for Sam's worry for his ex-wife. Knowing the trauma they'd both experienced, and the happiness they'd shared before, Singh admired Sam's immediate response to her peril.

Her only fear was that there was no way Sam would walk away from what they were heading into. Whoever the terrorist was who'd demanded his presence was unlikely to want a friendly handshake.

But if Sam did what he did best, then he would be walking straight back to a cell.

If he didn't, he would be coming out in a body bag.

This time there was no plan.

There was no back-up.

Singh drove silently, wondering how on earth Sam would survive this.

She turned off the M3 and joined the M25, speeding around the concrete loop that surrounded the city and caused a relentless stream of traffic jams during rush hour. The road was clear and as Singh approached junction sixteen, she turned off, joining the A40 at Uxbridge and hammered her foot down. Soon, they were racing through Wembley, with the magnificent arch of the football stadium bathed in a bright, blue light. Singh had always found the building striking but had never attended a football match in her life. The tribalism she'd witnessed based on supposed loyalty had put her off the sport, but the stadium always filled her with a strange sense of national pride.

Sam still hadn't said a word.

Singh had flashed him the odd, caring glance, but he stared silently ahead, his fists clenched. Sam had made numerous enemies on his rampage against the underworld, but this was something deeper.

This was a premeditated personal attack.

Judging by the fury in his eyes, Singh could tell he'd taken it as such.

Singh passed Baker Street station and the police cordon was so vast, she could see the bright blue lights already. By the time she got to Great Portland Street station, she was stopped by two police officers, who demanded identification. She flashed her badge, which was enough to get them nearer to the hospital.

The next time they might not be so lucky.

With the colossal hospital ahead, surrounded by an army of police cars, interested press and terrified spectators, Singh brought the car to a stop on the side of the road. With no traffic due to the police barricades, she had no fears of stopping on what was usually a gridlocked street.

The engine died and the only sound, besides the hustle of the standoff ahead, was the light patter of rain on the windscreen. Sam reached for his belt, but Singh shot her hand down and clasped his. Sam looked at her, saw the tear forming in her eye, and reached up to wipe it away.

'I have to go.' His words were calm, bristling with anger. 'You know I do.'

'I know,' Singh said, patting his hand. 'But just know that I could have.'

Sam drew his lips together in a warm smile, nodding his agreement. They could have been something.

Something worth fighting for.

But Sam's fight was elsewhere. They both knew that and as soon as they stepped out of the car, there would be no going back. Just another regret to add to a life full of them.

Singh leant over, kissed Sam gently on the lips and then recomposed.

'Right, let's do this,' she said, pushing open the car door. Sam soon followed, the rain crashing against his face as he locked eyes on the building that was holding his ex-wife, and then willingly walked towards the flashing blue lights that had hunted him for months.

CHAPTER TWENTY-SIX

After the initial shock of Mac's arrival had subsided, a subdued boredom had kicked in. Enraged that his demand hadn't been met straight away, Mac had yelled at a young teenage girl to stop crying, only adding to her fear. The following ten minutes were played out in deathly silence, until a senior nurse, a Jamaican woman with a kind smile, approached Mac, showing a steely bravery when threatened with a gun.

She'd pleaded with Mac to let them go, but if he couldn't, then she asked that the nurses and doctors be allowed to at least treat their patients.

Remembering the horrendous conditions of his own capture, Mac agreed, but warned every one of the consequences if they stepped out of line.

'This here...' he began, lifting his right hand. 'Is called a dead man's switch. It has been activated, meaning that the bomb strapped to this lady is live. Should I remove my thumb from this button, then this entire hospital will be blown to the ground. Now, I'm more than willing to die tonight. Is anyone else?'

Nothing but a terrified silence greeted his statement.

'Good. Let's all be sensible, and we may just see tomorrow.'

The staff continued as if nothing was happening and Mac admired their ability to work under such pressure. It was a part of their everyday lives but being ready to act to save a life carried with it as much anguish as being ready to take one. For Mac, it was easy. The part of him that held any empathy for others died in the same room as the man responsible for his captivity.

The rest of him would die alongside the man who had left him there in the first place.

As he slowly paced the corridor, Lucy sat by the door, looking longingly at the locked exit. Mac had made it clear to the receptionist that if she touched the button to activate it, he would put a bullet through the centre of her skull.

She wasn't paid enough to challenge his threat and Lucy stared at the non-existent path to freedom. As Mac returned to her end of the corridor, she looked up at him with red eyes, her tear ducts dried out with fear. Below her chin, the row of C4 explosives sat, ready to blow them all to kingdom come.

'Mac, you don't need to do this.'

'Shut up.'

'Sam doesn't even know you're alive. He'll be so happy to see you.' Lucy tried to add an element of hope to her words.

'He left me to die,' Mac spat, shaking his head as if he was being attacked by a wasp.

'Sam didn't know. Wallace told him you had died.'

Mac spun on his heel and lifted the gun, pointing it directly at her head. Lucy coiled back in fear.

'I said shut up,' Mac screamed, drawing the attention of the rest of the terrified hostages. 'I don't need you alive to carry that bomb, so shut your damn mouth.'

Lucy nodded frantically, cowering away from the gun.

Mac saw the terror in her eyes, looked at the gun, and then pressed the side of it to his head, as if wrestling with a horrible migraine. Whatever was happening, it wasn't good.

His mind was scattered, with different versions of his past washing over each other. It was as if his recollection of the truth had been stuffed into a washing machine and set to spin.

Sam had abandoned him.

Left him to die.

He didn't care. He saved himself.

Sam needed to pay. To experience real pain.

Like Mac had.

With a few concerned nurses apprehensively walking to their patient's rooms, Mac's inner turmoil was interrupted by a shrill buzz. His eyes scanned around, as if looking for an irritating bug until the receptionist drew his attention.

'It's the door buzzer. A man is there.'

Mac stormed over and looked at her screen. It wasn't Sam and he slammed his fist onto the desk, startling the young woman.

'I want to speak to him,' he demanded, and the woman shifted a small, thin intercom towards him and pressed the button.

'Who the fuck are you?' Mac said, watching the chubby man squirm.

'My name is Sergeant Peter Whitlow. I just want to talk to you.'

'Do you have Sam Pope?' Mac asked, knowing the answer. He watched as the negotiator adjusted his glasses, trying to maintain his composure.

'Not yet. But we are working on it.'

'Fuck off then.'

'Sir, we just want to talk. Also, I need to make sure the

hostages and patients are okay. If you let me in, we can work on bringing this to an end. I'm unarmed.'

The man held up his hands to the camera, showing Mac he wasn't lying. Mac nodded to the receptionist, who flicked the door open. With a buzz, it automatically swung inwards and Whitlow walked in, scanning the corridors, trying to absorb as much information as possible. He offered Lucy a reassuring smile then stopped still as he laid eyes on the horrifying burns that consumed Mac's face.

'Where is he?'

'Why don't we let these people go and we can discuss…'

A gunshot rang out, sending the entire ward into a panic. Whitlow screamed in agony, dropping to the floor and pressing both hands to the knee that had been shattered by the bullet. As blood pumped through his trousers, the man's face drained of colour and Mac squatted down beside him.

'This is non-negotiable.'

Mac tucked the gun into the back of his trousers and then grasped the back of Whitlow's shirt, dragging the wounded man across the corridor. As Whitlow moaned in pain, Mac hauled him up, then in one swift movement, shoved him as hard as he could through the glass window.

Whitlow hurtled down the three stories, followed by a rainfall of shattered glass. From the broken window, Mac could hear the screams of terror from outside, the sickening thud of Whitlow's death, followed by the delightful sound of the glass shattering. With no remorse for the life he'd just taken, Mac stomped back to the reception desk and pointed the gun at the receptionist, who froze in fear.

'Go downstairs and tell the police that if I don't have Sam here in the next hour, I'll start throwing a patient out every ten minutes. Do you understand?'

The young girl nodded frantically, and Mac jerked his

head to the door for her to go. He buzzed her out and watched as she ran. He shot a glance towards a mortified Lucy, who was staring at the smear of blood that lead to the window.

Mac smirked, knowing his message had been heard loud and clear.

The automatic door slammed shut and he waited for his revenge.

———

Stout watched from the crowded street; the rain illuminated in flashes of blue as the multiple cars blocked off the road. A sense of pride ran through him at the hard work of his team and he stood, agitated, waiting for Whitlock to emerge with an open dialogue to the man inside. Still waiting on the identity of the man to be discovered by his analytical team who were running facial recognition, he felt a sense of alarm rush through his body when he was told the name of the woman who had accompanied the terrorist into the building.

Lucy Farmer.

Sam Pope's ex-wife.

The pendulum had swung in the other direction.

Despite Ashton's theory of an accomplice, the fact the bomber had taken someone from Sam's personal life as effective bait told him this wasn't a plan to spring Sam from prison. Whoever this was, he wanted blood and Stout's job now was the limit the amount shed.

A large crash of glass was quickly accompanied by the sight of a bloodied Whitlock tumbling from the third floor of the hospital, the entire watching crowd holding their breath as the man crashed to the hard concrete below. Doctors and police officers rushed to the broken remains of the negotiator, as other officers did their best to quash the panic rising from the watching public.

Stout drew his hand to his head, mortified at the death of one of his officers. The option of sending in the ARU, armed and ready to go, was tempting, but there was no guarantee it wouldn't end in a massacre.

With their guns trained on the front door, the armed team gave the signal that someone was approaching and Stout marched towards the door. A blonde lady, pale with fear, emerged, the terror of sixteen assault rifles pinned on her threatened to overwhelm her.

'Lower your weapons,' Stout commanded, jogging the final few steps to the woman, who was shaking with fear. 'Are you okay?'

'He has a bomb. He has a bomb,' she repeated, as an officer brought a foil blanket which Stout wrapped around the woman.

'What happened up there?' Stout asked, glaring over his shoulder as Ashton joined him.

'He shot that man. He was only trying to help.'

Ashton shook her head.

'We need to send in the team, sir,' she demanded impatiently. 'Before this gets out of hand.'

'Thank you, Deputy. But I am in control of this situation.'

Ashton gestured to the crumpled remains of Whitlock, which was already covered with a sheet as EMTs carefully loaded the dead officer onto a stretcher.

'None of us are.' Ashton's cruel words were even more evidence that she was looking after herself. The last twelve hours had devastated her career, but she saw a clear opportunity to at least salvage her own reputation by attacking Stout's. Before the irate Commissioner could respond, a voice cut in.

'Let me go in.'

The two most senior figures in the Met Police turned, their eyes wide with shock as Sam walked towards them, having been guided through the cordon by DI Singh. Behind them, a group of officers had followed, watching on in awe at Sam's arrival.

'Officers. Arrest this man,' Ashton snapped, her face twisted in a bitter scowl.

'Stop.' Stout held his hand up to the officers and turned to Ashton. 'Take a walk.'

Sam met Ashton's glare without emotion, and she marched off into the rain, her hands shaking with fury. Stout watched her for a few moments, shelving their issues for later, before he turned back to Sam. Stout was impressed.

'Well, you're full of surprises, aren't you?'

'Sir, there are innocent people in there. He has my ex-wife. They have nothing to do with this.' Sam looked up at the shattered window. 'This is my fight. So, let me go in.'

Stout took a deep breath, his hands firmly on his hips as he contemplated the next move. He looked at Singh, who nodded her approval, as if underlining that Stout could trust Sam. The commissioner didn't doubt it. Although he was a huge advocate for removing Sam's one-man war on crime from the streets of his city, he never doubted that Sam held the nobility of a soldier.

He was fast running out of options and Stout knew it.

The terrorist wanted Sam Pope.

And here he was, willing to go in.

'Fine. But I need you to get those children out of there, do you understand?' Stout commanded. 'We know he's armed, and we know there is a bomb.'

'Anything else?' Sam asked, not taking his eyes off the window.

'The trigger.' The young receptionist peeked over her

blanket, nervous as all eyes fell on her. 'He said it was a dead trigger. His thumb was on it.'

'Jesus,' Stout exclaimed.

'What's wrong?' Singh asked, worried.

'It's a dead man's switch,' Sam interjected before Stout could. 'If he takes his thumb off of it, then the whole hospital will come down.'

'Sam…' Singh began, but she knew it was pointless. The man had Lucy in the firing line. Even if the ARU targeted their guns at him, it wouldn't stop Sam from trying to get to her.

'Good luck,' Stout said, before giving the order to the ARU to let Sam through. 'They'll be right behind you.'

'Keep them a floor below,' Sam demanded. 'He wants just me. Let's give him that.'

Stout nodded and stepped to the side; his attention pulled away by a frantic analyst who had raced towards them. Sam gave Singh a final look before he stepped forward towards the building, only halting when he heard the devastating words from the analyst.

They had discovered the man's identity.

Sam's wild suspicions about his attacker in Rome came true.

The man holding the hospital hostage. Who had strapped a bomb to his ex-wife?

His name was Matthew McLaughlin.

Mac.

Sam raced towards the doors of the hospital, ready confront a ghost from his haunted past.

CHAPTER TWENTY-SEVEN

TEN YEARS AGO...

The relentless heat of the sun bore down on the Afghanistan terrain like it held a grudge and Sam could feel the sweat dripping down the back of his shirt.

It had been two weeks since he'd been rescued by Theo and Marsden, their helicopter landing just outside of the war zone Sam had created.

A mission gone wrong.

Horribly wrong.

What should have been a simple elimination soon became a fight for survival, as a missile had sent Sam sprawling down the cliff face. The fact that he'd survived had been a miracle, and the sacrifice of a local doctor had been what had kept him alive. The doctor, Farhad Nabizada, had kept Sam alive, treating his wounds from the explosion, and eventually giving his own life to protect Sam and his children.

Tamir and Masood.

A local Taliban recruitment operation had laid siege to the doctor's home, then murdered the loving father in cold blood in front of his children.

Sam had avenged him, slaying the entire regiment.

He had asked Marsden, his commanding officer, to help find the children, but they'd vanished. Lost in the abyss of war.

But now, as Sam trudged across the stony cliff face from which he tumbled, he was searching for someone else.

Mac.

Mac was gone.

'Come on, Sam.'

Theo Walker, Sam's best friend and one of the finest medics in the team, rested his hand on Sam's shoulder in comfort. Sam stepped away, walking slowly to the scorched earth where the missile impacted.

'I can't leave him,' Sam stated, scanning the endless horizon in hope.

'We've been searching for days.' Theo sighed. 'Marsden has sent two choppers to find him. He's gone, Sam. Wallace has already confirmed it.'

Sam felt his fingers tighten into a fist and his arm shook with rage. He had promised Mac he would keep him alive and he'd failed. Despite everything Sam went through in the small village of Chikari below the cliff, he'd not been able to keep his promise.

Sam was built to survive.

Mac, sadly, had not.

'What if he is still out there?' Sam wondered out loud, before turning to face his friend. 'What if he needs us, right now? We can't just walk away. He's one of us.'

'Sam, Mac was a great soldier. But we all know the price we pay for this job. He died in the fight against oppression. The war on terror has a number of casualties, believe me, I've tried my best to lower that number.' Theo shook his head solemnly. 'But Mac died in the heat of battle. Don't take that away from him. And for the love of God, Sam, don't carry this burden with you. You did everything you could.'

Sam sighed.

Theo was right. It annoyed him how often he had to admit that.

With one final look towards the wasteland before them, Sam offered a silent apology to Mac, promising himself that he would do everything to honour the man's memory. Later that afternoon, he once again relayed the story to Wallace, who begrudgingly submitted Mac's death record into the system, declaring the young soldier KIA.

Sam had done everything he could.

But the guilt of the young man's death was something he knew he would never be able to wash away.

———

With each step of his boot echoing through the empty reception, Sam felt the unnerving emptiness of the building. Usually, the hospital would have been a hive of activity, but under the severe threat of an explosion, it presented Sam with a dark and ghostly atmosphere.

Like the world had ended and he was walking through its remains.

Rows upon rows of plastic seats sat empty, the coffee shop abandoned. There was nobody stationed behind the reception desk and Sam approached it, knowing his every move was being monitored from the outside. Sam climbed over the desk, dropping behind to the staff only area. His right hand was throbbing, and he checked the bandage which has stained red with blood.

Etheridge's handiwork wasn't holding.

Sam searched the drawers and found another roll of bandages and wrapped another layer around his wounded hand. It would do for now.

Taped to the desk was an itinerary of the numerous departments and wards which were dotted throughout the incredible medical facility and Sam ran through them. Handily, they were listed by floor and then in alphabetical order and it didn't take long for Sam to find the extension number. With over twenty patients on the ward under siege, the police had not disengaged the power to the building and Sam lifted the phone and welcomed the dial tone.

He tapped in the four digits and the phone began to ring.

———

The longer the wait, the harder it was for Mac to keep his mind straight. For a decade, he'd dreamt of this moment.

There was never a plan in place on how he would get to this point, but the thought of killing Sam, of putting him through his own hell, was what had fuelled his survival.

Waiting for them to present Sam to him was intolerable, and Mac felt like a petulant kid who couldn't wait for Christmas Eve to be over.

With his thumb pressed firmly on the trigger, he paced the foyer of the Teenage and Young Adult ward, fighting to keep control. Lucy still sat on the first chair of a row of five, and beyond her, nurses pottered between rooms, doing their best to keep the terrified patients calm.

The shrill ring of the phone cut through the silent tension like a knife and Mac raised his only eyebrow. Holding up the trigger as a warning for no one to do anything stupid, he rounded the desk and lifted the receiver.

'*Hello.*'

Mac froze.

Sam's voice drilled into his ear and an avalanche of memories flooded back. Their time together in the army camps, the lukewarm beer while hiking through rough terrain.

A genuine friendship.

But Mac gritted his teeth, refusing to offer the man a

greeting. Beyond the desk, Mac noticed Lucy's eyes light up in a misguided sense of hope. With no response forthcoming, Sam continued.

'*Mac? Is it really you?*'

Again, nothing. Mac held his jaw tight, pulling his charred lips into a thin line.

'*Jesus, I thought you were dead. They told me you were dead. I'm downstairs in the reception, but if you want me to come up and we do this face to face, then you need to let everyone else go. Okay?*'

Mac shuffled uncomfortably, his breathing loud enough to inform Sam he was listening.

'*Those kids are sick, Mac. They need to be treated somewhere safe. If you let everyone go, I promise you, I will come upstairs.*'

Mac scoffed.

Sam had made promises before and Mac valued them as much as he valued the lives of all the captives under his instruction. But Mac knew that Sam had a sense of purpose, one that he'd once admired.

One that he'd desired himself.

When Wallace told Mac that he needed him to track Sam down six months ago, he'd warned Mac of Sam's hero complex. That he would tear apart anything that stood in his way if it meant saving an innocent life.

This wasn't a negotiation.

It was a necessary move to get what he wanted. With his grip tightening around the phone, Mac finally spoke.

'Fine. But she stays. Then you have thirty seconds, or I will kill her.'

Mac slammed the phone down with a force that shattered its plastic coating. Lucy, having heard the ominous threat, looked hopefully towards the nurses, encouraging them to follow Mac's instructions. He strode into the centre of the corridor, with the trigger and his pistol held out for all to see.

A visual warning that he wasn't playing a game.

'You are all free to leave. Get out now.'

Confusion spread around the ward and Mac sighed, then blasted another bullet into the ceiling, ripping through the cheap panels and causing a light fixture to drop, entangled in wires. A scream of terror accompanied it and Mac's voice rose with his rage.

'Everyone out. Now!'

With the reality of the situation hitting home, the nurses and doctors leapt into action, helping their patients from their beds or chairs, and slowly, they began to file down the corridor. As a few of the teenagers shuffled past, holding their drips, Mac could feel their terrified stares.

In their eyes he was a monster.

He looked away, furious at where the road to redemption had led him.

If he was a monster, then he wanted the person responsible for making him so.

A cleaner who spoke little English, wheeled out a bed, under the guidance of a doctor who was whispering comforting words to a terminally sick teenager, who was slipping in and out of consciousness. As the final doctor approached the door, he turned back to Mac, nodding towards Lucy.

'And her?'

Mac aimed the gun at the young doctor's face.

'She stays.'

The doctor offered Lucy a sympathetic eyebrow raise, but his loyalty was to his patients and he turned and hurried towards the lift. The doors closed and it began its ascension. Mac would give them a minute or so to vacate the building.

Once it passed, he pulled Lucy from her chair and marched her thirty feet down the corridor and shoved her to her knees. Facing the door, Mac pressed the gun against the top of her skull, and she shook with fear. Tears ran down her cheeks, before crashing to the clean tiles below.

Mac began to count.

'Thirty…twenty-nine…twenty-eight…'

———

Sam held open the emergency door beside the revolving entrance and ushered the nurses and patients out as quickly as he could. They burst out into the rainy night, some of them shaking with fear, others infuriated that a situation like this had manifested.

The Armed Response Unit stood to the side, allowing police officers and other nurses to rush to the aid of the group, with the more seriously stricken patients quickly whisked away in ambulances, the sirens wailing as they headed to the nearest hospitals.

As the final doctor raced through the door, the ARU began to fall into position, but Sam looked to Stout and held up a hand, shaking his head.

'Stand down.' Stout ordered, much to the unit's disappointment and Sam shut the door. He didn't have long, and he burst into the stairwell, taking the steps two at a time. Lucy was still up there, no doubt terrified for her life and the child waiting for her at home.

Sam may not have been able to save their son, but he wouldn't allow Lucy's daughter to grow up without a mother.

Whatever it took, Sam was willing to sacrifice.

As he bounded up to the door, marked with a large *3* sign, Sam felt his heart pound.

Not a day had gone by that he hadn't beaten himself up about Mac's death. Sam had failed to keep him safe, and despite his best efforts, he never found his fallen friend.

There were no words he could offer Mac. Sam knew that.

He was out of ideas.

He was unarmed.

There was no plan.

All Sam had was himself, which is exactly what Mac had demanded. Whatever happened, Sam had to get Lucy out of the building.

Sam marched through the corridor, following the signs to the ward. As he rounded the final corner, he was welcomed by an already open door and he stepped through, ready to deal with the wrath of days gone by.

He saw Lucy first, on her knees, her eyes red, her cheeks wet with tears. Wrapped around her was a barbaric vest, lined with enough explosives to wipe them off the face of the earth.

Pressed against her blonde hair was a gun.

Sam stopped dead with shock at the horribly scarred face of the man holding it. The man's stare bore a hole through Sam, which felt like it knocked him off balance.

Sam could barely muster the words.

'Mac?'

'What's the matter, Sam? You look like you've seen a ghost.'

CHAPTER TWENTY-EIGHT

Sam took a few tentative steps forward, his hands held up in surrender. He scanned the corridor, but there were no details worth remembering. A friend he thought dead stood less than twenty feet away, with his ex-wife teetering on the edge of extinction.

No minor details could help him now.

The trade seemed simple enough.

'Mac. I thought you were dead.'

Mac lifted the gun and pointed it squarely at Sam.

'That's close enough.'

Sam stopped on the spot and his heart broke. Mac's youthful face bore the horrific scars of a man who went beyond his own pain threshold. Sam felt the tears begin to form in his eyes and he looked to Lucy, who looked on helplessly.

'Lucy, are you okay?'

'What do you think?' Mac spat; his familiar Manchurian accent brought back echoes of the night Sam almost died in Rome. 'This is your fault, Sam.'

'Mac, just let her go. She has nothing to do with this.'

'No, she doesn't.' Mac agreed, the gun still pointed at

Sam's chest. 'But imagine being put through more pain than humanly possible and knowing that you had promised you would protect her. That you would keep her safe.'

Sam took another step closer, the gap down to less than ten feet and Mac shifted the gun and pointed it at Lucy once more, causing her to weep loudly.

'I said stay where you are.'

'Okay, okay.' Sam held his hands up again. Above Mac, the halogen light was flickering, hanging from its wires, an errant bullet hole next to it.

'You left me, Sam. You left me for them.'

'I tried to save you,' Sam said.

'You abandoned me. Do you know what they did to me? They kept me in a fucking cage for years. They beat me, they cut me, pissed on me. They raped me. I was their pet, feeding on scraps while you were given medal after medal and got to live the life YOU wanted.'

Mac's voice was getting louder with each horrific memory, spit dribbling from his mouth as his crazed anger took over. He pointed the gun at Sam again.

'You promised me, Sam. Promised me you would bring me back.'

'Mac, they told me you had died. Wallace even signed your death certificate.'

Mac pointed the gun a few inches above Lucy's head and pulled the trigger. She screamed in pain, holding her ear as the bullet shattered the thin plaster wall behind her. Sam took a step closer in panic, but Mac lifted the gun once more.

'One more step and I'll blow her brains out,' Mac threatened. 'Wallace saved me. He pulled me out of that hellhole, and he gave me more than I ever thought possible. Then you killed him. You took that from me, too.'

'Wallace was a terrorist. And I didn't kill him.'

'Get on your knees,' Mac said coldly. Sam took another

255

step closer and Mac pressed the gun against Lucy's head. Blood was trickling from her hair, the blast from the handgun damaging her ear drum. 'Get on your fucking knees.'

Sam obliged.

'Can you please just let her go? She has nothing to do with this.' Sam caught Lucy's eye and offered her a smile, his undying love for her shining through. 'Everything is going to be fine. Just stay calm.'

'Do you know what it feels like to want to die? To dream that today is your last day on this planet?' Mac asked, enjoying watching Sam on his knees, begging for mercy. 'Every day I woke up in that cage, I begged whatever twisted God was watching that it would be my last. That when they dragged my naked body out into the sun, they would finally go too far. Do you know what that's like?'

Sam kept his eyes on Lucy, trying his best to keep her calm. He looked up at his former partner, shaking his head.

'Mac, I am sorry for what happened.'

'Answer my question.'

'Yes. I have. I felt that way for a long time. But like you, I made it out the other side. You don't have to go down this path, Mac. Put the gun down and let me help you.'

Mac chuckled and then broke into a sinister laugh, his grasp on his composure slowly dissipating.

'Help me? It's too late for that, Sam.' Mac turned the gun back onto Lucy. 'I prayed for death for seven years. You better start praying, too.'

Lucy's eyes widened in terror and Sam felt a tear roll down his cheek. There was no coming back from this. Mac was beyond salvation. All he wanted, regardless of the cost, was for Sam to suffer.

To pay for his alleged betrayal.

Think, Sam. Think.

Mac, with his eyes focused on the woman, regrettably straightened his arm, ready to absorb the impact of the gunshot.

'This won't make you a soldier,' Sam spat.

Mac stopped, slowly turning to face his nemesis, his eyes, wide with rage.

'What did you say?'

Sam, on his knees, knew that he was vulnerable. If Mac turned the gun on him now, there was nothing to stop him emptying the entire clip into his chest. With Mac unlikely to surrender, Lucy would no doubt be blown apart when Mac decided there was no other option.

But Sam had to try something. Anything.

'I said this won't make you a soldier. Soldiers don't kill defenceless people.'

'This isn't about being a soldier. It's about getting even.'

'Is it?' Sam slowly got to one foot and Mac spun his arm round, the gun aimed at Sam once more. Sam planted his other foot down and stood. 'You were meant to be a soldier, Mac. You told me you wanted the life I had. But you ran. You panicked and you ran. That's not what a soldier does.'

'Shut up,' Mac screamed, his eyes watering as he gritted his teeth. Inside, he was battling against his own broken mind. 'You left me.'

'No, you abandoned your post. And now you're showing how weak you really are by killing an innocent woman. If you really want to hurt me, Mac. Show me I was wrong. Prove to me that you were worth saving to begin with.'

'Fuck you. Fuck you,' Mac shouted over and again, his hand gripping the trigger. Lucy looked to Sam in bewilderment.

'You want to prove to me you're a soldier, then let her go. Give her the trigger, let her walk out of the door and then we can settle this. Like soldiers. You wanted me, Mac. Well I'm right here.'

Mac went frightfully still, his eyes closed. Sam shuffled tentatively, knowing this was the moment of clarity. Either a bullet was coming straight for him, or Mac's thumb was going to lift off the dead man's switch. Lucy shook, terrified of the precarious situation.

Eventually, Mac opened his eyes and held the trigger out to Lucy.

'Take this. Keep your thumb on this button. Now go.'

Mac slide the detonator into Lucy's shaking hand and slid his thumb out from under hers, locking it in place. Holding it like it was a glass sculpture, Lucy slowly rose to her feet, shot Mac a careful look, and then shuffled cautiously towards the exit. As she passed Sam, she glanced at him, a mixture of sorrow and fury before she continued towards the door. Sam watched her go, knowing the ARU would have assembled by the lifts, ready to burst in once the corridor was safe.

That didn't give him much time.

He needed to get Mac to surrender. As he turned back, he'd already begun his plea.

'Mac, we need to…'

A brick like fist collided with Sam's jaw, knocking him to his left. Sam spiralled and landed on his knee. He spat blood onto the tile and woozily got back to his feet.

'I've been waiting a long time to do that.'

Mac then threw another expert right hook, but Sam ducked, deflecting Mac to the side and then shoved him into the wall. Mac spun on his heel, fists up, ready to engage. Sam held his hands up passively.

'Mac, I can help you. But you need to stop.'

'Fight me,' Mac demanded. 'You owe me that, at least.'

Mac launched forward again, throwing lefts and rights, his Krav Maga training had clearly been effective. Sam, well trained in a number of hand to hand combat techniques, expertly blocked them with his forearms, before stomping forward and knocking out Mac's left foot. Off balance, Mac tried to swing another right, but Sam caught it, twisted the arm and then slammed Mac into the wall, pinning him against the cork noticeboard.

'It's over, Mac.'

Mac thrust his head back, his skull catching Sam above the eye, re-opening the gash that was held together by two strips of tape. Blinded as blood gushed over his eyeball, Sam stumbled back and Mac charged, ramming his shoulder into Sam's stomach and driving him into the opposite door. It swung open and Mac hurled Sam into the metal railing that surrounded the hospital bed. The impact caught Sam in the centre of his surgically repaired spine, and he rolled over backwards before dropping hard onto the tiles.

'Get up,' Mac demanded, stomping around the bed. Sam pushed himself to his knees, but Mac drove a solid boot into his ribs. Then another.

And another.

He threw one more vicious kick, but Sam blocked it. Blind with murderous rage, Mac threw another hard right, but Sam blocked it and instinctively drove his elbow into Mac's jaw. Stumbling backwards, Mac spat out a tooth, smirked, and then charged once more.

In the cramped room, Mac unloaded a flurry of strikes, and Sam tucked his head in and raised his arms, absorbing the blows. As Mac tired slightly, he drove in with another hook, but Sam deflected it, drove his knee into his adversary's ribs and then stepped to the side.

'I won't fight you, Mac.'

'You don't have a choice.' Mac swung the metal drip

stand, catching Sam in the hip. Stumbling backwards, Sam fell against the large, rectangular glass window that afforded the nurses a look into the room. Mac charged and as he approached, he leapt off his feet, slamming into Sam and sending them both careering through the panel. They collapsed onto the tiles, falling onto the shattered glass that had beaten them to the ground and they both groaned in pain. As Mac hit the ground, the SIG Sauer P226 spilled from his belt, landing among the shards. As both men worked to get their breath back, Sam could hear the approaching rumbling of the ARU's boots as they made their way towards the ward.

That meant Lucy had made it outside.

She was safe.

Mac lunged onto Sam, a thick, sharp shard of glass in his hand and he drove it towards Sam's throat. Sam managed to raise his arm, blocking Mac with his forearm, but Mac had the leverage and he climbed on top of Sam, pressing down with all his might. Sam strained his neck back, the blade only a centimetre from his Adam's apple and he looked Mac dead in the eye.

Mac said nothing.

Sam tried to drive his knee into Mac's spine, but Mac had him pinned.

A smile crept across Mac's charred face as the blade lowered, piercing the skin of Sam's throat, a trickle of blood falling out.

A gunshot echoed through the corridor.

As if hit by a train, Mac flew to the right, relinquishing his hold on Sam. The blade sliced across Sam's throat, but there wasn't enough pressure to cause anything but a slight cut.

Sam sat up in a panic, looking back towards the door where a member of the ARU was on his knee, rifle drawn up to his eye.

He was reloading. Sam leapt to his feet, standing in front of his fallen foe.

A man he'd once regarded a friend.

'Hold your fire,' Sam demanded. He turned and dropped to his knees, examining the bullet wound that had ripped through the top of Mac's chest, shattering his collar bone. Through gritted teeth, Mac was groaning in agony, his hand pressed against the wound to stop the bleeding. Sam reached down underneath Mac's arms and helped him to his knees, uttering that he would be okay.

But as Sam tried to haul him to his feet, Mac refused to move, dropping back onto his knees, his head bowed in defeat.

There was no fight left in him.

Sam knelt in front of him and rested his hand on the side of Mac's face, cupping it tenderly. Mac slowly lifted his head, locking eyes with the man he'd hated for over a decade.

A man he'd held responsible for all the pain that had created the monster he'd become.

But the truth was, Sam didn't know.

Wallace had told him Sam had left him for dead. Hadn't cared.

But he had. He still did.

With his energy levels dropping through blood loss, Mac slumped his head forward and pressed it against Sam's. Their bond had been reforged, albeit only slightly.

'I'm sorry, Mac. I'm so sorry,' Sam said quietly. 'This time, I'm taking you with me.'

Mac shook his head and pushed himself back. Sam looked at him with confusion.

'All I've known for ten years is pain. Pain and anger.' Mac let go of his shoulder and pressed his arm to the ground behind him. 'I'm sorry, Sam. But without it, I don't exist.'

'Mac, what are you saying?'

Without answering and with his final strands of energy, Mac pushed himself to his feet, drawing the handgun from behind him and aimed it directly at the armed men who had lined the corridor behind Sam. Despite Sam's cries of horror, three gunshots exploded behind him and the bullets ripped through Mac's chest, sending him jolting backwards before collapsing onto the glass.

Sam scurried across the sharp shards, ignoring the pain and leant over Mac.

With his chest a bloodied mess and his eyes closed, Sam knew he was dead, but he still called out his name. Guilt shook through his body and he rested his hand on his friend's chest, the devastation of what had happened to him hitting with as much velocity as the bullets that sent Mac to his grave.

Sam began to cry and as he was surrounded by the ARU, he pulled the dog tags from his fallen comrade's neck, clutched them in his blood-soaked hand, and allowed himself to be marched back to his impending incarceration.

CHAPTER TWENTY-NINE

Singh had watched with bated breath as Lucy had emerged through the emergency door of the hospital, flanked either side by the armoured officers who had escorted her carefully out of the building. One of the men had both hands clasped around her hands, indicating the trigger was secure.

A palpable panic spread through the street, with Stout demanding that the cordon be moved back, asserting his authority in a way that would be missed when he stepped down. As everyone scurried away, Stout sent two bomb defusal experts towards Lucy and Singh held her breath as they slowly lifted the bomb over her head, freeing her from her explosive chains. Carefully, they transitioned the dead man's switch into the gloved grip of the brave officer who then instructed his teammate to remove her from the scene.

Moments later, the expert confirmed that he'd defused the bomb and to the relief of everyone, the switch had been deactivated.

Despite the promise of safety, Lucy seemed hesitant to move, jerking her neck back to look up at the building.

Sam was still in there.

Singh shared her concern.

As she was ushered towards the cars, Singh and Commissioner Stout approached her, with Stout wrapping his warm jacket around her shoulder.

'You are safe now, Mrs Farmer,' he assured her; his words full of clarity.

'Lucy?' A voice called out from the crowd and she raised her head. Tears of relief began to fall as she saw her husband, Nick, stood at the edge of the cordon and as the rain lashed down upon her, she raced through the swathes of officers to embrace him. Singh made to follow, but Stout gripped her shoulder with a firm hand.

'Let her go,' Stout said. 'We'll talk to her when this is over.'

'Sir, we need to know what the situation is.'

'Our Armed Response Unit is in place. They'll be moving in shortly.' Stout noticed the concern on Singh's face and smiled. There was clearly more than a professional interest at stake. 'Don't worry, Singh. They know who the target is.'

Before Singh could respond, a gunshot echoed from the building, causing a shriek of excitement from the street. Singh's heart raced and she took a step forward. Stout shook his head and demanded an update into his radio.

Three more shots echoed out and Singh burst into action, ignoring Stouts calls for her to stop. She burst through the emergency door and into the derelict reception of the hospital, scanning the room until her eyes fell on the stairwell. As she began to climb the steps, she heard the clattering of footsteps above her and she stopped, waiting in trepidation as her armed colleagues descended towards her.

Sam was among them.

Singh took a breath.

Despite moving gingerly, and with blood pouring from his eye and neck, he seemed fine as he approached her, but she could see the devastation on his face. She made her way down the stairs and back into the reception, allowing the officers to filter out and Sam emerged, shuffling with his hands once again cuffed behind his back.

'Sam,' she called to him. He didn't respond.

Sam took three steps towards her and then buried his head in her shoulder, allowing himself a moment of grief. Singh held him tightly, closing her eyes and stroking the back of his hair. The last six months had told her that he didn't fear prison. Sam was more than willing to pay the heavy price of his actions.

He pulled away and looked her in the eyes, nodded, and then for the second time in the space of a month, he allowed Singh to lead him out of a building in cuffs, but this time, there was no rampant excitement at his capture.

As they took their first step down the steps, the ARU stood to the side, forming a guard of honour for Sam and to Singh's shock, they saluted. Sam stopped, taken aback by the show of respect and he nodded his thanks to them.

They took another step and an audible clap went up and as they moved cautiously towards the police cars, an echo of applause spread throughout the onlookers, all of them showing their appreciation for Sam's bravery. Singh squeezed his arm, her eyes watering at the overwhelming response for Sam.

With half his face covered in blood, he scanned the approving audience, nodding to them with a slight movement of his head.

Two figures stood ahead of them.

Deputy Commissioner Ashton glared at Sam, her arms crossed and a look of disgust across her face.

Commissioner Stout, however, was joining in with the

applause. Singh brought Sam to a stop and he stood, back straight, shoulders steady.

Like a soldier.

'Thank you, Sam,' Stout said with a smile. 'You saved a lot of people tonight.'

'Not all of them, sir.' Sam's words hung heavy with sadness. 'He was my friend and I failed him.'

'You did everything you could.' Stout reassured him, leaning over and opening the backseat of the nearest car. 'And I will do likewise.'

Sam managed a smile.

'Thank you, sir.'

Singh helped Sam into the back of the car and then closed the door. As she turned to the driver's door, Ashton pushed it shut.

'I assume you have an explanation for all of this?' Ashton snapped. 'Otherwise, I'll have you arrested right now.'

'Deputy Commissioner, stand down,' Stout commanded, much to her chagrin. 'Singh, take Sam back to HQ. I'll be along shortly.'

'Yes, sir,' Singh replied, looking Ashton dead in the eye as she did. She slipped into the seat, slammed the door, and turned the key. With the blue lights flashing, she turned the car towards the watching crowd and they parted like the Red Sea. Carefully navigating her way through, she couldn't hide the smile as they applauded.

'Looks like you have yourself a fan club.'

Singh smirked, shooting a glance at the rear-view mirror. But Sam didn't respond. Looking off into the distance, Sam was too busy mourning a fallen comrade to even register the adulation.

As the car disappeared down Euston Road, Ashton stared at the appreciative crowd with disillusionment. Sam Pope was a convicted criminal, a man who had killed

266

numerous people. Yet he'd just commanded the respect she'd craved and it felt like a disgrace to Wallace's memory. Stout's voice broke her thoughts.

'I guess I don't need to tell you I expect your resignation on my desk by the morning?'

Ashton turned on her heel, her face screwed in anger.

'You are making a mistake, sir,' she pleaded.

'Not anymore.'

Commissioner Stout shook his head with disappointment, then turned back to the busy crime scene, hurling out directions to bring it to a close. Over his shoulder, Ashton watched as paramedics brought out Mac's dead body, shielded from the public with a white sheet. Slowly, the nurses, doctors, and police officers worked in unison to return the patients to the hospital and Stout stood, casting his eye over proceedings.

Soon, everything would return to normal.

But for Ashton, things would never be the same again.

————

Marie brought two cups of tea into Stout's office and laid them on the desk. Singh thanked her kindly then glanced at the time.

The woman worked round the clock.

Stout's office was surprisingly low key. The furniture was of the finest quality, with the large, oak desk the centrepiece of the room. But beyond a few bookcases and a plethora of framed certifications that lined the walls, there wasn't too much else of note. The floor to ceiling glass windows offered a spectacular view of the city, lit up like a painting. The beauty of the city always caught Singh by surprise, and she stared out over the Thames at the bright lights beyond.

'That's better,' Sam said with satisfaction, sipping the

warm tea and then reclining back in the chair. Singh smiled, knowing Sam was holding on to as many comforts as he could. It was unlikely he would end up buried underground in a maximum-security prison, but they both knew his freedom had a time limit.

Whatever Stout wanted to speak to them about would be the final conversation Sam had as a free man.

The on-site doctor had tended to Sam's wounds and rebandaged the others, surprised by the competency of Etheridge's stitching, which drew a chuckle from Sam. Singh had watched as they looked over his beaten body and she was reminded once again of what he'd been through.

What he'd put himself through.

It was another stark reminder that their time together would never last.

The door flew open and Stout strode in, removing his sodden raincoat and sliding a hand through his thinning hair.

'Apologies for keeping you waiting.'

'No worries, sir,' Singh said, receiving a warm smile from the commissioner. He turned his attention to Sam.

'How are you holding up?'

'I've had worse nights.'

Stout chuckled. There was a clear respect between the two men, despite their opposing ideals.

'Well, I and the city of London can't thank you enough. What you did took extreme courage and I can only offer my condolences at the loss of your friend.'

Sam nodded meekly; the thought of Mac's death still too fresh to expand on. The door behind them closed and Singh swivelled. A well-built, middle-aged man stepped in, dressed in a resplendent suit. His dark hair, tinged with grey flecks, was combed neatly to the side and his strong jaw was clean shaven.

Whoever he was, he screamed money, and he walked confidently to the commissioner and shook his hand.

'Director Blake.' Stout introduced him to the room. 'Thank you for coming.'

'My pleasure.' Blake's words were clear and concise. Singh immediately ascertained that confidence wasn't a hard attribute for him to find.

'Sir, what's going on?' Singh asked, shuffling in her seat. Sam watched on with interest. Blake clasped his hands together and walked to the front of the desk, casually leaning against it.

'Detective Inspector, have you ever heard of Directive One?'

Singh looked towards Stout in confusion and then shook her head. Blake smiled warmly and continued.

'I wouldn't have thought so. We operate in pockets that the government do not want a presence, ensuring we stay out of the public and professional eye.'

'You're a spook?' Sam chimed in, drawing a wry smile.

'That's a pretty crude word, but you're not far off.' Blake spoke confidently. 'We operate as a small yet essential operation to ensure matters of national and international security do not escalate. There are a lot of situations that do not reach the public surface and we are the ones who make sure of it.'

Again, Singh looked to her commissioner.

'Sir?'

'Just listen, Singh,' Stout said, sat back in his chair with his fingers clasped together. Blake continued.

'In light of today's events, and the events of the last six months, we would like to extend the invitation to you both to join Directive One. Lord knows we could use people like you.'

'People like us?' Sam asked wearily.

'Those who put the right thing above all else. We abide

by the law, but we are given a certain *leeway* shall we say? Your fight against crime, Sam, is something we've followed since you outed Inspector Howell. Singh, ever since you worked diligently to help take down Wallace, you've been on our radar.'

'Are you offering me a job, sir?' Singh asked excitedly.

'Haven't you wanted to do more, Singh? There is only so much you can do with all the red tape in the force.' Blake smiled. 'Commissioner Stout is in agreement with me.'

Singh looked to the commissioner who nodded.

'You're tailor-made for it, Singh.' Stout confirmed. 'You'd be a hell of a loss for us, though.'

Blake turned back to them both and shrugged.

'What do you say?'

'I'm in.' Singh's response was immediate.

'Hard pass.'

All eyes fell on Sam, who casually sipped his tea. Singh looked confused, Stout shocked. Judging by the look on Blake's face, he wasn't used to being turned down.

'Excuse me?'

'Let me guess. This will require us giving up all forms of identity, residence, the works. Then we would be assigned undercover missions, where the only directive is to ensure it's completed. How am I doing?'

'That's correct,' Blake said, patting down his immaculate blazer in frustration. 'Directive One operates off the radar so to speak.'

'No offence, but I've already been part of a shady elite government group and it's not a road I want to travel again.'

Singh turned on her chair, resting a hand on Sam's arm.

'Sam, this is a way out.' Her eyes were wide with hope. 'You're still facing life in prison.'

'She's right,' Blake said cockily. Sam shrugged.

'My fight is over.' Sam put his empty mug on the desk and turned to Singh. 'Good luck, Amara. Thank you for everything you've done for me.'

Speechless, Blake stood, adjusting his tie. He nodded a thank you to the commissioner and turned to Singh.

'We will be in touch.'

Blake shot a glare at Sam before striding out of the office. Singh turned to Sam in dismay, but Sam winked at her, catching her off guard. Stout let out an audible yawn and leant forward on the table.

'It's late. Singh, why don't you head home. And keep this to yourself. Those guys don't exactly like gossip.'

'Yes, sir.' Singh stood, before resting her hand on Sam's shoulder. 'Goodbye, Sam.'

He reached up and squeezed her hand.

'Good luck.'

Singh marched to the door, wiping a tear from her eye, before stepping out of Sam's life. Sam felt a small twinge in his chest, knowing he would miss her. But she needed to break away from him. His fight would only bring her down and now she had the opportunity to do more than she ever imagined. Singh was a tremendous fit for the role, but Sam hoped that she was smart enough to see when the agenda wasn't about the freedom of others.

Every government had an agenda.

Sam's fight was for the people.

For justice.

With a resounding sigh, Stout reached into the cabinet beneath his desk and returned with two glass tumblers. He followed it up with an expensive Scotch.

He shot Sam a smile.

'We can sort out your transfer tomorrow.' Stout unscrewed the cap on the bottle. 'You look like you could use a drink?'

'Very astute, sir.'

Stout chuckled, poured out two generous helpings and then slid one across to Sam. As surreal as it was to be toasting with the Commissioner of the Metropolitan Police, Sam took a sip of the warm liquor and looked out over the city.

He thought of Mac and mourned his passing.

He thought of all the criminals he'd taken out and the lives he'd saved.

He thought of Jamie, and how the public and police had treated him like a hero.

Ignoring the conversation that Stout was trying to initiate, Sam looked at the skyline and for the first time that evening, he felt a smile creep across his face.

CHAPTER THIRTY

It was a surreal experience waking up unemployed.

Ruth Ashton had followed Stout's advice and sent her letter of resignation through to his office the moment she'd returned home. In less than twenty-four hours, her career had fallen from an unprecedented high to rock bottom. It seemed an age ago that she was stood in front of the media, waxing lyrical about the effectiveness of the Met under her careful management and the incredible bust of Chapman's drug empire was compelling evidence.

But Ashton hadn't seen the full picture and although Stout had given her the dignified option of jumping before she was pushed, it had left a bitter taste in her mouth.

There was no applause as her career ended.

No nods of respect.

No thanks.

Those had been reserved for Sam Pope, a convicted killer who had broken out of prison.

As she'd watched the public applaud him for his bravery, she'd decided they didn't deserve her sweat and tears, the lifetime dedicated to making their city a safer place.

When Stout had overruled her, offering Sam his thanks, she decided that he no longer deserved her loyalty.

With sleep out of the question, she'd returned to her isolated life and poured numerous glasses of the strongest alcohol she could find. There was no loving husband to wrap herself in during her crisis. Nor were there any kids to band around her, to thank her for doing all she could.

The closest she'd come to love was with a deceased general who had been outed as a global terrorist.

Brought to his end by Sam Pope.

As she fell further into a drunken stupor, Ashton began to angrily connect the dots.

The common thread that ran through her miserable life was Sam Pope. He had been the architect of her downfall and had stripped every modicum of happiness from her life. Drunkenly vowing her revenge, she'd fallen asleep across her dining room table, waking the following morning with a stiff neck and a thumping headache.

Somehow mustering the energy to head for the shower, Ashton allowed the warm water to run over her body for nearly forty-five minutes. It allowed her to cry without facing the reality of actually doing it, the water crashing against her face and wiping the tears away.

It took her a while to realise she was mourning.

Wallace.

Her career.

Her life.

An hour later, surrounded by glasses of orange juice and enough paracetamol to start a small pharmacy, she began to scribble notes down on a notepad, drawing connecting to lines as her brainstorm began to take shape.

Her career with the Metropolitan Police may have finished but she would, if it took her the rest of her life, find a way to get her revenge on Sam.

She just had to find it and without the pressures of the

Met on her shoulders, she had all the time in the world to do so.

———

'Are you okay, dear?'

Anna stopped a few paces ahead of Harris, looking back with concern. The spring morning had offered a wonderful sunshine, which basked the beautiful lake with a blinding shimmer. For years, Harris and his wife had enjoyed strolls around it, often leading to hikes up the hilly terrain. But with his health in decline, Harris could only manage one lap around the lake. Two at a push.

Harris offered her his best smile.

'All good, here.'

Anna beamed at her husband. They had been married for over thirty years and she felt as much affection for him that day as she did the moment she'd met him. Back then, he was a hunky soldier and was the talk of her friends, who all paired off with office men. But as the years went by and Harris returned to the UK, he impressed her even more by his diligent work in rehabilitating convicts.

But the Ashcroft assignment had changed their lives.

Sworn to secrecy, they'd become guarded around friends and she'd been adamant that it was the stress and pressure of running such a facility that had exacerbated his MS.

But they didn't need to worry about that anymore.

Harris's retirement had been confirmed that morning, a day after the entire prison was decommissioned. Anna had wept in his arms when he'd returned, her husband shaking from the bullet with which he'd ended Sharp's life.

There would be an investigation, one which Harris had demanded himself and as a man of the utmost integrity, Anna was sure he would be cleared of any wrongdoing.

But until then, she was just pleased to have her husband back.

She waited until he shuffled beside her and then slid her hand into his, smiling warmly as he gently rubbed his finger against her wedding ring.

'It's beautiful, isn't it?' Anna said, looking out over the water.

'It's good to be home.'

Anna tilted her head against his shoulder and then the two of them continued their stroll around the lake.

Eight guards had died during the riot, and a further seven of them had been critically injured. Along with over ten prisoners found dead, including Chapman and his crew, Harris knew that the investigation would be a long and arduous experience.

The government would sweep it under the rug and the rest of the guards who had operated under Sharp's misguided regime were also facing the full strength of the law. They would be sent down, and along with the other inmates, they would be scattered UK wide across numerous prisons.

No one would ever know the truth.

The thought of that did eat away at him, but Harris knew his priorities needed to be elsewhere. His treatment plan for his multiple sclerosis had been enhanced, with stronger medicine being recommended to keep him mobile.

They couldn't cure it.

All he wanted was to move on, spend the rest of his years with his wife, and try to live as comfortably as possible.

With the warmth of the sun covering everything with a joyous glow, he held Anna's hand tightly and they shuffled around the lake, happy to be spending another day together.

After a few drinks with the commissioner, Sam had thanked him for his hospitality. Stout had been surprisingly understanding of Sam's mission, acknowledging that at times he even envied the freedom with which Sam operated. But having dedicated his life to the letter of the law to such an extent that he ended up leading it, he would never condone the actions Sam had taken.

There was a justice system for a reason and despite Sam's selflessness and bravery, there could be no walking away from the path he'd gone down.

Both of them accepted that, but Stout did imply he had a few favours to call in before he stepped down. Due to Sam's courageous actions that night, Stout would push for him to see out his sentence in a minimum security facility, offering him more freedom and a real chance of rehabilitation.

Perhaps even the chance for parole.

Stout escorted Sam through the New Scotland Yard building to the holding cells and told him that the next day he would be transferred to HMP Huntercombe near Nuffield, on the outskirts of Oxfordshire. A category C prison, which would afford Sam more freedom than Ashcroft ever did, along with a safer environment. Stout promised him he would talk to Judge Barnes personally, to push for a transfer to a category D prison, where Sam would be offered the freedom of the prison, along with the chance to keep his head down and maybe see the other side of a cell again.

Sam shook his hand and with the horror of Mac's death heavy on his mind, settled down for a rough night's sleep.

The following morning, Sam was woken by two officers who allowed him the opportunity of a shower before his transfer. They bundled him out through the back of the building, out of the public eye, and signed him over to the transport guards who seemed in awe of their prisoner.

'This isn't another switcheroo, is it?' Sam joked, although his audience were clueless as to his ordeal at Ashcroft.

As part of the Met's 'Green Initiative' the secure van was electric powered, and Sam stepped into the back and settled down for the near fifty-mile journey. Despite the heavy traffic, it only took them an hour to make it through to the M40 at Denham, which they stayed on for a few junctions, passing through Beaconsfield, Handy Cross, and Lane End until they turned off at junction five.

As they entered Nuffield, Sam felt the smoothness of the road change, the narrow country lanes causing a number of stops as the large van pulled into the predeter-mined gaps to allow cars through.

On the home stretch, one of the guards rattled his knuckles against the metal partition, yelling to Sam that they were twenty minutes out.

Before Sam could respond, he felt the engine of the van die and the vehicle roll to a stop.

It wasn't unexpected.

Sam had enemies and he'd wondered if an irate officer or an Ashton sympathiser would tip someone off to his route. Luckily, the officers in charge of the journey had allowed him to sit in the back uncuffed, realising that he wasn't a threat.

Sam could hear them bickering in the front seat, with little confidence that either of them would survive an attack.

As one of them got out of the van, Sam heard the sick-ening thud of a blow to the head, and then the officer colliding with the side of the van. More shouting, as the attacker demanded the other officer get out of the car and Sam knew it was at gunpoint.

Protecting Sam wasn't worth the officer's life, which Sam agreed with and he stood in the back of the van, ready to try his best to whatever onslaught was awaiting on the other side of the door.

Two sets of footsteps crunched on the ground around to the back of the van and with the electric system fried, the officer shook as he put the key in the door.

Another sickening thud, and Sam heard the man crumble to the ground.

Sam steadied himself, fists clenched.

He was born to survive.

The door swung open, and Etheridge, holding an assault rifle in one hand, pulled off the balaclava that had shielded his identity.

'Hello, handsome.' Etheridge smiled. 'If you could see the look on your face.'

'What the hell?'

'I'll explain on the way. Chop chop.'

Hesitantly, Sam stepped out the back of the van, looking around at the two unconscious officers. Etheridge shrugged, told Sam he felt bad about them both, and asked Sam to help him move them from harm's way. After lining both men on the grassy hillock that ran alongside the road, Etheridge set off through the woodlands, followed by a guilt-ridden Sam.

He had made peace with going to prison.

To finally pay the price for his war on crime.

Etheridge's response was simple.

'The world needs you to keep fighting, Sam.'

After five minutes of jogging, Etheridge slowed the pace, his busted knee stiffening and he walked through the trees. Sam caught up to him, baffled by the rescue mission.

'How the hell did you do all this?'

'With this.' Etheridge held up a small, black remote. 'It's like an EMP. Pretty good.'

Sam looked at him blankly, carefully stepping over a fallen branch.

'An electro-magnetic pulse. Essentially, this button fried their electrical system. There's no nuclear or radiation damage and it can only emit the pulse within a few feet. Worked though.'

Etheridge carried on walking, stepping through a large bush and onto a quaint village road, with no path for pedestrians and numerous cottages lining the road. His car was parked on a patch of grass and he tossed Sam the rifle.

'It's not loaded,' Sam said, knowing from the weight.

'Correct,' Etheridge said, hopping into the driver's seat.

'What if they'd been armed?'

'Then I'd have been up shit creek. Now get in.'

Sam cast one final glance back to the woods, tossing the idea of turning himself in over in his mind like a pancake. With a deep sigh, he pulled open the door and dropped into the passenger's seat. As Etheridge started the engine, Sam turned and looked at his friend who had crossed too many lines to make his way back.

'Why did you do this for me, Paul?' Sam asked. Etheridge smiled, slid the car into the gear and pulled out onto the road.

'It was the right thing to do.'

GET EXCLUSIVE ROBERT ENRIGHT MATERIAL

Hey there,

I really hope you enjoyed the book and hopefully, you will want to continue following Sam Pope's war on crime. If so, then why not sign up to my reader group? I send out regular updates, polls and special offers as well as some cool free stuff. Sound good?

Well, if you do sign up to the reader group I'll send you an EXCLUSIVE copy of the Sam Pope prequel novella, THE RIGHT REASON, absolutely free. (This book is not available anywhere else!)

You can get your FREE copy by signing up at www.robertenright.co.uk

SAM POPE NOVELS

For more information about the Sam Pope series, please
visit:

www.robertenright.co.uk

ABOUT THE AUTHOR

Robert lives in Buckinghamshire with his family, writing books and dreaming of getting a dog.

For more information:
www.robertenright.co.uk
robert@robertenright.co.uk

You can also connect with Robert on Social Media:

facebook.com/robenrightauthor
twitter.com/REnright_Author
instagram.com/robenrightauthor

Cover by Phillip Griffiths

Edited by Emma Mitchell

Made in the USA
Monee, IL
08 October 2020